GAZING UPON
THE DEAD

ROGER MORRISON

Gazing Upon The Dead
© Roger Morrison 2018

National Library of Australia Cataloguing-in-Publication entry (pbk)

Author:	Morrison, Roger, author.
Title:	Gazing Upon The Dead/Roger Morrison
ISBN:	978-1-925680-60-7 (paperback)
	978-1-925680-61-4 (ebook)
Subjects:	Fiction--Mystery and Detective
	Fiction--Crime

Published by Roger Morrison and Ocean Reeve Publishing
www.oceanreeve.com

REEVE
PUBLISHING

For Sharon.

Thank you.

PROLOGUE

Anna hadn't been frightened. At first, she was simply surprised. But now she became angry. Very angry.

'How dare you threaten me!' she snarled.

She tossed her book aside, slammed her wine glass down on the side table, and rolled quickly off the bed.

'Get out!' she yelled.

As Anna aggressively began to move forward she could see that the intense dark eyes held an anger that matched her own. And then she halted. She could now see something else; something that unnerved her. There was not only anger in those eyes. There was also madness.

Suddenly there was a swift movement, almost a blur, and something hard struck her ribcage. She didn't utter a sound as she began to fall. Anna was dead before she reached the floor.

CHAPTER ONE

Probationary Police Constable Stewart Braddock had been excited when the call came in. He had never seen a dead body. However, when he and PC Sam Johnson had reached the house, he'd been instructed to wait downstairs while Johnson and Locke, the house's owner, had gone up to the bedroom. Braddock had been quite disappointed.

When Johnson and Locke eventually returned from the upper floor, Detective Sergeant Broadhurst, three Scene of Crime Officers and the pathologist arrived. After they had gone upstairs, Braddock realised that of all the people in the house, he was the only one who had not seen the body.

Braddock craned his neck and looked into the house's living room. Johnson was sitting talking with Locke. It doesn't take two coppers to watch things down here, reasoned Braddock. Surely it wouldn't matter if he went up and had a quick look. So, overcome with curiosity, Braddock began to climb the stairs.

From the top, Braddock could see into the bedroom. He saw the white-coated pathologist and DS Broadhurst, but they didn't see him. The pathologist had her back towards him and Broadhurst, although facing in Braddock's direction, was looking downwards. As he approached the doorway Braddock looked downwards also.

When Braddock saw the woman lying on the floor he involuntarily uttered a loud rasping sound. Broadhurst immediately looked up. Seeing the colour draining from Braddock's face, she hastened across the room and grabbed his arm. Holding it firmly with her nitrile gloved hand, she said, 'Sit down, Stewart. On the floor.'

Braddock had no hesitation in following Broadhurst's order. He knew that he had been headed in that direction anyway.

As she guided Braddock's head down between his knees, Broadhurst raised her own head and called out, 'Constable Johnson! Get up here!'

Heavy boots could be heard coming up the stairs. Soon the solidly built Johnson appeared. If he was surprised to see Braddock sitting on the floor with Broadhurst squatting next to him, Johnson's face didn't show it.

'Take him outside, Sam.' Broadhurst stood and Johnson leant over and placed his hands under Braddock's arms.

'Put your arm around my shoulder, son,' Johnson said gently as he helped Braddock stand up.

Broadhurst returned to the bedroom and Johnson slowly walked Braddock towards the stairs. Johnson said, 'Don't worry, son. It happens to all of us. When I saw my first corpse I spewed all over the crime scene. I can tell you,' he chuckled, 'the detectives weren't happy.'

When they were half-way down the stairs, Johnson said, 'You can "stand guard" in the front yard, Stewart, and prevent anyone not involved in the investigation from entering the house.'

Braddock did not reply. He'd be pleased to get out of the house. When he'd joined the police force, he had naturally expected to see dead bodies. What he hadn't expected was that they would affect him so drastically.

'It will do you good to be outside,' Johnson added. 'You'll feel much better once you've had a breath of fresh air.'

As soon as he exited the building, Braddock took a deep breath of "fresh air". But it was far from comforting. The air was too warm. It had been warm when he'd been leaving for work that morning. Unusually warm. Especially for England. He'd complained to his mother but she had laughed and said, 'When I was a girl in Sydney this would be a normal winter's day.' He'd laughed then. But he certainly wasn't laughing now.

It was a "scorcher" of a day. And here he was, standing outside, receiving the brunt of it. He could feel the sweat pooling in his armpits and running down inside the back of his shirt collar. It was causing his shirt to stick to his lean body. Braddock turned his thin face upwards and squinted at the sky. Not a protective cloud to be seen. Yes. He was uncomfortable but knew he would be more uncomfortable if he was upstairs looking at that dead body.

The young constable thought that he might be able to ignore the heat – and perhaps forget about the body upstairs – if he talked to somebody. But Johnson had returned to the house's living room and the white-garbed scene of crime officer, who had been fingerprint dusting the front door and the hand rail at the bottom of the stairs, had obviously moved higher up and was now out of sight.

Braddock then thought that maybe it would help ease his discomfort if he focused on his surroundings. But looking around, he quickly realised that there was nothing of interest to see. Unlike the front yards of other semi-detached houses on this side of the street, this one had no beds of colourful flowers to look at and no low brick fence over which he could watch passing cars or pedestrians. This house had a front yard that was completely paved and bare and was bordered on three sides by a tall, thick hedge.

Admittedly, there was a gap in the hedge where the low front gate was hinged. This allowed him a limited view of the outside world. But vehicles and pedestrians passed by this narrow opening so quickly they barely registered on his retinas. He thought that if he blinked, most of the vehicles wouldn't register at all.

It was then that all discomfort suddenly disappeared. Braddock drew himself up to his full height and stiffened to attention. A tall, broad-shouldered man had appeared at the gap in the hedge and was now leaning down to open the gate. The constable instantly recognised him. This man was very easy to recognise.

Detective Chief Inspector Julian Walker was wearing his usual dark grey suit, a lighter grey shirt and today, a very pale grey tie. His closely cropped hair and his eyes were also grey. Although he had a broken nose that twisted sideways, it was the steel grey eyes that were the salient facial feature. It was obvious why he was known to many of those upholding the law – and to some of those breaking it - as "the Grey Man".

'Good afternoon, sir,' greeted Braddock, quickly stepping to one side as Walker's imposing figure neared the entrance to the building.

'Good afternoon, Constable,' Walker replied in a friendly tone.

Walker stopped and focused his unusual eyes on the face of the uniformed man. For a brief moment, Braddock imagined he was undergoing a brain scan. He would later muse about how useful those eyes must be in an interview room.

'Constable Braddock, isn't it?'

'Yes sir,' replied the young officer, pleased that the chief inspector had remembered his name. Especially since they had met only once previously.

'So, Constable Braddock. Who's inside?' Walker asked.

Braddock took a deep breath and replied as if reciting a prepared speech. 'David Locke, the chap who reported finding the body, and who claims to be the owner of the building, is in the sitting room with Constable Johnson. The deceased female, Anna Gruber, who Locke claims is - or rather was - his fiancée, is in the front bedroom on the second floor. DS Broadhurst, Doctor Simons, and two scene of crime officers are up there as well. A third scene of crime officer, who has just checked the front door, is currently dusting the staircase rail for fingerprints, sir.'

As Braddock exhaled, Walker smiled and said, 'What's your first name, Constable Braddock?'

'Stewart, sir.'

'Well, Stewart,' said Walker, 'I can see that you have a good memory for names and an organised mind for details. Those are valuable assets for a policeman. I'm sure you'll go far in the force.'

'Thank you, sir,' said a beaming Braddock.

4

Walker had noticed that the young constable was perspiring heavily. Not being vain enough to assume it was due to his presence, Walker said, 'Why don't you move inside, Stewart? It's way too hot to be standing out here.'

Braddock again said, 'Thank you, sir,' but didn't move.

'What's the matter, son?' asked a puzzled Walker.

'Constable Johnson said I was to stay in the yard, sir,' explained Braddock. He did not feel inclined to disobey Johnson's instructions a second time.

Walker laughed. 'Well, stand in the doorway. That's shaded and technically it's not inside.' Then Walker winked. 'And if Constable Johnson says anything, tell him I gave you a direct order.'

Braddock smiled. 'Yes, sir,' he said and followed Walker up the front steps.

Once he was on the threshold, Braddock turned to face the yard and assumed a rigid stance.

Looking back over his shoulder as he reached the bottom of the stairs, Walker said with a smile, 'Keep up the good work, lad.'

At that moment, Walker actually envied the work that Braddock was doing. Performing sentry duty seemed preferable to the work that Walker was about to do. Walker liked being a detective but he did not like the first task in a homicide investigation: the inspection of the body. The dead body that had so adversely affected Braddock would also affect Walker. But it would affect Walker in a much different way.

CHAPTER TWO

When he reached the top of the stairs, after squeezing with some difficulty past an overall-wearing scene of crime officer, Walker had no trouble finding his junior partner. Broadhurst was standing just outside the open doorway leading to the bedroom. At some point since Braddock's visit, crime scene tape had been placed across the doorway. Broadhurst was staring vacantly into the room and talking into a mobile phone.

Walker noted that Broadhurst, tall, narrow-waisted and broad-shouldered, was wearing not only her usual navy blue trouser suit, but also light blue booties over her shoes.

Hearing Walker approach, Broadhurst turned her face towards him and nodded a greeting. The nod caused a few strands of her thick, burgundy coloured hair to escape from its fastenings and fall over her face; a face that, although slightly pock-marked as a result of adolescent acne, was favourably accentuated by large, dark brown eyes.

Walker responded to the greeting with a smile and a nod of his own. Broadhurst, while continuing to speak into the phone, quickly moved aside so that her boss could see into the room.

Walker slowly scanned the room from the doorway. It was quite big. The wall in front of him was dominated by a wide, floor to ceiling window that overlooked the main road. It was flanked by heavy, chocolate coloured curtains. To his left was a neatly made double bed with two side-tables. On the bed cover, which matched the curtains in colour, lay an open paperback book. On one of the two varnished, dark wooden side tables stood an empty glass and a near empty bottle of wine. Nothing else. Taking up most of the wall facing the window, and matching the side tables in colour and texture, was a built-in wardrobe. The only other piece of furniture was a long, low, narrow chest of drawers that sat directly in front of him against the right wall. It too was dark brown and varnished and, like the rest of the furniture in the room, looked very expensive. The walls, which were bare, had been painted white. The room's minimalism of colour – and lack of bright colours - appealed aesthetically to Walker.

Eventually Walker turned his eyes downwards. Even after more than twenty-odd years on the force he still had an intense dislike for, as he put it, "gazing upon the dead". Blood, gore, mutilation, even dismemberment – none of these bothered Walker. What disturbed him was the absence of life.

Broadhurst, who was watching him closely, alone knew how Walker was feeling. She knew that he was feeling very uncomfortable. But she also knew that, unlike Braddock, Walker was not feeling light-headed. And just as well, she thought. She would find it almost impossible to support someone of his size if his legs suddenly went rubbery. No. She knew that seeing dead bodies did not make Walker faint. Seeing them simply caused him to be incredibly – almost unbearably – sad. And she was well aware that, although Braddock would eventually be unaffected, Walker would probably always feel this way.

On a white tiled floor, between the bed and the chest of drawers, lay a blonde-haired woman. Walker guessed she was in her late twenties or early thirties. She was attractive but detracting from her beauty was a nose that, while small, was globular rather than pointed. Her clear, pale blue eyes were staring widely at the ceiling. Her full lips were opened and formed a perfect circle. The overall facial expression was one of utmost amazement.

Walker moved his eyes from the face to the body. He saw that it was fully clothed, dressed in tight blue jeans and a short-sleeved, white blouse. He also observed that the only evidence of blood was a small, circular mark that stained the blouse just below the left breast.

Walker now raised his eyes to the face of the thin, grey-haired, bespectacled woman who was standing next to the body and staring at him. Doctor Ann Simons, like the two scene of crime officers in the room, was wearing white overalls as well as the mandatory blue gloves and booties.

'Afternoon, Doctor,' Walker said to the pathologist as he pulled gloves and booties from his coat pocket and donned them before stepping under the tape and into the room. 'Not much blood on her, is there?'

'Good afternoon, Chief Inspector,' replied Simons as she turned her eyes down towards the body. 'No, there's very little blood. But that doesn't mean she was killed elsewhere, if that's what you're thinking. I've only made a cursory examination but there seems to be only one, small, puncture wound. Whatever made it may have pierced her heart and killed her instantly. If that was the case, then once the heart stopped there would, naturally, be no pumping of blood.'

'A gun?' asked Walker.

'As I told your sergeant, I don't think she was shot,' said the pathologist. 'I haven't examined the wound itself yet but the hole in the blouse is quite small; small enough to help explain why there is no blood spatter and so little seepage. That in itself does not exclude the possibility of a small calibre firearm being used of course, but if you look very closely at the point of entry in the blouse you'll see the edges of the material come outwards not inwards. That would indicate that whatever penetrated the body was pulled out after entry. I'll be able to tell you more about the cause of death once I've carried out the post-mortem.'

'So she was stabbed,' said Walker, 'and whatever was used to stab her is missing.' He surveyed the room again before continuing. 'Has the room been searched?'

'I've checked it out, sir. There's nothing here,' announced Broadhurst as she closed her mobile phone. 'I'm going to search the rest of the house and I've just arranged for some uniforms to be sent here to do a thorough search of the outside areas.'

Walker nodded his approval and then asked, 'Has she been turned over? I know it's unlikely, but the weapon might be underneath her.'

'We haven't moved her yet, Chief Inspector,' replied the pathologist. 'We were waiting for you to arrive.'

'Okay. Well, if the photographs have been taken, let's roll her over now.'

Broadhurst walked over to the body and, with the help of the pathologist, gently turned it over on to its stomach. Walker took a quick look at the floor and the victim's back.

'No weapon and no blood on the back of the blouse,' said Walker, more to himself than to the others. 'You can roll her back over.'

Once the body was in its original position, Broadhurst retreated to the doorway. Walker took a couple of steps back as the pathologist began unbuttoning the buttons of the victim's blouse and one of the scene of crime officers moved in to take fresh photographs.

'If you were to make a rough guess, how long do you think she's been dead?' Walker asked the pathologist.

The doctor stopped what she was doing and placed her hands around the victim's throat. 'At a rough guess I'd say she died no more than seven hours ago. Rigor appears to have just started in her neck. I'll be more definite after I've carried out the PM.'

Walker looked at his watch. It was a quarter past three. 'Thanks, Doctor. I'll look forward to reading your report.'

Walker had half turned away when a red-coloured object passing by outside the window was momentarily caught by his peripheral vision. This was accompanied by the low rumbling sound of a heavy vehicle. Walker turned back and faced the large window. 'Were the curtains of that window already pulled aside when you first entered the room?' he asked the scene of crime officers.

'They were open when we came in but we weren't the first to enter,' said one of the white-garbed men who was dusting the chest of drawers for fingerprints. Both he and his stouter companion were unknown to Walker.

'PC Johnson and the victim's fiancé, Mr. Locke, were here before I arrived,' said Broadhurst. 'Johnson wouldn't have touched anything but maybe Locke opened the curtains when he found the body.'

'Let's go and ask him,' said Walker as he turned and strode towards the doorway.

CHAPTER THREE

In the middle of another white tiled and white walled room, a dark-haired man sat on a black, hard-leather lounge. His lowered face was covered by his hands and his elbows rested on his knees. At right angles to the lounge were two black, hard-leather chairs. One of these was currently occupied by Constable Johnson, whose round, closely shaven skull Walker immediately recognised. A glass-topped, black-legged, coffee table was positioned in front of the two men.

'Mr. Locke?'

The dark-haired man raised his head when Walker spoke and a somewhat startled Constable Johnson turned his head and rose to his feet. The soft-soled shoes worn by both Walker and Broadhurst had allowed them to enter the room silently.

'I'm Detective Chief Inspector Walker and this is Detective Sergeant Broadhurst.'

Locke did not reply to the introductions. He watched as Walker reached for the empty chair and effortlessly moved it to another side of the coffee table. It now faced Locke. Walker sat down and studied the man.

David Locke was in his late thirties, guessed Walker. His dark hair was thick and wavy and brushed back. He had full, protruding lips and a large, fleshy nose but the most noticeable facial feature were the eyebrows. They were very dark and extremely bushy. They almost hid the equally dark eyes. He was solidly built and wore a light blue, short-sleeved shirt, navy-blue jeans, and black sneakers.

Broadhurst withdrew a notebook and pen from the black shoulder bag that she always carried and seated herself in the chair vacated by Johnson. The constable had moved to stand by the doorway through which the detectives had entered.

'I'm sorry to intrude on your grief, Mr. Locke, but it's essential that I ask you some questions - and ask them without any delay,' said Walker.

Locke nodded.

'Is your name David Locke and are you the owner of this building?'

Locke nodded again.

'The name of the woman upstairs is Anna Gruber and she was your fiancée?'

'Yes,' said Locke, who seemed to shudder slightly.

'I noticed she wasn't wearing a ring. Is it missing?'

'No, we hadn't bought one yet.' Locke sighed. 'As always, Anna wanted the best and none of the local jewellers had anything she liked. We were going down to London to buy one next week.'

Walker paused briefly before asking his next question. 'You rang the police station at five past two. At what time did you find Anna?'

'Not long before then.' Locke now became slightly agitated. 'I could tell she was dead. She was so still. I ran to the phone straight away.'

'Did you open the bedroom curtains?'

Locke looked at Walker as though puzzled by the question. 'No,' he said. 'They're always open. Anna hated having them closed. Even at night when we were getting undressed for bed.' Locke frowned. 'She said if people wanted to look in, it didn't bother her. And that we were up too high anyway for people walking past to see in.'

'It bothered you?' asked Walker.

'A little. I was concerned about the neighbours across the road watching us but I don't like to argue,' Locke replied quietly.

The interview was suddenly interrupted by a babble coming from outside the building.

'Ah! The media have arrived,' said Walker. He turned in his chair so that he could see Constable Johnson. 'Please go and tell Constable Braddock to stand at the front gate and keep them out of the yard.' He thought that the hedge enclosing the front yard should be high enough to stop them climbing in anywhere else. It should also provide some shade for Braddock.

As he was about to turn back to continue the questioning of Locke, Walker noticed the very large, black, flat-screen television and sophisticated speaker system attached to the wall that Locke was facing. Very nice – and very expensive, thought Walker. He slowly surveyed the rest of the room. A couple of low black cabinets stood at both ends of the room and a black desk and office chair filled one corner. Against the wall behind Locke stood a large, frosted glass fronted bookcase. It too was black. Walker had noticed this particular piece of furniture as he had entered the room but, at the time, he had given it little attention. The only bright colours in the room came from three frameless, abstract, oil paintings positioned on two of the walls. Walker didn't like these. Too many colours and way too bright for his taste. Nevertheless, he assumed that they, like the other furnishings he had so far seen, would have cost a lot of money.

Locke noticed Walker making an appraisal of the room. He said rather nonchalantly, 'All designed by Anna. She had the whole place tiled and repainted. And she had me buy all new furniture when she moved in.'

'What is your occupation, Mr. Locke?' asked Walker.

'I own a craft shop.'

'So what, may I ask, brought you home so early in the day?'

'I come home every day around twelve o'clock to have lunch with Anna. My shop is only about two hundred metres away up the main road. Next to the bakery.'

'I don't understand, Mr. Locke,' Walker said with a puzzled expression on his face. 'If you arrived home at twelve how come you didn't call us until nearly two?'

'I didn't come home at twelve today,' Locke said quietly. 'My assistant in the shop had a dental appointment this morning and was supposed to come into the shop just before twelve.' Locke's voice now contained a hint of anger. 'She didn't arrive until nearly one so I didn't get home until about five past.' His voice lowered. 'When I arrived here I called out to Anna. And when she didn't reply I assumed she had gone out in a huff because I was late.' Locke now seemed calm again. 'So I made myself a sandwich and a cup of tea and read the paper – I figured she wouldn't be away long. She'd cool off and come home. Anyway, when she hadn't shown up by a quarter to two I decided to go back to work. I went upstairs to clean my teeth and … and,' Locke's voice began to crack, 'that – that's when I found her.'

Walker waited while Locke took a tissue from his pocket and blew his nose. He then asked, 'Why didn't you ring Anna from the shop to tell her you would be late?'

'I did,' replied Locke, looking directly at Walker. 'I didn't ring her on the house phone because she never answers it. She only uses her mobile. But when I rang her on the mobile a couple of times there was no answer. I rang her again on the mobile when I got home - when I thought she wasn't here. But I still got no answer.'

'Didn't you hear it ring somewhere in the house?'

'No. I guess she must have had it turned off because she didn't want to talk to me.'

'Because she was angry about you being late?'

'Yes,' Locke replied very quietly. He lowered his head and his eyes were now concealed by his eyebrows.

'Anna didn't have a job, Mr. Locke?'

'She hasn't worked since she came over from Germany. She had a high ranking position over there and refused to work here unless she could find a job of equal standing.'

'She wouldn't work with you?'

Locke looked up at Walker. His eyebrows shook and moved upwards. 'Oh no! She'd never work in a shop.'

'What time was it when you opened your shop this morning, Mr. Locke?

Locke shrugged. His eyes returned to the floor. 'Same time as I open it every morning. Nine o'clock.'

'When I arrived, I noticed a red Porsche parked out front,' said Walker. 'I also noticed that its personalised number plates ended with the letters "AG". Am I correct in assuming it belonged to Anna?'

Locke nodded.

'If Anna never worked how could she afford such an expensive car?' asked Walker, knowing what the answer would be.

'I bought it for her,' Locke replied and then added, 'for her birthday.'

'Why would you think Anna had gone out when her car is here?'

Locke's eyes returned to Walker. 'When I came in - and there was no answer to my call - I thought she had walked down to the river. She often does that on a warm day. It's not far and she likes the exercise.'

Walker was about to ask another question when they heard a noise at the front door. He heard Johnson's heavy footsteps as he left the room, and then again when he returned seconds later.

'The men from the mortuary are here, Chief Inspector,' said Johnson.

Walker nodded and turned his attention again to Locke.

'When did Anna come over from Germany?' Walker asked.

'She came over about three years ago to marry Richard Morris,' replied Locke. 'He's an artist. She left him nearly a year ago and moved in with me.'

'Morris?' said Walker, 'I thought her surname was Gruber.'

'That was her maiden name. She said she kept it when she got married because she didn't like the name "Morris".'

Walker paused for a moment before speaking again. 'Can you think of anyone who might have wanted to harm Anna? Was she on bad terms with anyone?'

'I don't think she knew anyone in England. Only Morris.' Locke's voice rose and he frowned at Walker. 'And he was very angry when she left. Threatened to have me beaten up.'

'Do you know where I might find Mr. Morris?'

'He lives a few doors down. The other side of the co-op. The semi-detached with the bright yellow door.'

'Anna didn't have far to carry her belongings then when she moved in with you,' Walker commented.

Locke said nothing. He lowered his head.

'Speaking of belongings. Have you noticed if anything belonging to Anna - or to you - is missing, Mr. Locke?'

'I haven't looked.'

Walker thought for a moment. He then stood up and said, 'I think that's all the questions I have for now, Mr. Locke.'

Broadhurst closed her notebook and was rising to her feet when they heard the sound of voices at the front door. Again, Constable Johnson left the room. And again, he returned moments later.

'The officers you requested from the station have arrived, DS Broadhurst,' Johnson announced.

'How many, Constable?' Walker asked.

'Four, sir.'

'Four? There must be no work to be done at the station.' Walker shook his head. Their station was small. Too small. Commanded by a superintendent, it housed only three plain-clothed detectives and ten uniformed personnel. And now six of those uniforms were in attendance at this one crime scene.

'Alright then, tell them to report to DS Broadhurst for their assignments. And tell Constable Braddock to stay at the gate.' Johnson began to turn towards the door but stopped when Walker added, 'After you've spoken to the men I want you to come back here and stay with Mr. Locke while the scene of crime officers check out this bottom floor – and don't let anyone else come in here until after they have finished.' Johnson waited this time to make sure that Walker had finished giving him instructions. He hadn't. Walker said, 'After the scene of crime officers have gone you can make Mr. Locke and yourself a cup of tea and then accompany him while he checks to see if anything is missing.'

Johnson departed and Walker then turned and spoke to Broadhurst. 'Get one of the officers to check with the neighbours – especially those living directly opposite – to see if they heard or saw anything. Another two officers can search for the missing weapon. Make sure they look in the front hedges, neighbours' gardens, rubbish bins, street drains and then out back once the techs have finished out there. You know the drill.'

'What about the fourth officer?'

'He – or she - can assist you in a house search. And while you're searching for a weapon, Paige, see if you can find Anna's mobile. Also look at letters, papers, flyleaves of books and anything else that may reveal the names of people with whom she had contact.'

'Did Anna have a computer?' Walker asked Locke, whose head was still lowered.

'Yes,' he said, without looking up at Walker. 'She had a laptop and there's a computer that we both used in the office upstairs.'

'We'll have to take the laptop away and I'd like you to give DS Broadhurst the password of your computer,' Walker said, wondering if the computers were still there. He paused before speaking again. 'And for elimination purposes I'll need to have your fingerprints taken by one of the technical officers when they come down to examine this level.'

Walker watched Locke for a moment before he spoke again. 'One last thing, Mr. Locke. When you arrived home was the front door locked?'

'No, it was unlocked.'

'Didn't that make you think Anna was at home?'

Locke sighed and looked up at Walker. He said, 'Anna never locked the door when she was at home or when she went out. I spoke to her about it once and she got quite angry. She said whatever thieves took could easily be replaced and - ,' Locke paused and his face reddened as his eyes looked downwards, 'she said a rapist would provide her with an exciting experience.'

Walker raised his eyebrows. He then looked around the room again before speaking. 'Well that's all for now, Mr. Locke. We will talk again later. My condolences for your loss.'

Walker moved over to the doorway where he waited while Broadhurst wrote down the computer password now being recited by Locke. When she was finished and walked over to join him, Walker said quietly, 'I'm going up to the shop to have a word with Mr. Locke's assistant. After you've finished here I'd like you to check out the CCTV.'

CHAPTER FOUR

When Walker exited the building he was enveloped by warmth. He looked up briefly and saw that the sun still had a fair distance to travel before it reached the horizon. Ah, he loved mid-summer.

His feeling of contentment was short-lived. He was assailed by a sudden increase in noise as many of those jammed outside the gate recognised him. When he reached the gate he saw that there were not only journalists crowding the footpath but also curious members of the public. We're a nation of busy-bodies, mused Walker.

Walker said an inaudible farewell to Constable Braddock as he closed the gate behind him and stepped into the noisy gathering. He recognised most of the media representatives but ignored their questions. A few of them thrust microphones in front of his face but no-one attempted to block his path. Realising that some would probably follow him if he walked the short distance towards the shop, he turned left to where his car was parked.

A red, double-decker bus that was passing in front of him, slowed for a nearby bus stop. Walker came to an abrupt halt and turned to face the crowd. He'd had an idea. He slowly scanned the many faces watching him until he saw the one he was seeking. Raising his hand, he beckoned to a blonde-haired woman, whose heavily starched and brilliantly white blouse, expertly applied facial make-up, and stiffly lacquered hair left little doubt as to her role in the media. Holding a large microphone aloft, she struggled to force her rather shapely figure through the bodies in front of her. She was accompanied by a thin, long-haired man who was also struggling. He was having difficulty keeping the large camera on his shoulder as he was jostled by those around him.

'Sarah,' Walker said to her when the couple finally reached him. 'I would like to make a statement.'

With a surprised but pleased expression on her face, the blonde raised her microphone higher so that it would catch the tall man's forthcoming words. As her companion fiddled with his camera, Walker mused about how annoyed his boss would be when he learned of this unauthorised interview. Superintendent Terry Sheen would be further aggravated by the fact that it was not his face on the television screen.

'A woman has been murdered,' announced Walker when the camera man was ready and the small crowd had quietened, 'and we are appealing to the public for help. We would like to hear from anyone who was on the upper deck of the red bus travelling between Essex University and the Colne River at any time today. Please telephone, or come into, the Wivenhoe police station.' He paused, said 'Thank you,' and turned away.

Multiple questions noisily erupted but all remained unanswered as Walker resumed the short walk to his car.

CHAPTER FIVE

Walker's Chrysler was not grey but it was a subdued colour. It was brown. It was old but comfortable. With the seat adjusted as far back as it would go there was sufficient room for his long legs. The only problem with it was parking. Nowadays most of the parking spots available on the roads seemed to be suitable only for Minis. Fortunately, on this particular afternoon, in the space available directly opposite Locke's shop, he could have parked a truck.

He locked his car and leisurely crossed a road that, at that moment, carried surprisingly little traffic. A dark green sports car reversing into a parking space outside the bakery and a red double-decker bus disappearing in the distance were the only signs of movement.

Locke's shop had been easy to find. It had the words "THE CRAFT SHOP" painted in large blue letters on its wide front window. Hanging from the inside surface of an adjacent clear glass door could be seen a sign which a woman had been turning. The sign now read, "Closed".

Walker looked at his watch. Ten minutes to five. The assistant was closing the shop early. She apparently assumed Locke was not returning.

When Walker reached the door, she looked up at him and shook her head. He reached into his inside coat pocket and pulled out his warrant card. She paused to read it through the glass and then opened the door. She stepped aside as Walker entered and then closed the door behind him.

Walker stopped and stood motionless. He was confronted by a plethora of colour. Displayed in several rows on a huge rack facing the door were balls of knitting wool of every conceivable colour. Gaudy colour had always offended Walker's sensibilities but here the gaudiness was so abundant it was mesmerising. He found it difficult to turn his eyes away.

'How can I help you?'

The spell was broken and Walker turned to face the woman. As he had noticed through the front door, she was tall, slender, and not unattractive. Probably aged in her early thirties, she had short, curly, dark brown hair and large, very dark brown eyes. She was wearing a white t-shirt and dark brown slacks.

'I'm Detective Chief Inspector Walker. And your name is?'

'Denise Richards.' The assistant looked puzzled. 'The owner is not here at the moment.'

'I know,' said Walker. Obviously Locke had not telephoned after Walker had left. 'I've just come from him. Are you Mr. Locke's assistant?'

The look of puzzlement was replaced by one of concern. 'Yes. What's happened? Is David okay?'

Walker ignored her question. 'What time did Mr. Locke leave the shop today, Ms. Richards?'

'About one o'clock – why?'

'Was that usual?'

'No – he usually leaves about twelve but today I was late coming in. Please tell me what's happened.'

'Anna Gruber, Mr. Locke's fiancée, has been found dead.'

'What?!' Richards' face expressed firstly surprise, then relief, and then confusion, before finally flushing with anger. 'Fiancée?! He didn't tell me he was going to marry her!'

Noting that the assistant was more concerned about Locke's relationship with Anna than with Anna's death, Walker then asked, 'Where were you this morning, Ms. Richards?'

'It's Miss – and I was at the dentist's. Why?'

'What time was your appointment?'

'Ten-thirty.'

'You went straight from your home to the dentist's?'

'Yes.'

'How long were you there?'

'I arrived just before ten-thirty. The dentist saw me at eleven. And he finished just before twelve.'

'And did you come straight here from the dentist's?'

'Yes – I mean no. I went home to feed my cat. I remembered I had forgotten to feed her this morning – I was nervous about going to the dentist – so I went home after my appointment before coming here.'

'Apart from the cat and yourself, does anyone else live in your house, Miss Richards?'

'No! Why are you asking me these questions?'

'Because Anna Gruber was murdered.'

'What – and you think I might have done it?' Richards seemed horrified.

'We are interviewing everyone connected with her, Miss Richards. Did you speak to a neighbour, or did anyone in the street see you, when you left your home to go to the dentist? Or when you went home after your appointment?' asked Walker.

'No. I didn't see anyone – I don't think I did.' Locke's assistant was now obviously becoming flustered.

'What is your relationship with your employer?' asked Walker.

'What? What do you mean?'

'Would you say you are friends?'

'Yes. I'd like to think we are.'

'Why do you think then that he didn't tell you about his engagement to Miss Gruber?'

'I don't know.' Richards looked annoyed.

'Were you ever more than friends with Mr. Locke?'

The assistant sighed and averted her eyes. 'Yes. Until he met Anna we were in a very close relationship.'

'How well did you know Anna?'

'I only saw her a couple of times. She rarely came into the shop. I think she thought she was too good for this place.'

'So you didn't like her.' This was a statement rather than a question.

'No, I didn't,' admitted Richards glaring defiantly at Walker. 'From what David told me, I think she was a selfish, arrogant gold-digger.'

That's being honest, thought Walker, before speaking again. 'Well, that's about all for now, Miss Richards. Oh, would you please write down for me your address and phone number – and the name and address of your dentist.'

While the assistant wrote down the requested information on a scrap of paper Walker found himself, almost compulsively, looking again at the wool rack. His attention however, was once again diverted. Not this time by the assistant's voice but by the metal container standing on the counter adjacent to the rack. Shaped like a miniature umbrella stand, the container was filled with a large number of knitting needles. Like the wool, the needles came in a wide variety of colours. The brightly coloured plastic needles may have initially caught his attention but it was the silver ones on which he now focused. He lifted one out and examined it. It was made of steel and was long and narrow – and tapered to a point at the end.

CHAPTER SIX

'The super wants to see you, Chief Inspector,' greeted the Desk Sergeant as Walker entered the police station.

'And a good morning to you too, Sergeant,' replied Walker with a smile. 'The superintendent's in rather early, isn't he?' He knew that his boss rarely arrived at the station before nine and it was now only just past seven-thirty.

'He's going away tomorrow for a three day police conference in Brighton,' said the sergeant who always seemed to know everything that was going on. 'He's probably wanting to get all of his paper work out of the way.'

'Is that right?' said Walker. 'Who's in charge while he's away?'

'That I don't know,' said the sergeant, obviously disappointed that he didn't have this particular piece of information. 'Probably some higher-up from another station.'

'Well good luck to him, whoever it is. I don't envy anyone having to do the paperwork, even if it is only for three days.'

Walker lingered by the counter. He had known Bob Williamson for many years and always enjoyed his company. Also, he was in no hurry to see the superintendent.

The sergeant was a large, friendly man who had a round face with high, prominent, pink cheeks and small, dark, laughing eyes. His hair, which was cut so that it sat only on the very top of his head, was straight and black, a colour that Walker suspected had been obtained from a bottle. He was overweight to the extent that his stomach placed an enormous strain on the buttons of his tunic when it was closed. It was for this reason, to the annoyance of Superintendent Sheen, that his tunic was seldom closed.

'By the way, we've had a bit of response to your television show,' said the sergeant, holding up a wrinkled sheet of note paper.

'Well, I would appreciate it if you would hand the list of names to DS Broadhurst when she arrives, Sergeant,' said Walker, knowing that Paige habitually arrived at the station at seven forty-five.

'I certainly will, Stanley,' said Williamson, imitating Oliver Hardy, a silent film star whom the sergeant both admired and resembled.

Walker laughed and looked around the surprisingly empty foyer. He then walked over to the large notice board that was attached to the wall opposite the desk sergeant's counter. He appeared to be looking at a particular sheet of paper but he wasn't really seeing it. His thoughts were elsewhere. He abruptly turned to face the front desk where the sergeant was now reading a newspaper.

'Bob, you've lived in this area for many years. What do you know about "The Craft Shop" and its owner, David Locke?'

The sergeant looked up and thought for a moment before speaking, 'The shop's been there for a long time. It used to be run by an elderly woman named Mrs. Southern. Locke was her assistant. When she died a couple of years back, Locke took over the shop. She had no family that I know of so I presume she left it to him.'

'Was she wealthy?' asked Walker. 'Did Locke inherit any money from her?'

'She was as poor as a church mouse. The shop seemed to have few customers and she lived in a small rented cottage down by the river.'

'What do you know about Locke?'

'Oh, he's a local lad. Comes from a working class family,' replied the sergeant.

'Well he seems to be doing all right. Certainly spends plenty of money,' said Walker.

The sergeant thought for a moment and rubbed his chin with his thumb and forefinger. 'I never thought about that. I don't think that shop has many more customers now than it used to. Perhaps a few more tourists nowadays. That is a puzzle.'

'Yes, it is,' Walker said thoughtfully. 'Thanks Bob,' he added as he turned and began walking slowly up the corridor towards the superintendent's office.

CHAPTER SEVEN

'Morning, sir,' said Walker after being invited to pass through the open doorway. The superintendent never closed the door to his office. Walker thought his boss was either slightly claustrophobic or, more likely, he simply did not want to miss seeing or hearing anything that went on outside his room.

Superintendent Terry Sheen, wearing his usual dark blue uniform, sat behind a large, paper covered desk. Aged in his fifties, he was of medium height and of average build but had a slight pot-belly. He wore rimless spectacles that were always positioned slightly below small, squinting, brown eyes. He had straight, thinning, sand coloured hair that, regardless of how often he pushed it back, was always falling over his forehead. He looked up at Walker with the usual slight scowl on his face.

'Good morning, Chief Inspector,' he responded rather grumpily to Walker's greeting.

'What did you want to see me about, sir?' asked Walker, hoping it was not – but fully expecting it to be – about his television interview.

The superintendent surprised him. 'I've added a new member to your team. With DC Osborne on leave, you will probably need a replacement to help you solve the murder of the young woman.' His voice had now become more pleasant. 'How's that investigation going by the way?'

'I interviewed a couple of people yesterday and will be talking to someone of interest today. We'll be able to do more once we have the pathologist's report,' replied Walker. He then asked, 'Who's the new team member?'

'DC Peter Kent.' Sheen's eyes momentarily dropped, as they habitually did, to watch as he flicked imaginary dust from the sleeve of his spotless, well-pressed uniform.

'Peter Kent? A DC? You mean our quiet PC has been promoted and has finally left the radio room?' asked Walker.

'Yes, he has,' replied the superintendent. 'And it's about time. He's been in there nearly ten years. He'd still be there if I hadn't had a word with him.'

'Ten years? How old is he, sir?'

'Thirty-two,' replied Sheen who always knew the personal details of all members of his station.

Walker was surprised. He'd assumed Kent was younger. Not only because of his physical appearance but also because Walker was aware that Kent still lived with his mother.

'He should have applied for promotion long ago,' continued Sheen. 'He's a very bright lad. Did exceptionally well in the exam. And he knows quite a lot about computers, I've been told.'

'Well that could be useful,' said Walker. He had always liked Kent. He was quiet, polite and keen to please. Walker knew not only that Kent was single and lived with his mother, he also knew that Kent was popular with his colleagues who usually referred to – and addressed – Kent as "Superman". As well as having the same surname as that fictional character's alter ego, Kent was also known to be extraordinarily fond of comic books.

'Yes, well I told him to report to you at eight,' said the superintendent, picking up his pen and looking down at his papers; an action that appeared to be a dismissal of Walker.

As Walker turned to leave the room the superintendent spoke again. 'Oh, by the way. I saw you on television. Very clever, thinking of the buses.'

Walker turned back to face the superintendent and smiled. The smile quickly disappeared however, when the superintendent added,

'Because I admire your ingenuity and leadership qualities so much, I'm placing you in command of the station for the next three days while I'm away attending a police conference.'

Walker quietly groaned as he thought of the paperwork the job entailed. He said, 'Thank you, sir,' and, with a frown on his face, again turned to leave the office. His downturned mouth turned upwards as he closed the door behind him. He was amused by the thought of the superintendent's annoyance at having to further interrupt his work by getting up and crossing his room to open the door. Sometimes very petty actions could be very satisfying.

Walker suddenly realised he was hungry. He hadn't yet had breakfast. An unpleasant image of a desk covered by paperwork was replaced by a very pleasant image of a plate covered by fried eggs, bacon and sausages. He looked at his watch and saw that it was a quarter to eight. Instead of heading for his office he turned and walked briskly in the opposite direction, towards the stairs leading down to the canteen. Continuing to envision a hot, appetite-satisfying meal, Walker told himself that, if he was a little late reaching his office, Broadhurst would keep Kent entertained.

CHAPTER EIGHT

It was ten to eight. Today Broadhurst was five minutes later than usual arriving at the room her colleagues commonly referred to as the "incident room" and which she had once laughingly described as a "room free of incident".

The room was small. It contained only three desks, one of which belonged to Broadhurst, another to DC Osborne, and one which had been vacant for some time. The doorway through which she entered was part of the wall that formed a backdrop for Broadhurst's and Osborne's cluttered desks. The wall opposite was taken up by a window and filing cabinets, while a whiteboard and the unused desk filled the wall to the right. To the left was a glass wall and wooden door separating Walker's small office from the rest of the room.

Even if Walker's office door had been closed, Broadhurst would still have been able to see the figure standing at Walker's desk with his back towards her. He was as tall as she was but much heavier. He had thick, curly, dark brown hair and was wearing what looked like a new, but not well-fitting, dark blue suit. She was wondering who he might be when he apparently sensed her approach and turned to face her.

'Superman!' a surprised Broadhurst exclaimed. 'What are you doing here? And in a suit!'

'Good morning, ma'am. I was told by Superintendent Sheen to report to DCI Walker's office. I've been appointed to your team,' the new DC replied.

'Well bless my soul! You! A detective!' Broadhurst said. 'And don't call me "ma'am".'

'How would you like me to address you?'

'Call me "Sarge" when we're on duty and "Paige" when we're not.' Broadhurst then held out her hand. 'Anyway – congratulations on your promotion. It's about time you moved up!'

'Thank you, ma'am – I mean Sarge,' said the DC, with both his thin-lipped mouth and his dark eyes revealing his pleasure as he shook Broadhurst's hand.

Broadhurst leaned back and, making it obvious that her eyes were focusing on Kent's waistline, said, 'You've put on weight since I last saw you.'

Kent, a trifle embarrassed, smiled and self-consciously patted his stomach. 'Mum's cooking,' he said.

'So you're going to help me and the DCI "fight for truth, justice, and the American way"?' said Broadhurst as she placed on Walker's desk a large plastic bag she had been carrying.

'Yes – but I'd prefer the British way,' Kent replied with a smile.

'Well, welcome to the team, Superman.'

'Thanks,' Kent said. He then paused before asking, 'What's it like working for the "Grey Man"?'

'Good,' replied Broadhurst without any hesitation. 'He's always fair. And he's usually friendly,' she paused before adding, 'but he might not be so friendly if he heard you refer to him as "the Grey Man". He's aware people use that nickname but I don't think he likes it. Once, when we overheard a uniform refer to him by that name, he told me that "the Grey Man" was the nickname of an American serial killer.'

'Oh - well I won't call him that anymore,' Kent assured her. Then he said, 'Sergeant Williamson told me that he's really clever.'

'Well, the "Grey Man", as you called him, certainly has plenty of grey matter. He's actually got a Master's degree from Oxford.'

'Really?' said Kent. His face expressed surprise. 'Sergeant Williamson didn't mention that.'

'Maybe it's one of the few things that Bob Williamson doesn't know.'

Kent smiled but then his face took on a puzzled expression. He asked, 'So why is the chief inspector a copper then?'

'His degree is in history and he says that all you can do with that is teach. He told me he'd rather catch criminals than educate them.'

Kent smiled again. 'Does he lose his patience with his slower witted colleagues?'

'I hope you're not referring to me,' laughed Broadhurst. She then spoke in a serious tone, 'No. He's a very patient man. He can get angry with his superiors but I've never seen him lose his temper with anyone. I also know he hates to have to use violence on anyone.'

'I suppose his size makes other people think twice about using violence on him,' said Kent. 'But how did he get the broken nose?'

'He told me his nose got broken when he was caught at the bottom of a rugby ruck,' replied Broadhurst before adding 'and don't think his size always prevents our customers from taking a poke at him. A complaint was made against him some years back. One of our guests claimed Walker threw him down the stairs when he was being escorted to the cells. Fortunately there was a witness. He told the complaints board that this idiot, arrested for being drunk and disorderly, had thrown a wild punch at Walker but missed. The momentum of the punch carried the fool head over heels down the stairs. Walker was cleared but he's not very fond of the complaints board.'

Kent was about to say something when he noticed the approach of the man he and Broadhurst had been discussing. Although the DS had her back to the doorway she knew from the sudden change of expression on the DC's face that Walker was about to join them.

CHAPTER NINE

After shaking hands with his new DC, congratulating him on his promotion and welcoming him to the team, Walker led him over to the empty desk in the incident room. Broadhurst followed closely behind.

'This can be your desk, Peter,' said Walker. 'It has an extra computer terminal that you may find useful.'

'And it has a very large drawer in which you can keep your "Superman" comics,' added Broadhurst with a smile.

Kent returned her smile. 'Actually Sarge, I prefer "Spiderman" to "Superman". Far more entertaining with his emotional vulnerability and angst.'

Walker laughed. 'Well let's hope the guilty party in our murder case has some angst. It might make it easier to catch him – or her.'

'Her?' said Broadhurst, giving Walker a curious look.

Walker then told them about his meeting with Locke's assistant. 'Locke was in a serious relationship with Miss Richards before he replaced her with Anna. I suspect she's still in love with him – and I know she had an intense dislike for Anna. Also, she can't confirm her whereabouts either before or after her dental appointment.' Walker gazed at the window as he thought about the assistant. He then turned his eyes back to Broadhurst and asked her about the previous day's weapon search.

'I found nothing in the house and the uniformed officers found nothing in the front or back yard, neighbours' yards, front street or back lane,' she replied.

Walker told them about the steel knitting needles. 'A possible weapon. We'll know once the pathologist has finished.' He paused. 'So, as they say in the American crime films, our Miss Richards not only had motive, and possible opportunity, she also had possible means.'

Walker pulled out a chair from the remaining desk and sat down. He invited the others to do likewise. Before Broadhurst took a seat, she removed a piece of paper from her bag and handed it to Walker.

'Bob Williamson gave me this to give you, sir. It's the names and numbers received so far of travellers on yesterday's buses,' she said, before adding, 'Bob said calls are still coming in.'

'Thanks, Paige,' said Walker, taking and looking at the piece of paper. 'We may get lucky. One of them may have seen something.' He then looked up at Broadhurst and asked, 'How did the door-to-door canvassing go?'

'According to the officer, none of the neighbours saw or heard anything.'

'Disappointing,' he said. 'What about CCTV? Have you managed to get the tapes?'

'No point, sir. The camera covering that area was turned off.'

'What?!' exclaimed Walker.

Broadhurst shrugged. 'It seems it's been off for a while. The council told me that the low crime rate in this village doesn't justify the expense of operating it.'

'Pardon me for interrupting, sir,' said Kent, 'but I heard that for some time now local councils right across England and Wales have been turning off and removing some of their CCTV cameras as a cost saving measure.'

Walker muttered a curse and shook his head in disgust. He then lowered his eyes once again to the paper Broadhurst had given him.

Walker appeared to be studying the names on the paper and several long moments passed before he spoke. 'By the way, Paige. Did you find Anna's mobile phone?'

'Yes, I found it in the pocket of a jacket hanging up behind the front door. I left it on your desk,' she replied, 'And her laptop's there too. I tried last night but had no luck breaking into either of them.'

'Never mind. Our new DC may have more success. He's the electronics genius, according to the Superintendent,' Walker said jokingly.

Kent's face reddened but he said nothing.

'Locke appears to have been very generous with Anna,' said Walker, kindly taking the attention off Kent.

'Yes, he does,' said Broadhurst. 'During my search I found dozens of bottles of wine in his kitchen – mostly French and all expensive. I should know!' she laughed, 'I love wine but I've never been able to afford those labels. Anyway, when I asked Locke about them he said he'd bought them for Anna. It seems he only drank beer.'

'That bottle we saw in the bedroom – was that an expensive wine?' Walker asked Broadhurst.

'It was,' replied Broadhurst. 'A bottle with that label usually sells for around fifty pounds. And speaking of expensive labels in the bedroom, there are some very high-priced ones on the clothes in Anna's wardrobe.'

'Expensive wine, clothes, furnishings, and car. All for Anna – and all paid for by Locke,' said Walker. He paused and thought for a moment before saying, 'He's certainly spent a lot of money in less than a year and according to Bob Williamson that craft shop is not a highly profitable business.' Walker told them about his conversation with the desk sergeant. 'Of course, Locke may have won the pools but I think Bob would have known about that. I think we need to find out more about Mr. Locke's finances.'

'Maybe he sells something other than crafts – and maybe whatever it is has a link with Anna's murder,' said Broadhurst.

'It's a possibility,' replied Walker. He was about to say something else when they were interrupted by a knock on the panelling near the open doorway.

Constable Johnson entered and handed Walker a sheet of paper. 'Sergeant Williamson said to give you this, sir. A couple more bus travellers.'

'Thanks, Sam,' said Walker. 'By the way, did Locke notice anything missing?'

'No, sir. I told him to call the station if he does eventually find that something's been taken.'

'Good,' said Walker.

As Johnson left the room, Walker turned to the other detectives. 'Peter, I'd like you to try and get into Anna's mobile and laptop and check her recent messages and emails.'

'Yes, sir.'

'Paige, you can make some phone calls. Call the lab and see if the SOCOs found any unknown fingerprints or any other useful forensics. I'd also like you to ring Miss Richards' dentist to confirm the time she was there.' Walker paused before adding, 'Then start on the bus travellers.'

'Right, sir,' replied Paige. 'I presume you are going to visit Anna's ex-husband.'

'I am,' said Walker, rising from his chair. 'I rang him last night and arranged to meet him this morning.'

CHAPTER TEN

Richard Morris's small front yard was partly paved with grey stones and contained a tiny garden bed. The plants currently dominating this garden bed, and growing between the paving stones, were weeds. The yard was surrounded by a low brick fence that allowed the bright yellow front door to be clearly visible to all those passing by. Too visible, thought Walker, as he rapped it twice with his knuckles.

When there was no response, Walker knocked again, more loudly this time. Finally, Walker heard someone on the other side of the door say, 'Who is it?'

'Detective Chief Inspector Walker. Here to see Mr. Morris.'

Following the sound of a bolt being unlatched, the door opened slightly. A taut security chain prevented it from opening any further. From the narrow gap, a pair of very dark eyes stared at Walker's face. Walker held out his warrant card. The eyes glanced at it and then, rather anxiously it seemed to Walker, made a quick survey of the street.

'Are you Richard Morris?' asked Walker.

'Yes,' came the reply.

The door closed while the chain was detached. It was then re-opened, wider this time, by a thin, very tall, dark-haired, olive-skinned man, whose dark eyes were accompanied on his lean face by a narrow nose and a thin-lipped mouth. He was wearing jeans and a matching blue, denim shirt. He quickly stepped aside and gestured to Walker to enter. Once Walker was in the hallway the man closed and bolted the door behind him.

Walker was ushered into a living room, the neatness of which was in sharp contrast to the outside yard. It was almost a replica of the room where Walker had spoken with Locke. Here however, the colour combination was not black and white but brown and white, the combination used in the bedroom where Anna's body had been found. It was obvious to Walker that Anna had once lived here.

There was only one picture on the wall. This was a large, cubist painting where the only colours used by the artist were white, brown and a little black. This appealed to Walker. He realised that bright colours would enter the room only when the big television set was turned on.

Morris sat down in one of four, matching, dark-brown, leather chairs and waited, unspeaking, for Walker to seat himself.

'You are Anna Gruber's ex-husband are you not, Mr. Morris?' asked Walker, staring intently at the other man.

'Yes,' replied Morris, glancing briefly at Walker before turning his attention to the front window.

'Why did she call herself "Anna Gruber" and not "Anna Morris"?'

'She wanted to keep her German name. Said something about it giving her a sense of identity.' Morris continued to look towards the window.

'How did you feel about her becoming engaged to Mr. Locke?'

'Engaged?' Morris seemed surprised. He turned his dark eyes away from the window. Walker had his full attention now. 'That's rubbish! She wasn't going to marry him!' snorted Morris, screwing up his long, narrow nose. 'She still loved me and was coming back to me!' Then, scowling, he added, 'She wouldn't have left in the first place if it hadn't been for that bastard!'

'How was he responsible for her leaving?' asked Walker.

'Whenever he saw her in the street he would ask her into his place for a glass of wine and Anna could never refuse an offer of wine. They became friends and then, when we had a small, silly squabble, the next thing I know she's moved in with him.' The scowl was now replaced by a smug expression as Morris said, 'She told me a couple of days ago that she'd had enough and was coming back.'

'What was the squabble about – the one that caused her to leave you, Mr. Morris?'

'Oh, the usual thing. Money. Anna liked to spend and I didn't have much at that time.' Morris had again turned his attention to the front window.

'What do you do for a living? Is it correct that you are an artist?'

'A black and white artist. I don't use paint – I only work in pen and ink.'

'Is there much call for that type of work nowadays, Mr. Morris?' asked Walker.

'Certainly!' Morris turned his eyes back on Walker. He was clearly annoyed by the question. 'I make some money illustrating text books but I also do a little bit of advertising work and sell a few cartoons to men's magazines. I also draw a weekly comic strip for the local newspaper. It all adds up.'

'Where were you yesterday, Mr. Morris?' said Walker, abruptly changing the subject.

'I was here all day. Working.'

'Did anyone see you?'

'No. I live and work alone.' Morris was now strumming the fingers of his right hand on the arm-rest of his chair.

This man is obviously very nervous about something, thought Walker as he spoke, 'Only a couple more questions, Mr. Morris, and then I will leave you to get back to your work.'

Morris said nothing but looked sharply at Walker as if he thought the detective had italicised the word "work".

'How did you meet Anna?' asked Walker.

Morris's expression altered. His eyes again shifted from Walker's face but this time he wasn't looking anxiously at the window. His eyes now appeared to be looking at something over Walker's head and in the far distance.

'I was in Germany for a black and white artists' convention. Anna worked for the company that catered the event. She was wandering around supervising things when we met. It was love at first sight. She resigned from her job, came over to England, and we were married six months later.' He then glared at Walker and added angrily. 'And we'd still be married if it wasn't for Locke.'

Walker asked Morris a couple more questions, then thanked him for his indulgence and politely took his leave. As the yellow door closed behind him, Walker wondered what it was that was making Morris so nervous.

CHAPTER ELEVEN

Kent was tapping away on his computer's keyboard and Broadhurst was writing something in a notebook when Walker entered the incident room. He was carrying two containers of tea and two packets of sandwiches.

'Lunch, people,' he announced, handing over the food and drink.

Broadhurst and Kent thanked Walker who seated himself in Osborne's chair. As they unwrapped their sandwiches, he began informing them of his meeting with Morris.

'So, Morris said Anna still loved him and was returning,' he concluded, 'but Locke told us Anna loved him and that they were getting married. One of them must be telling porkies.'

'Unless it was Anna lying to both of them,' said Kent, after taking a sip of his tea.

Both Walker and Broadhurst looked at Kent who went on to explain, 'Anna, it seems, was romantically involved with someone else. A chap named Malcolm Cook.'

'Ah!' said Walker, 'You managed to break into her computer.'

'Yes,' replied Kent, 'There is quite a lot of romantic correspondence between Anna and this Cook.' He paused. 'Now all I have to do is find out who Cook is.'

'Good work, Peter,' said Walker.

'Thanks, sir, but there is something else. Somebody has hacked into Anna's computer before me. And quite recently.'

'It has to be Locke!' exclaimed Broadhurst.

'Very interesting,' said Walker. 'If it was Locke, and he found out about Cook, he certainly would not be very happy.'

The trio were quiet for a moment before Walker spoke again, 'How did you go with your calls, Paige?'

'Richards' dentist confirms the times she gave you, sir,' replied Broadhurst, 'and the forensics team did find one thing of interest at Locke's house. On the frame of the door leading to Locke's bedroom there was one clear set of prints that belonged to neither Locke nor Anna. It's been run through the system and you'll never guess who the prints belong to …,' Broadhurst paused for effect and then grinned. 'PC Stewart Braddock!'

'Braddock?' Walker raised an eyebrow. 'Surely he would have known better than to touch anything.'

'When he saw Anna's body he nearly fainted. He probably touched the door frame as I was helping him to sit down.'

'You were there when Braddock first saw the body? I thought that he and Johnson arrived at the house before you did.' Walker was puzzled.

'They did,' said Broadhurst. 'They responded to Locke's phone call and were the first at the scene. But apparently only Johnson went upstairs to the bedroom with Locke. When I arrived all three were downstairs. After Doctor Simons and the techs arrived, Braddock's curiosity must have gotten the better of him and he came upstairs to see Anna's body. However,' Broadhurst paused and gave a sympathetic smile, 'it seems that the sight was too much for him.'

Walker, who empathised with the young constable, said, 'Let's not tell anyone about this.' He looked directly at each of his officers before adding, 'Not even Braddock.'

Kent said, 'Yes, sir,' and Broadhurst nodded agreement.

Walker then changed the subject by asking Broadhurst about her phone calls to bus passengers.

'None of those I called provided any useful information, sir. However, just before you came in, I took a call from a woman who claims to have seen something.' She glanced at the piece of paper on her desk. 'A Mrs. Margaret Hetherington. Yesterday she was riding on the top deck of the bus travelling from the university to the river and says she saw a dark-haired man in Anna's bedroom.'

'What time was this?' asked Walker.

'She was a little vague, sir. I think it might be best if we went and spoke to her in person. She lives near the university and says she will be home all afternoon.'

'Alright,' said Walker. 'You and I will go and see her now.' He then spoke to Kent. 'Peter, find out all you can about this Cook character and then I'd like you to try and find out where Locke does his banking.' As Walker rose from his seat he added, 'We'll need to get a court order to look into his accounts. I just have the feeling he's involved in something he shouldn't be.'

CHAPTER TWELVE

Walker had no trouble finding the address. It was the last stone cottage in a row of small, similar cottages that nestled alongside the narrow road leading to the university. On one side of this cottage lay a broad, un-mowed, grass field in which two horses were silently grazing. Across the road from the field, the grass was sparser, shorter and more brown than green. Partly shaded by numerous trees, this area was the beginning of a parkland that, further along, merged with the university grounds.

Like the previous day, it was very hot. The sky was cloudless and there was no hint of a breeze. The only movement was the occasional shifting of their hooves by the horses in the field. It was also very quiet. The only sound to be heard was the distant caw of a crow.

The top of the hedge that surrounded the cottage was level with Walker's waist. This permitted the detectives to have an uninterrupted view of the front yard as they approached the gate. A lawn, which, like the hedge, was obviously professionally maintained, was broken up by a number of small circular garden beds. From all of these, nurtured by rich, weed-free soil, sprouted dozens of white roses. Their scent, mingled with that of freshly mowed grass, filled the air.

When they entered the yard they came across more white roses. They had been planted along both sides, and for the full length, of the stone path that they had to use in order to reach the front door.

The door, framed by a vine covered trellis, was opened by a short, thin woman wearing, what Walker had once heard someone call, a twin set. The dark green, woollen, matching top and cardigan, which

Broadhurst thought must have been most uncomfortable to wear on such a hot day, was accompanied by a brown woollen skirt that reached well below the woman's knees. She was also wearing a pair of brown, flat-heeled shoes and, around her neck, a strand of large, imitation pearls. With her lined face and thin, permanently curled white hair, she appeared to be in her seventies. She stared curiously at the detectives with pale, watery, blue eyes, from behind rimless, thick-lensed glasses.

'Mrs. Hetherington?' asked Walker.

'Yes, that's right. Can I help you?'

'I'm Detective Chief Inspector Walker and this is Detective Sergeant Broadhurst. Sergeant Broadhurst telephoned you earlier about your bus trip yesterday and we've come to ask you some questions.' Walker and Broadhurst showed the woman their identification.

'Oh yes! Yes!' Mrs. Hetherington's expression changed from curiosity to pleasure. 'Come in! Come in!' she cheerfully exclaimed, stepping back to allow them entry.

Both Walker and Broadhurst had to crouch down considerably in order to pass through the doorway without hitting their heads. They then proceeded to follow the woman along a dark, narrow hallway.

The room they entered was a small sitting room, made even smaller by the amount of furniture it contained. Against, or close to, the walls were cabinets, a chest of drawers, a sideboard, a bureau, a glass-fronted bookcase, and a small table supporting an equally small television set. On, or in, most of the furniture were dozens of ornaments, predominantly made of clear glass or pewter. In the centre of the room, and nearly touching the other furniture, stood a sofa, two armchairs and a round wooden coffee table. On this table sat a glass vase containing white roses. Walker suspected that without the pervading scent of the roses, the air in the room would smell quite dank. Especially as the one small window of the room looked to have been permanently closed.

Walker and Broadhurst were told to be seated by Mrs. Hetherington as she left the room.

The detectives lowered their long frames into the two armchairs, both of which had antimacassars, and settled themselves comfortably. They then allowed their eyes to roam the room in a leisurely, more detailed examination of the contents of the many cabinets.

Broadhurst suddenly emitted an obviously false gasp of shock and raised her eyebrows in an exaggerated manner. Walker saw what she was looking at, closed his eyes tightly in an equally exaggerated manner, then shook his head and laughed. He knew Broadhurst was well aware of his dislike of bright colours and so was not at all surprised by her antics. On a single shelf of the cabinet that was the focus of her attention, and contrasting sharply with the very subdued colours found elsewhere in the room, stood a row of gaudily painted Toby jugs.

Mrs. Hetherington re-entered the room carrying, with some difficulty, a large, silver tray, laden with a teapot, sugar bowl, milk and cream jugs, a container of jam, a plate of scones, empty plates, cups, knives and spoons. Walker jumped to his feet to relieve the elderly woman of her load as Broadhurst, just as quickly, jumped to her feet and moved the vase of roses to a small space on top of a nearby cabinet. Walker then carefully placed the tray on the coffee table.

Eyeing the scones, Walker decided the questions could wait awhile. He watched silently while Mrs. Hetherington poured their tea.

Broadhurst, who had obviously also been salivating at the sight of such a splendid afternoon tea, said, 'Those scones look appetising, Mrs. Hetherington. I presume you made them?'

'Thank you, dear. Yes, I did,' Mrs. Hetherington replied. 'And I mustn't forget to make some more in the morning. Harry will probably be home tomorrow and he loves my scones.'

'Is Harry your husband?' asked Walker.

'Yes. He's away on a fishing trip.'

While Walker smeared jam and cream on a scone he asked, 'You travelled down to the river yesterday on the red bus didn't you, Mrs. Hetherington?'

'Yes,' she smiled. 'I got the days mixed up. I thought Harry was due back then.'

'And you travelled on the upper deck of the bus?'

'Oh yes, I always ride up there,' said the elderly lady as she added sugar to her tea. 'You can see so much more than you can when riding downstairs.'

Walker took a bite of scone and allowed Broadhurst to ask the next question.

'You know the house in which the woman was killed, Mrs. Hetherington?' asked the sergeant.

'Oh yes. The one near the co-op with the very high hedge.'

'And from the bus you could see into the room on the second floor of that house?'

'Yes. The windows on the top floor of the bus are level with the window of that room. And the curtains are always open when I go past,' the elderly lady replied. 'The only person I usually see in there is a blond woman, but yesterday I saw a dark-haired man.'

'Are you sure it was a man?' said Walker. 'Your bus was moving.'

'The bus always slows down there because of the stop outside the co-op.' Mrs. Hetherington took a sip of her tea before continuing, 'I couldn't see a face but this person was tall. Too tall to be a woman.'

'Sergeant Broadhurst here is tall – taller than many men,' Walker pointed out.

'Well, yes,' the elderly lady conceded, 'but I'm fairly certain it was a man.'

'Do you know what time it was when you passed the house, Mrs. Hetherington?' asked Walker.

The woman took a moment to think before answering, 'No, I'm sorry. I don't wear a watch.'

'Was it morning or afternoon?' asked Broadhurst.

Mrs. Hetherington looked embarrassed. She placed her cup on the table and bent over to pick up a small crumb from the carpet before replying. 'I'm sorry. I don't know.'

The detectives glanced at each other and Walker was about to say something when the elderly woman suddenly spoke excitedly. 'Bill would know. Bill the bus driver. I spoke to him as I always do, when I got on the bus! Why don't you go and talk to him?' she said, before adding, 'The bus depot is in Flanders Street. It's not far from here.'

The detectives thanked the woman for the tea and scones and left the cottage. Once they were on the front footpath Walker asked Broadhurst for her thoughts.

'She's old, she appears to have weak eyesight, and her memory's not good. She can't remember what time she was on the bus even though it was only yesterday,' said Broadhurst.

'She's not too old to climb the bus stairs to the top deck,' said Walker, 'and I doubt she would sit up there if she couldn't see. Having weak eyes may make it necessary to wear such thick lenses but I suspect those lenses allow her to see very well. Didn't you notice how she spied that small crumb on the floor?' They climbed into Walker's car. 'Let's go and see if we can find this driver, Bill. He might be able to tell us the time of her trip.' As Walker started the car he added, 'Hopefully he will be at the depot and not out driving a bus or clocked off for the day.'

CHAPTER THIRTEEN

The bus depot was in a large, tarmacked area enclosed by a high, wire fence. It consisted of a big front yard, a huge frontless shed that resembled an aircraft hangar and, adjoining the shed, a small glass-fronted office. Walker presumed that a driveway on the other side of the shed led to employee parking. In the shed there was one red, double-decker bus that was currently receiving attention from a man in greasy overalls and in the yard were two other apparently serviceable buses awaiting drivers.

Walker and Broadhurst entered the office and showed their identification to a big, orange-haired, multi-studded woman who was sitting behind a desk operating a computer. Her body weight was such that Walker marvelled at the strength of the chair supporting her. Peering at them with intense dark eyes through spectacles that may have been borrowed from Dame Edna, she politely asked how she might help them.

'We are looking for a driver named Bill,' said Walker.

'We have two drivers named Bill,' the woman told them. 'Do you know the route of the one you're looking for?'

'He was driving between the university and the river yesterday,' Walker replied.

'Oh, that would be Bill Welsh.' The woman suddenly looked like she had placed something unpleasant in her mouth but she remained friendly as she continued speaking. 'He's the only driver on that route. You've just missed him. He's on a break at the moment and I think he's gone home. He lives nearby.'

Walker was about to ask the woman for the driver's home address when she jumped to her feet and, with surprising speed for someone of her size, brushed past them and raced to the door. She had apparently spotted the old Vauxhall that had come from the rear yard and was now slowly heading towards the front entrance.

Placing the thumb and forefinger of her right hand between her lips, the woman emitted a loud piercing whistle and the Vauxhall braked to a sudden halt.

'That's him! You've got him!' she said, obviously pleased that she was able to be of help.

Walker thanked her and the detectives walked towards the car. As they approached they could see a reddish, square-shaped face framed by the driver's window. Small, hostile, pale blue eyes watched them intently.

'Mr. Welsh?' said Walker as he reached the Vauxhall's front door.

'Yeah. Who're you?' The frowning man spoke through a lipless, down-turned mouth.

Walker didn't like the man. Holding his identification out so that it almost touched the driver's small, porcine nose, Walker said, 'I'm Detective Chief Inspector Walker and this is Detective Sergeant Broadhurst.'

'What do y' want?' said Welsh in an unfriendly voice.

Broadhurst frowned and thought to herself how much the man's personality matched his face. 'And they call us "pigs",' she muttered to herself as Walker responded to the man's question.

'We'd like to ask you some questions, Mr. Welsh,' said Walker calmly. 'Please turn off the engine and step out of your car.'

Welsh grunted, reluctantly turned off the car's ignition and opened the door. He slowly climbed from the driver's seat and stood stiffly in front of the detectives. He was short, fat, and wore a poor-fitting toupee.

'Do you know an elderly woman named Mrs. Hetherington?' asked Walker. 'We believe she was a passenger on your bus yesterday.'

'"Mad Maggie"?' Welsh suddenly appeared to relax and the ends of his thin mouth moved upwards to form what was probably a smile.

'My only half – decent passenger. Always giving me fresh cake. Treats me respectful like, but she's as mad as a hatter.'

The two detectives stared at him with bewilderment on their faces. Neither said a word.

'Ah!' said Welsh with a sneer. 'I can see you don't know her story.'

'No we don't,' said Walker. 'Why don't you tell it to us?'

'Well, several years ago her husband - Harry his name was - went out fishing in a small boat. The next day they found the boat floating upside-down a couple of miles out to sea but Harry's body was never found.' Welsh paused. 'Maggie tells herself he's still out there fishing.' He laughed. 'She goes down to the wharf every day to see if Harry's returned. She usually goes down twice a day, early morning and just after lunch.'

'And yesterday?' said Walker.

'Twice she went down to the wharf yesterday.' He shook his head and chuckled. 'Caught the eight forty-five in the morning and the one forty-five in the afternoon. She usually stays down there until I return the following trip.'

'Are you sure of the times?' Broadhurst spoke for the first time.

Welsh looked at her as if he'd been insulted. 'Of course I am. Maggie travels at the same times every day and my bus is never late.' He looked up at Walker. 'Why are you asking about her?'

Walker stared at the man for a moment without replying. He then said, 'Thank you, Mr. Welsh,' turned abruptly, and started walking away.

'Hey!' shouted Welsh. 'I know you! You were on the telly last night.' His almost invisible eyebrows rose as realisation suddenly came to him. 'You think "Mad Maggie" might've seen something from my bus! Well good luck with that,' he sniggered.

'What a waste of space he is,' Broadhurst said when they were out of earshot. 'I've met his type before. Loud-mouthed bullies who claim they've never taken a backward step but who quietly slink off when someone stands up to them. I'll bet he weakens your opposition to violence.'

Walker smiled but said nothing.

CHAPTER FOURTEEN

When they returned to the incident room, Walker went straight into his office to catch up on some paper work while Broadhurst told Kent about the visits to the witness and the bus depot.

'A nice old lady,' said Broadhurst, 'but, as we learned from her very unpleasant bus driver, she's completely away with the fairies.'

'So she can't be relied upon as a witness,' said Kent.

'I have my doubts but the DCI seems convinced she did see someone tall with dark hair in Anna's room. The problem of course is we don't know when.' Broadhurst sighed before speaking again. 'I know it's only been one day since the murder but we don't seem to be making a lot of progress.'

'Well, I've found out a couple of things,' said a grinning Kent.

Broadhurst looked at him then turned her head and summoned Walker.

'What have you got for us, Peter?' asked Walker as he joined them and sat on the absent Osborne's chair.

'Well, first of all, I've identified Malcolm Cook. He's a solicitor and his office is on the main road not far from Locke's craft shop.' He paused but continued before Walker could say anything. 'I've also located Locke's bank and had a look at his account.'

Walker interrupted. 'His account! How did –?' The inspector stopped and slowly moved his head from side to side. 'Never mind. I don't want to know.'

'There's not much money in it,' continued Kent, 'but quite a bit has been going in and out every two months in the past year. A lot of what goes out is sent by international bank draft to a company in Mexico City.' Kent looked at his note pad. 'It's called "Articulos De Arte".'

'Art supplies,' said Walker. 'Interesting. Paints, brushes, canvasses and so forth. I wonder why he has to purchase those materials from Mexico. Import costs would be high and surely it would be difficult to make a profit. I can't see him selling too many art materials from that shop anyway.' He paused for a moment, apparently lost in thought. 'I think we'll have to visit Locke's shop on some pretext and see the size of his stock of art supplies and also note what prices he puts on them.'

'If Locke is sending large amounts of money to Mexico on a regular basis for the purchase of something illegal, and not for art supplies, it seems to me that he would have visited that country at least once to establish an ongoing business connection,' said Broadhurst. 'Perhaps we should check his passport?'

'We don't want to arouse his suspicions just yet,' said Walker, 'but we could ask him for Anna's passport as part of our ongoing enquiries. If he's made any visits to Mexico in the last twelve months I doubt he would have left Anna behind.'

'I saw Anna's passport amongst her papers while searching Locke's house,' said Broadhurst, 'but I didn't check its contents. I could call in and get it from Locke on my way home tonight and bring it into work in the morning.'

'Good,' said Walker, 'and also in the morning I'd like you to attend Anna's post-mortem.' He paused before adding, 'While you're there, Peter and I will visit Mr. Locke's shop.' Walker then looked at his watch and rose from the chair. 'And now I'm going down to the pub for a big plate of roast beef and a glass of stout. Anyone want to join me?'

Kent looked a little embarrassed as he replied. 'I'd like to join you, sir, but tonight mum's making me one of her steak and kidney pies and I told her I'd be home.'

Walker smiled. 'That's okay, Peter,' he said. 'Some other time.'

'All this talk of roast beef and steak and kidney pies has made me hungry,' said Broadhurst. 'I'll join you, Inspector.'

CHAPTER FIFTEEN

As Doctor Simons prepared to carry out the second stage of the post-mortem, Broadhurst's eyes wandered slowly over the body lying face-up on the stainless steel table. Anna's nakedness, extreme paleness, lifelessness, and even the unnatural hole in her chest, had no effect on Broadhurst. She felt absolutely nothing. This had not always been the case, of course. She remembered her first post-mortem. Her reaction then had been very similar to Braddock's in Anna's bedroom.

Broadhurst had seen many corpses since joining the police force. So too, she thought, had Walker. But she had become used to them whereas Walker probably never would. She knew that a childhood experience, one that would probably be merely fascinating for most children, had been life changing for young Walker. That was why he always avoided post-mortems and sent her. And, as far as she was aware, their superiors had never reproached him.

Broadhurst looked around the room. Anna's corpse was, at that moment, the only one occupying a table. There were probably other bodies lying on stainless steel shelving behind the thick, stainless steel doors that covered one wall at one end of the room. Broadhurst looked at these doors and then at the other walls, the ceiling, the floor, and the tables. If Anna hadn't been on one of the tables, Broadhurst thought, the room would have held strong appeal for Walker. There was a total absence of bright colours.

Broadhurst's scrutiny of the room was disrupted and her attention brought back to Anna by the bright light reflected briefly from the scalpel now in Doctor Simons' gloved hand.

As the scalpel penetrated the skin, Broadhurst thought about the earlier stage of the post mortem; the removal of Anna's clothes and the scraping of her fingernails. Broadhurst was not really expecting that an examination of the clothing and scrapings would reveal DNA or other evidentiary transference. The killing appeared to have been too quick and clean. She believed the only physical contact made between killer and victim was with the weapon. She was far more optimistic about what would be learned from an examination of Anna's wound.

CHAPTER SIXTEEN

When Walker and Kent entered Locke's shop, Walker was surprised by the owner's height. At the time of the initial interview Locke had remained seated and his upper body had given no indication as to how tall he really was. Now, standing in his shop, it was revealed that he was almost as tall as Walker.

The plan was for Walker to keep Locke occupied while Kent wandered around the store and see if he could find anything even remotely suspicious. Kent's intention was, of course, to focus on the art related merchandise.

'How are you coping, Mr. Locke?' asked Walker, deliberately standing with his back towards the wool display.

'I miss her terribly. Especially at night when I'm alone in that house. It's so quiet and empty,' replied Locke sadly. He was watching, with little interest, a plump, elderly woman who had just entered the shop. He then turned his eyes to Walker and asked, 'By the way, why did you need Anna's passport? When I asked your sergeant, all she said was that you wanted to see it.'

'In an investigation like this it helps to know as much about the victim as possible,' said Walker. 'A passport not only confirms date of birth and nationality, it also tells us when the owner has left the country and to where they have travelled. In Anna's case, if she had made any recent trips to Germany, it may be that we have to look to that country to find a reason for her death.' Walker knew that he was rambling but needed to keep Locke occupied. He was trying to think of things to say. Fortunately, Locke came to his rescue.

'Are you making any progress?' Locke asked.

'Well, as a result of the television appeal, we do have a witness but that's all I can tell you at the moment,' replied Walker as he glanced to see where Kent was. 'It's still early days. We'll find the killer, Mr. Locke. That I can promise you.'

Locke lapsed into silence. His eyes looked downwards and his bushy eyebrows almost concealed his thoughtful frown. Walker, desperate to keep the conversation continuing, began asking Locke already answered questions about Anna's background and life in England.

Kent had been relieved when the plump woman had entered the shop. He had hoped that she would require the full attention of Miss Richards who, it seemed, had been keeping a close watch on him.

The assistant's interest in Kent did appear to be diverted by the customer who apparently had a number of questions to ask. Kent had finished scrutinising all the art supplies in the shop, and their prices, and was now focusing on a closed door at the back of the shop. He ambled in that direction and, when he thought the assistant's attention was on the customer, reached out and turned the door's handle.

'Can I help you, Constable?' The assistant had obviously not given all of her attention to the plump woman.

'Just looking for the lavatory,' said Kent, opening the door and making a quick study of the room. All he could see was a filing cabinet, a sink, a table and two chairs. There was no stock.

'Over there,' said the assistant, pointing to a doorway further along the wall. This doorway had no door and the fact that it led to a wash room had already been ascertained by Kent.

'Thanks,' said Kent. He closed the door to the stock room that contained no stock and began walking towards the doorway that had no door.

When he emerged from the wash room a short time later, Kent walked straight over to Walker, indicating he had finished his search.

As Walker was about to take leave of Locke, the shop owner's bushy eyebrows suddenly moved upwards and he said, 'Oh, by the way, Chief Inspector.' Locke spoke with an excitement that indicated he had just remembered something that he considered important. 'I've been meaning to call your station. I finally finished going through Anna's things and found that there is something missing. A drawing.'

'A drawing?' said Walker. He watched Locke's face closely. The excitement in Locke's voice surprised him. He sounded much less sad than he had earlier.

'Yes, an old drawing of two boys.'

'Really?' said Walker. He was more interested in drugs than drawings. Was this a "red herring"? He had no intention of being side-tracked by Locke. 'Have you looked everywhere in the house for it?'

'I haven't gone through the attic yet but I don't think Anna would have kept it there,' said Locke.

'Well, when you've completed your search, and if you still haven't found it, give me a call,' said Walker. He stared at the closed storeroom door for a moment before looking once again at Locke.

'Thank you for your time, Mr. Locke. We'll keep you up to date on our progress.' Walker then said, 'Bye for now,' and, followed by Kent, made for the exit of the shop.

When they were seated in Walker's car, Kent told Walker all that he had observed. 'Plenty of paints, brushes and canvasses. Also pencils, charcoal, paper and easels. But all reasonably priced and there is no stock out back. There's not a single box in that other room.'

'The extra stock must be kept somewhere,' said Walker. 'He probably has a lockup nearby.' Walker reached for the ignition before adding, 'I doubt very much that Anna's car is left on the street. Too valuable. I'll wager that wherever he keeps the car is where he stores his additional art supplies.'

As the Chrysler began to move away from the side of the road, Walker said to Kent, 'When we get back to the station, Peter, I'd like you to find out what property Locke owns – or perhaps rents.' Walker glanced at his watch. 'Firstly, however, I think we should get something to eat. I had a very light breakfast and I'm starving.'

CHAPTER SEVENTEEN

Broadhurst had returned from Anna's post mortem by the time Walker and Kent reached the police station. She was eager to report what she had learned.

'Anna *was* stabbed,' she said as the other detectives took their seats. 'And,' she enthusiastically informed them, 'she was stabbed with a very thin, very sharp instrument.'

'Ah! Then it could have been a knitting needle,' said Walker.

'No,' said Broadhurst. 'Whatever it was, it had a small hilt as indicated by some bruising on the skin next to the wound. Also, it tapered all the way from the hilt to the tip and, most interesting, it was neither cylindrical like a needle nor flat like an ordinary knife blade. It was square!'

'What could that be?' said a puzzled Walker.

'A medieval stiletto,' said Kent.

Both Walker and Broadhurst stared so sharply at Kent that his face reddened.

Broadhurst finally uttered what both she and Walker were wondering, 'How do you know that?'

'I've seen a picture of one,' replied Kent.

'Where?' asked Walker.

Kent's face reddened even more. He looked down at the floor as he replied. 'In a comic book.'

In anticipation of being mocked for this revelation, Kent hurried on with his explanation, 'I've been reading a series of American comic books titled "True Horror Crimes" and each issue has one full page devoted to weaponry. There's a large drawing of the weapon and information about it written underneath. One of the pictures matches perfectly what the sergeant just described. The text said that when they were first made in the late fifteenth century the cross-section shape of most blades was triangular but some were round, some were diamond shaped and some were square. I'm sure it will tell you all of that on Wikipedia.'

Broadhurst immediately swivelled her chair and started tapping on her computer keyboard but Walker continued to look at Kent. He had a look of puzzlement on his face when he spoke, 'Where did you get those comic books from, Peter? I thought all comic books with the word "horror" on their covers were banned in Britain by the "Children's and Young Person's Harmful Publications Act" of 1955.'

'Oh, you can't buy them from a newsagent,' said Kent. 'The only place you can buy them across the counter in England is in a specialist comic book shop. The one I go to is in Colchester.'

Walker sighed and shook his head slightly. Before he could say anything else, Broadhurst began speaking excitedly. 'Here it is! Peter's right! This drawing fits in with what the pathologist said exactly! It also says here that the weapon was favoured by assailants because it drew very little blood and did not leave the victim's blood on the assailant. That helps explain why there was so little blood in Anna's bedroom.' She began printing off a copy of the drawing.

'Good work, Peter,' said Walker.

'Thank you, sir.'

'What did the pathologist say was the time of death, Paige?' Walker asked, as Broadhurst attached the printed drawing of the knife to the whiteboard.

'Between eight-thirty and nine-thirty a.m.'

'Ah! That means Mrs. Hetherington could have seen the murderer,' said Walker.

'And it doesn't rule out any of our suspects. Locke, Morris, or Miss Richards,' said Broadhurst.

'No, it doesn't,' said Walker. He rose and walked over to the whiteboard. Using a black marker pen, he began writing.

Looking at what he had written, Walker began speaking. 'Time of death: eight-thirty to nine-thirty. Mrs. Hetherington's bus trips: eight forty-five and one forty-five. Richards' time of arrival at dentist: ten-thirty. Locke's opening of shop: nine o'clock. Morris's whereabouts between eight-thirty and nine-thirty: unknown.'

'Richards could have killed Anna after Locke had left for work and before she went to the dentist,' said Kent.

'Or Locke could have killed Anna before leaving to open his shop,' Walker added. 'We must remember also that these times are not exact. The buses could have been late regardless of what the driver says. Also, the times given are for when the bus left the depot. Not for when the bus passed Locke's house.'

'And Locke could also have been late opening his shop,' said Kent.

'Mrs. Hetherington may not have seen anyone on the first trip and on the second trip saw Locke when he found Anna's body,' said Broadhurst.

Walker thought for a moment before asking, 'What else did you learn at the PM, Paige?'

'Well, Anna was healthy except for her liver. That was a mess. But we have to wait for the blood test results to see just how much alcohol, or if any drugs, were in her system,' said Broadhurst. 'Also, she had not eaten for some time. There was no food in her stomach. And finally, there was no sign of recent sexual activity.'

'None of that helps us much,' said Walker.

'Oh! One other thing, sir,' said Broadhurst. 'I've had a look at Anna's passport. It's got an American visa in it and she's made two visits to the United States in the past twelve months. Both times landing at Los Angeles airport.'

'And Mexico?' asked Walker.

'Both times. She has stamps for return entry into the US.'

71

'We need to find out where Locke stores his art materials,' said Walker. 'Get onto that, Peter.'

'Yes sir,' said Kent, turning to his computer.

'By the way, sir,' said Broadhurst, 'When I called in at Locke's home last night to get Anna's passport, his assistant was there. She was in the lounge room and had a drink in her hand.'

'Well Locke told me he especially misses Anna at night when he's alone in the house,' said Walker. 'Looks like he's found a way to ease his grief.'

'Do you think they may both have been involved in Anna's murder?' asked Broadhurst.

'I don't know. They're certainly both suspects,' said Walker. He looked down at his watch. 'And speaking of suspects, you and I are now going to visit Mr. Cook. His secretary gave us an appointment for three o'clock.'

CHAPTER EIGHTEEN

The solicitor's rooms took up the entire top floor of a small, two-storeyed, grey-brick building. Access was gained by opening a clearly marked door at street level and climbing a narrow stairway. The door and stairway adjoined an optometry business that took up all of the building's remaining space on the lower floor.

Cook's secretary, who had identified herself as Mary Sutton when Walker had telephoned earlier requesting a meeting with Cook, sat behind a desk sorting through a number of folders. She looked up as the detectives entered.

'May I help you?' she enquired. She was a small, thin, plain-faced woman of indeterminate age, with straight, grey hair that just covered her ears. She wore thick-lensed, rimless glasses over hazel eyes and had a very small mouth. From what they could see of her clothing from their side of the desk, she was wearing a navy jacket over a pale blue blouse.

'I'm Detective Chief Inspector Walker and this is Detective Sergeant Broadhurst. We're here to see Mr. Cook.'

'Oh yes. Please wait a moment while I tell Mr. Cook you are here.' She rose and went to the door behind her. She knocked twice before opening the door, entered, and then closed the door behind her. Walker noted that large gold letters on the door, like on the one downstairs, clearly stated Cook's full name, university attainments, and profession.

When she emerged from Cook's office, Sutton closed the door behind her and pointed to the chairs placed against the wall opposite her desk. 'Please take a seat. Mr. Cook will see you shortly.'

Walker and Broadhurst walked over to the chairs and sat down. Broadhurst picked up one of the ancient magazines piled neatly on a side table and began flipping through the pages. Walker slowly scanned the room.

Walker became fidgety. Broadhurst had finished with the magazines and was looking towards the secretary. Miss Sutton seemed to be totally oblivious to their presence.

Walker looked at his watch. It was after three-fifteen. He had arranged to meet the solicitor at three.

'Miss Sutton,' said Walker.

At the sound of her name, the secretary quickly looked up at him. She appeared a little surprised to hear his voice.

'Does Mr. Cook have someone in there with him at present?' Walker asked.

'No,' replied the secretary.

'Is he on the telephone?'

'No.' The secretary was beginning to frown.

'Perhaps he's gone to the lavatory?'

The secretary said nothing. She was now looking flustered.

'Then we'll see him now,' said Walker. He stood up, walked past the startled woman and reached for the knob of the door leading to Cook's office. Broadhurst, trying hard to suppress a smile, followed closely.

The man sitting behind a large, mahogany desk in a thick-carpeted room had longish, side-parted, jet-black hair that Walker thought was probably dyed. He had thick lips, narrow, dark eyes, and wore black-framed glasses. These sat upon what was his most distinguishing facial feature, a rosacea, or "gin blossomed", nose.

Well, thought Walker as he stared at the nose, I can see one interest you shared with Anna.

'What do you want?' said Cook, without looking up from the papers in front of him.

When he received no response, Cook looked up. The scowling expression on his face turned to one of surprise when he realised the intruders were strangers and not his secretary. The surprise quickly became anger.

'How dare you interrupt me when I'm busy working!' he said angrily. He rose swiftly to his feet, revealing that he was very tall. It seems Anna liked her men tall and dark haired, Walker thought. And, he also thought, yet another person fitting Mrs. Hetherington's description.

Cook also had very narrow shoulders. The shoulders, plus a substantial paunch, could not be concealed by the expensive, dark, pin-striped suit he was wearing. He also wore one of those pink-striped, white-collared shirts seemingly favoured by men of the legal profession, and a crimson necktie.

'I'm busy working too,' said Walker calmly, 'and I've no time for games.'

Intimidated by Walker's stare, Cook calmed slightly. 'Well, what do you want?' he said, as he slowly resumed his seat.

Walker turned and closed the office door before speaking. 'We want to ask you some questions about Anna Gruber.' Before Cook could reply, Walker and Broadhurst sat down, uninvited, in the two plush chairs that fronted Cook's desk.

Cook glared at them for a moment and then said in a supercilious tone, 'Miss Gruber was a client and I can't reveal information given to me in confidence.'

'Anna Gruber is dead so you can, and you will, answer my questions. Either here or down at the police station.'

'How dare you speak to me in that manner!' snarled Cook. His voice had risen again. He was now sitting up very straight with his red nose getting even redder. 'I'll have a word with your superior!'

Walker had had enough. He had noticed the man wore a wedding ring so, assuming Cook's spouse was still alive, and still married to Cook, he said, 'Then I'll have a word with your wife about your relationship with Anna.'

'What are you talking about?' asked Cook. He now spoke a little less loudly and the bluster had diminished slightly. Walker knew he had assumed correctly.

'We've seen the e-mails and phone messages, Mr. Cook,' said Walker, thinking how this man must be related to the bus driver. 'If you'll calm down, lose the arrogant attitude, and answer my questions, it's possible your wife won't find out.'

Cook looked surprised and stared at them with his mouth open. Finally, he calmed down. 'Alright,' he said in a much quieter voice, 'What is it you want to know?'

'How did you meet Anna?' asked Walker as Broadhurst removed her notebook from her bag.

'I met her when she and Richard Morris came to see me about the drawing up of a marriage contract.'

'You are talking about a pre-nuptial agreement?' said Walker. 'I thought they weren't legally binding in England.'

'They're not, but it is very unusual for judges not to uphold them,' replied Cook.

'Who did this agreement favour?'

'It very much favoured Anna. Richard was the one with the assets.'

'Was it Morris's idea to have the contract drawn up?'

'No,' said Cook. 'I believe it was Anna's idea.'

'Why do you think Morris agreed to such an arrangement?' asked Walker.

'He loved Anna and she refused to marry him if he didn't sign such an agreement. She was leaving a well-paying job in Germany and wanted some guarantee of security if the marriage didn't work out.'

'Was Morris happy about the contract?'

'No,' replied Cook. 'I don't believe he was.'

'What were the exact terms of the contract?'

'I'm sorry,' said Cook, 'but that I can't tell you without Mr. Morris's permission.'

Walker decided not to push the matter any further and abruptly changed the subject. 'How did you get romantically involved with Anna?'

Cook looked down and coughed before speaking. 'When I had finished drawing up the agreement she visited this office on her own to see that it was worded to her satisfaction. We had a drink together and things went on from there.'

'So, you were having sex with Anna before she married Morris and throughout their marriage?' asked Walker.

Cook studied the top of his desk. 'Yes, but the marriage was very short-lived.'

'And your relationship with Anna continued after she moved in with Locke?'

Cook finally looked a little shame-faced. 'Yes,' he admitted.

'Were either Morris or Locke aware that Anna was having a sexual relationship with you?' asked Walker.

'Neither did, as far as I know.'

Broadhurst then spoke. 'Pardon me for interrupting, Inspector, but I would like to ask Mr. Cook a question.'

'Be my guest,' said Walker, motioning towards Cook with an open hand.

'Mr. Cook,' she began, 'When you learned that Anna had been killed, did it not occur to you that either Mr. Morris or Mr. Locke may have killed her because of her relationship with you?'

Cook was silent for a moment. 'It did,' he finally admitted. He was now studying his finger nails.

Broadhurst frowned. 'Well, don't you think you had a duty to come to us and tell us about your relationship with Anna?'

'I didn't dare tell you,' said Cook who now looked directly at Broadhurst and became very animated. 'I didn't want my wife to find out. Elizabeth's a very jealous woman. She even selected my secretary, for God's sake!'

'Well then,' said Walker as he stood up, 'Let's hope for your sake she doesn't find out.'

As Walker and Broadhurst were about to leave the room, Walker spoke again. 'Where were you on the morning that Anna died, Mr. Cook?'

'Here. In my office working.'

'Was your secretary here? Did you see clients?'

'I honestly don't recall,' said Cook. 'Ask her. She'll be able to tell you.'

Walker nodded and he and Broadhurst walked out the doorway, leaving Cook sitting gloomily at his desk.

Mary Sutton's recollection of events on the day Anna died was far better than Cook's. The secretary told the detectives that she had not arrived at work until twelve because she'd been having trouble with her dementia-suffering mother. She also informed them that Cook had had no appointments scheduled for that morning. As far as she knew he had spent the morning drawing up a will for an elderly, bed-ridden client.

When they were sitting in Walker's car Broadhurst said, 'Another tall, dark-haired suspect.'

'Yes,' said Walker. 'No alibi and, as far as motive is concerned, perhaps he feared Anna was going to tell his wife. Or, more likely, that Anna wanted to end the relationship and he didn't.'

'The messages "Superman" found on Anna's phone and computer do show that Cook's feelings for Anna were intensifying while Anna's feelings for Cook were fading,' said Broadhurst.

'So,' said Walker. 'Motives and suspects abound.'

Walker sat thinking for a moment before he turned on the car's ignition. He then eased the car out into the traffic and said, 'I'll drop you back at the station.'

'Oh,' said Broadhurst. 'Where are you going?'

'Not that it's any of your business,' said Walker with a smile, 'but I'm going home. I have an engagement.'

'Well I hope your engagement is very satisfying,' said Broadhurst, also smiling.

CHAPTER NINETEEN

'Going home, Superman?' asked Broadhurst as she met up with Kent in the police station car park.

'Yes,' said Kent, 'the DCI said I could leave early.'

'I know. I was with him when he phoned you.' Broadhurst smiled and was about to move on when she suddenly remembered something. 'By the way,' she asked. 'Did you find out where Locke might keep Anna's car?'

'I think so. Locke owns two houses. The one he lives in and another which has a garage behind it. I found out that he rents out the house but keeps the garage for himself.'

'How did you find that out?'

'A couple of phone calls.'

'Good work, Peter,' said Broadhurst. She smiled again and then turned in the direction of the police building and started walking.

'Thanks Sarge,' said Kent. 'Say – where's the chief inspector gone?'

'Home,' she said, turning her head and speaking over her shoulder without slowing her pace. 'I think he's entertaining a lady tonight.'

'Oh,' said Kent, thinking how wonderful it would be if he was entertaining a lady tonight.

'Well, bye for now. I'll see you nice and early in the morning,' said Broadhurst as she continued on her way.

'Bye Sarge,' said Kent, watching Broadhurst until she reached the entrance to the police station. He considered her to be very attractive.

He thought for a moment that he would like to be entertaining her that night.

Kent was now alone in the car park. As he walked towards his car he admonished himself for having such thoughts about Broadhurst whom he thought of as "Paige" but still addressed as "Sarge". The idea of having a relationship with her was ridiculous. Not only was she senior to him in rank, she was also a couple of years older. Anyway, she probably had a boyfriend. And why would she, or any other girl for that matter, be interested in him? He had an old car, wore cheap clothes, was overweight, lived with his mother, and most people considered him to be a nerd.

As he opened the door of his old Saab, Kent thought about improving himself. He would upgrade his car and get himself some nice clothes. He could afford it. The small cottage in which he lived was owned, mortgage-free, by his mother and she would not allow him to pay rent. His only expenses, apart from petrol, were gas and electricity, which, in spite of his mother's objections, he insisted on paying. And he'd lose some weight. That would be difficult, he realised, as he thought of his mum's cooking. He'd just have to go to the gym. It had been a while since he'd done any serious exercise.

Kent also knew that he might not be considered a nerd if he spent less time sitting down at a computer and more time outdoors, particularly at work. He resolved to change things. He would start tonight.

CHAPTER TWENTY

Walker had shaved and showered and was now dressed in freshly washed, tight fitting jeans and a polo shirt. The shirt was light grey. Walker had smiled when he selected the shirt. He liked the colour grey because it reminded him of the scenery that had surrounded his childhood home. But he wasn't obsessed by it. He continually chose to wear the colour because he found it very satisfying to maintain the public image it had accidentally helped create. Contrary to what he knew many thought, he was not displeased with the nickname that had become associated with this image. He was actually pleased because of the social visibility it provided; a visibility he had so desperately wanted as an unseen child.

Walker's childhood had not been altogether unhappy but it had been lonely. His parents had both been writers and, not long after the birth of their only child, had moved from England to an old, isolated, stone house in the Scottish Highlands. There had been no other children living nearby and no school which he could attend. He had been educated at home by a visiting tutor but this man had been very reserved and spoke to the young Walker only when giving him lessons.

Walker's parents had also seldom spoken to him. They had been absorbed by their work and left their young son to his own devices. He had even eaten alone, in a room that his parents rarely entered. The food had been prepared by an elderly, surly woman who lived in a nearby farmhouse and who called into their house three times a day. She had not spoken to Walker when serving him his meal. The only sounds Walker could recall from his childhood were the old songs that had been occasionally played on a record player and had echoed softly throughout the house.

Outside the house, the mountainous surroundings had seemed to be constantly shrouded by mist; a moist fog that made everything seem grey. It also made everything very wet; a wetness which limited the opportunities for Walker to venture outdoors and explore. This limitation had increased the area's allure for an inquisitive young boy.

Then had come the discovery of the fawn. Walker had been ambling through an unfamiliar, dense, and particularly green, forest on one of the dryer days when he'd stumbled upon a young deer, laying wide-eyed and motionless on the grass. It was dead but totally unmarked. Walker had stood beside it for what seemed an eternity, unable to turn his eyes away. He had been overcome by an unbeliev-able sense of despair.

Eventually the young Walker had returned to his home. The discovery of the fawn had not lessened the attraction of his immediate surroundings but it had made him determined to never again enter that particular forest.

Spending considerable time indoors because of the weather, the young Walker had filled his leisure hours with reading. And he had continued with this pastime until he had read every book that was in the house's huge library. There was fiction – literary classics ranging from "The Adventures of Tom Sawyer" to "Wuthering Heights" – and non-fiction – text books covering every subject from anthropology to zoology, with a special emphasis on history. Perhaps surprisingly for a young boy, Walker found particular enjoyment in reading the history books.

Not surprisingly, Walker had had no difficulty being admitted to Oxford to read history. And because he had already accumulated much of the knowledge required for passing his courses, Walker found that he had time for other pursuits. He had been attracted to Rugby because it was a team sport and satisfied his long yearned for interaction with other males of his age. He was already very tall but a little lean for playing contact sport. So he had been very pleased when one of his teammates had introduced him to the weight room and power lifting. He soon discovered that this type of training, combined with a large intake of meat, eggs and dairy products, created the size and strength necessary for survival on the rugby field.

Involvement in sport however, eventually began to interfere with Walker's studies. He'd been awarded a Bachelor's degree with honours but his Master's was not distinguished enough to allow him to pursue a PhD. When he'd first entered university, he'd had thoughts about lecturing at a university. His Masters however, was only good enough for teaching in schools. And he had no desire to follow that career path.

Walker had then decided to join the police force. He considered policing a respectable and exciting profession, fairly well-paid and with opportunity for advancement. It would also allow him to spend time outdoors. For him this was the profession's major attraction. What he hadn't considered was the occasional contact the job would give him with the dead. At that time he had not yet become aware of the psychological effect of his earlier discovery of the fawn.

Walker's parents were both deceased by the time he graduated from Oxford. It turned out that neither had been very successful as a writer and the old house carried a heavy mortgage. He had not inherited much. There were the books, but most of these he had sold rather than attempt to transport them to his Oxford flat. The only other thing left to him had been his mother's unused cutlery set.

Some of his mother's cutlery, and his recently purchased serviettes and placemats, were now laying in their appropriate places on Walker's small dining room table. A chicken was browning nicely in the oven and vegetables were cooking on the hob. Walker stood and looked through the large kitchen window at his tree-filled, but flower-free, back yard. Through the trees, and beyond his low fence, he glimpsed Crockleford Heath. He loved this cottage. He purchased it not long after his divorce and when he had first been transferred to Essex. It had a mortgage but this would hopefully be paid off by the time he retired.

Walker thought of his divorce. He had married not long after leaving university and soon after entering the police force. The marriage had been brief. He had nothing in common with his ex-wife and they had produced no children. He had not seen or heard from her in years. He thought of the few relationships he had been involved in since his divorce. None of these had been very satisfying and none had lasted very long, the last one ending over two years ago. This time however, he believed things would be different.

Jenny Haysom worked in the Essex University library. That was where Walker had met her. She was tall, slender, and very pretty. She had long, brown, wavy hair, blue eyes and a smile that, when offered to Walker, made him feel like an infatuated schoolboy. It also turned out that, apart from a fondness for crime fiction, the reading of which Walker considered to be a complete waste of time, she shared his interest in history and lack of interest in music.

Perhaps because of his early life, Walker's interests had always been visual rather than auditory. He did own a small CD player but very few CDs and all of these contained pre-Beatles songs from the late 1950s and early 1960s. He tended to play them only when he had company and then only very softly as a background to conversation. This was the music that had been played in his childhood home and he often wondered if his purchase of these CDs had been motivated by nothing more than nostalgia.

Walker's thoughts returned to Jenny. They had been seeing each other socially for only two weeks. They had been to a restaurant and an art gallery but neither one of them had yet been inside the other's house. This evening however, Jenny was visiting his home for dinner. And hopefully, thought Walker, for something more. So far, the only intimacy between them had been a shaking of hands and, following their second outing, Walker had given her a brief peck on the cheek.

He did not for a moment believe that Jenny lacked passion. She was obviously waiting for him to make the first move. That he hadn't yet done so was due to an unfamiliar awkwardness on his part; an awkwardness that, he surmised, was due not only to his long period of solitude, but also to the awesome effect Jenny had upon him. Since the first time he had seen her he had fantasised about them spending an entire night together. And, thought Walker now, tonight could be the night.

Walker's excitement was suddenly increased by the sound of the front door bell. He hurried down the hallway and was immensely pleased by what he saw when he opened the door. Jenny, wearing a white, short-sleeved top, blue jeans and a broad smile, was carrying two bottles of wine. She had driven to his place and Walker knew that she would not drive home after drinking. Tonight, would be the night.

CHAPTER TWENTY-ONE

It was nearly midnight when Kent drove down the main road of Wivenhoe. He passed Locke's house, which he recognised by its tall hedge, and noted that there were no lights showing from the second floor. Locke may have gone out or perhaps he was in bed asleep.

Kent passed the dimly lit co-op and then saw the yellow front door of Morris's house. It was illuminated by the bright street light. Two doors further down, this block of semi-detached houses ended. It was separated from the next block by a narrow road.

The Saab turned into this road and immediately slowed. The speed indicator dropped further as Kent again turned left and eased his car into a narrow lane running parallel to the main road.

The car had just passed the rear of the co-op when Kent turned off the headlights, applied the brake and shut down the engine. He could see a faint light emanating from what was probably an open garage doorway about one hundred and fifty metres ahead and on the left side of the lane.

Telephone calls to the Lands Department and to local real estate agents had proved enlightening. So too had a map on the internet. The semi-detached houses on the main street all had back yards bordering the lane until they neared the area where Locke's shop was located. The last half dozen or so houses located just before the business buildings had rear lock-up garages instead of back yards. As Kent had told Broadhurst, he had learned that Locke owned one of these properties and that, although he had rented out the house, he had kept the garage for his own use.

Kent stepped out onto the tarred surface of the lane. He eased the door back until it was almost closed and left it resting against the catch. Whoever was up ahead in the garage probably hadn't seen his car's lights, but in the still night air they would almost certainly hear the noise of a slamming car door.

It was still very warm and Kent was aware of perspiration trickling slowly down his back as he slowly moved forward. Apart from the illumination coming from the garage, the lane was in complete darkness. Kent felt safely concealed from the eyes of anyone who might emerge from the garage.

As Kent came close to the open garage door, the first thing he saw was the tail end of Anna's red Porsche. He could hear the slight sounds of movement coming from inside the garage, apparently from the rear.

Kent eased his head around the edge of the doorway. The source of the light was a bulb attached to a black rubber cord hanging from the rear wall. He could see the back of a dark-haired head bobbing around under the light. The owner of this head was obviously crouched down as his or her body was concealed by the Porsche. This unknown person was responsible for the sounds of movement.

Kent inched forward a little more. He noted that along the rear wall, stacked high, were a number of large, cardboard cartons. He was trying to read the printing on the white label attached to one of the boxes, when he heard a faint sound behind him. Before he could turn his head, he felt a short, intense pain and darkness overwhelmed him.

CHAPTER TWENTY-TWO

The sound of birds chirping outside his bedroom window awakened Walker. Laying on his back, he opened his eyes to see a room full of bright sunlight. He was momentarily puzzled because usually when he woke it was still dark. Then he became aware of the faint scent of perfume and his confusion evaporated. He turned his head and saw the beautiful face, wide-eyed and smiling at him.

'Good morning, Detective Chief Inspector Walker. I trust you slept well.'

Walker smiled back. 'I certainly did. And not surprisingly.' He could feel himself becoming aroused. This surprised him considering the amount of activity they had engaged in during the night.

'I'm pleased to hear you are refreshed,' Jenny said, watching the bed-sheet rise above Walker's pelvic region. She added, 'I can see you are ready to resume where we left off in the early hours of the morning.'

Walker laughed and then emitted a sudden gasp as, under the sheet, Jenny's moving hand reached its objective.

'I must say that if we ever go camping we won't need to take a tent-pole.' Jenny spoke softly and Walker saw her moistening her lips with her tongue before her head disappeared under the sheet.

CHAPTER TWENTY-THREE

It was eight o'clock. Walker was later than usual arriving at work but he didn't care. As he stepped from his car onto the surface of the police station's car park he imagined that the earth's gravitational pull had considerably lessened. Throughout the drive from home he had not been able to stop smiling. He was happy, almost euphoric. He should be focusing on the case but all he could think about was Jenny. Obviously, he laughingly mused, his brain had released a lot of dopamine.

Upon entering the police station both Walker's smile and thoughts of Jenny disappeared. A short, plump woman, wearing a plaid skirt and, despite the growing heat, a maroon cardigan, was standing in the foyer with Broadhurst and the desk sergeant. Although the woman had her back towards Walker, it was obvious she was very distressed. Bob Williamson, whose head was in profile, appeared extremely concerned. And Broadhurst, who was facing him, wore an expression that closely resembled panic.

'Chief Inspector!' called Broadhurst when she spotted him. 'Peter's missing!'

The plump woman quickly turned to face him. Her long grey hair was pinned up but a couple of strands had come loose. They fell down across her round, tear-stained face. When Walker came close to the woman, her blue, tear-filled eyes stared up at him in a manner that suggested she believed he was the Messiah.

'Chief Inspector Walker! Thank God!' she exclaimed. 'You'll find him!'

Broadhurst introduced the quietly sobbing woman as Peter's mother and repeated to Walker what she and Williamson had just been told, 'Peter went out last night but didn't return home.'

Walker placed a hand under Mrs. Kent's elbow and guided her towards the chairs that lined one wall of the police station foyer. He then turned to Broadhurst and asked an obvious question, 'Have you tried his mobile?'

'Yes, but it's apparently been turned off.'

Walker sat down beside Mrs. Kent and softly said, 'Now tell me everything about last night.'

'After we had our dinner and washed up we sat down to watch television as we do every night. Peter had been very quiet at dinner and I noticed he seemed a bit restless while we were watching the telly.' She paused and wiped her nose with a small white handkerchief. 'When I asked him if anything was wrong he said that you were working on a very difficult case and that he felt he wasn't doing enough to help. It was now our bedtime but instead of going to bed, Peter got his coat and said he was going out. When I asked him where he was going, he said there was something he had to look at for you, Chief Inspector.' She gave a small sob and then said, 'Then he left and I haven't seen him since!'

'Ah!' Broadhurst suddenly spoke excitedly. 'I bet I know where he went. The garage!'

'What garage?' Walker asked. He was puzzled.

'The garage where Locke keeps Anna's car!'

Walker quickly stood up. 'What's the address?'

Broadhurst immediately looked unhappy. 'I don't know,' she said. Then her eyes widened as her excitement returned. 'Maybe he's got it on his desk!'

For such a big man, Walker could move very quickly when he felt he had to. Before Broadhurst could utter another word, he was half way down the corridor.

Having only been with them for a couple of days, Kent had, fortunately, not yet managed to acquire too much clutter on his desk.

Walker noted that Kent's notebook was not there but did find a piece of paper on which there was doodling. A row of squares had been drawn on one side of two parallel lines. The first square contained the letter "S", another square further down the row contained the letter "G", and the final square contained the letter "H". Walker stared at the drawing and thought hard. Then, suddenly, realisation struck him. This was a map and the letters made sense. The "H" square was Locke's house, the "S" was Locke's shop, and the "G" was Locke's garage. He raced out of the incident room.

CHAPTER TWENTY-FOUR

The Chrysler was travelling well above the speed limit. A grim-faced Walker was driving and an anxious Broadhurst was sitting next to him, clutching her seat belt. A moist-eyed Mrs. Kent was perched nervously in the rear with both hands gripping the back of Broadhurst's seat. Walker had not spoken a word since he had hurriedly ushered the two women into his car at the police station but, as the Chrysler swerved left off the main road and into the narrow side street, Broadhurst guessed where they were going. The lane into which the car now veered was the lane that had been searched for a murder weapon three days earlier.

They all lurched forward as Walker brought his car to a sudden halt. Directly in front of them, and only a few metres away, was Kent's Saab. It was standing where Kent had left it the previous night, far enough out from the bordering fence to prevent Walker's Chrysler from making any further progress along the lane.

Walker and Broadhurst quickly climbed out of Walker's car while Mrs. Kent struggled with the Chrysler's rear door handle. Walker made a cursory inspection of the Saab. Then, without speaking, he turned and sprinted along the lane. Broadhurst took hold of Mrs. Kent's arm as the two women followed him.

Walker soon found out what Kent had learned. He saw that, while most of the main road's semi-detached houses had rear yards adjoining the lane, those up near Locke's shop had lock-up garages. One of these, Kent had discovered, belonged to Locke. But which one?

Walker saw Kent before he had passed the second garage. Kent was lying quite still, on his side, partly concealed by a garbage bin. The hair at the back of his head was matted by what was obviously congealed blood.

Walker crouched down and was examining Kent's wound when Broadhurst and Mrs. Kent finally arrived.

'Is he alive?' Mrs. Kent gasped. 'Oh please God, let him be alive.'

The quietly sobbing woman dropped to her knees next to her son. She was now close enough to hear what Walker had heard moments before. The sound of gentle snores.

When Mrs. Kent began gently stroking her son's cheek his eyes suddenly opened. They opened wider when he saw the three faces staring down at him. Then he felt the pain at the back of his head. Uttering a low groan, he briefly closed his eyes again.

Kent raised himself onto one elbow and, with the hand of his other arm, sought the source of his pain. He grimaced as his fingers made contact with the wound.

Kent's eyes shifted and he took in his surroundings. Memory of events of the previous night quickly returned. He looked up at Walker and said, 'There were several large cardboard boxes at the back of the garage, sir. And someone with dark hair was kneeling down in front of them. The Porsche stopped me seeing who it was or what they were doing.' He grimaced again. 'I remember trying to get closer and then I heard a noise behind me. That's all I remember. Someone must have snuck up and hit me hard.'

'We have to get you to the hospital, Peter,' said Walker.

'I'll be okay, sir. It's only a headache.'

'Nevertheless,' said Walker firmly. 'You're going to the hospital. You may have concussion.'

'I've found something, sir.' Broadhurst had lifted the lid and was looking inside the garbage bin. She then put on gloves, reached into the bin and pulled out half of a house brick. The red stain that could clearly be seen on one end was obviously blood.

'Good,' said Walker. 'You've found the assault weapon.'

'Yes, but it's unlikely we'll be able to get any prints off it,' said Broadhurst.

'That doesn't matter,' Walker said. 'Bag it.'

Walker turned to Kent. 'Which garage is the Porsche in, Peter?'

Kent indicated the one on the other side of the garbage bin. It was now closed and secured with a large padlock.

'Give Sergeant Broadhurst the keys to your car, Peter,' said Walker.

Kent sat up and, without saying anything, searched for his keys.

Walker then turned to Broadhurst and said, 'Bring the Saab up here please, Paige, and drive Peter and his mother to the hospital.'

Broadhurst nodded, took the keys from Kent, and began walking back towards the cars.

Mrs. Kent was now sitting next to her son on the narrow curb at the side of the lane. She was examining her son's wound. Walker watched them for a moment and then said, 'You two wait here,' before hastening to catch up with his sergeant.

'What are you going to do, sir?' Broadhurst asked when she realised that the inspector was now beside her, matching her brisk stride.

'I have to get something from the boot of my car.'

Broadhurst glanced at him. 'You're not going to do what I think you're going to do, are you, sir?'

'Why not?' replied Walker. 'A policeman has been assaulted so this is a crime scene. I don't think I need a magistrate's permission to look in Locke's garage. Anyway,' he grinned, 'I'm pretty certain it was open when we arrived.'

Broadhurst gave a little smile and a slight shake of her head but said nothing. She was reaching for the handle of the Saab's open front door when Walker spoke again. 'After you've taken Peter and his mum to the hospital, meet me at Locke's shop.'

Walker was about to move on to his car when he stopped. He'd had another thought. 'On the way back from the hospital, Paige, call in at the station and get Constables Johnson and Braddock to come to Locke's shop in the van.'

As Broadhurst drove up the lane to pick up Kent and his mother, Walker found what he was looking for in the Chrysler's boot. He didn't know what it was called. All he knew was that it was normally used to remove a hubcap when changing a flat tire. This should do the job, thought Walker as he balanced the iron tool in his hand.

It took considerable effort to break the padlock. When it finally snapped, Walker tossed it aside and opened the garage door. He looked around. There wasn't much to see. The Porsche was there and Walker could see the now extinguished light globe hanging on the back wall behind it. The light globe was however the only object at the rear of the garage. As Walker had expected, the cardboard boxes were no longer there.

CHAPTER TWENTY-FIVE

Walker stood aside so that a middle-aged woman wearing a bright floral sun dress could exit the shop. She was of average height, solid, wore her bluish grey hair tightly curled and had a round face that, to Walker, was very familiar. Where did he know her from? A frustrated Walker unsuccessfully pressured his memory.

'Why, hullo Chief Inspector. Fancy seeing you here!' She leaned towards him conspiringly and said softly, 'I'd love to stop and have a chat with you but I'm running late for work. I've been talking for too long already to those lovely people in the shop.' She laughed, shifted the parcel she was carrying under her arm, and said, 'I'll see you later,' as she scurried away.

'Bye, Doris!' said Walker, mentally kicking himself. As soon as she had spoken her first words he had recognised her as the woman who usually served him in the station canteen. Previously he had only seen her in a white hat and white coat.

When Walker entered the craft shop both Locke and his assistant were at the front counter.

'Good morning, Mr. Locke, Miss Richards,' said Walker pleasantly. 'I see Doris is one of your customers.'

'A very good customer,' said Locke. He was smiling; something Walker hadn't seen him do before.

'And a very good talker,' Walker said, smiling back at Locke.

'Yes, when she comes in she always stays quite a while.' Locke laughed for a moment and then spoke to Walker with a more serious expression on his face.

'How may I help you, Chief Inspector?' he asked, 'Or have you come to give us a progress report?'

'One of the reasons I'm here, Mr. Locke,' replied Walker, turning his expression serious also, 'is because Detective Constable Kent was assaulted last night outside your garage.'

Locke and Richards both seemed genuinely surprised and Locke, whose bushy eyebrows had momentarily risen very high, said, 'I'm sorry to hear that, Chief Inspector.'

'You both seem surprised,' said Walker. 'Is that because you didn't know the assaulted man was a policeman? Or is it because you thought we didn't know the location of your garage?'

Locke was about to speak when Walker continued, 'And would you also be surprised, Miss Richards, if the fingerprints on the bloodied piece of brick we found in the garbage bin turned out to be yours?'

Richards' face paled. She remained silent for a moment but soon reacted to Walker's intense stare.

'How did you know it was me?'

'I didn't, but it was an easy guess. There were two people at the garage last night. I figure your boss was the one inside lifting boxes. And as you two seem to be "joined at the hip", as the expression goes, it's easy to figure out who was outside giving my sergeant a whack on the head.'

'I didn't know he was a policeman,' she blurted out. 'I thought he was a thief – someone intending to steal the Porsche!'

'Then why didn't you call the police after you knocked him unconscious?'

'I panicked – I thought I had killed him. Is he alright?'

'Hopefully he will be fine,' said Walker. 'But you will be charged with the assault of a police officer. There will be some other officers here soon and one of them will formally arrest you and escort you to the police station.'

Richards appeared to stumble. She reached for a nearby stool and rather shakily sat down. She raised her hands to cover her face.

Walker turned to face Locke. 'The other reason I'm here, Mr. Locke, is to find out what happened to the cardboard boxes that were in your garage last night.'

Locke looked startled for a moment but quickly composed himself. 'Oh, they're in the back room, Chief Inspector. They contain stock for the shop.'

'Would you mind showing me?'

Locke replied with a confidence that both puzzled and disturbed Walker. 'Not at all, Chief Inspector. I'd be very happy to do so.'

Walker was about to insist that Richards join them when the front door opened and Broadhurst entered the shop. She was followed by Johnson and Braddock. Walker silently hoped that he had not requested the presence of the two constables needlessly.

'Hello, Sergeant,' said Walker. 'You were quick.'

'I dropped Kent and his mother at the hospital's front door. He's steady on his feet.'

'Good,' said Walker. 'Miss Richards here has admitted assaulting him. Please bring her with you to the store room.' He then spoke to the uniformed officers, 'You men wait here and don't allow anyone else to enter the shop.' Finally, he turned to face Locke and gestured for the shop owner to lead the way to the storeroom.

Walker counted seven large boxes. Each carried a label showing they originated in Mexico.

'Why go to the trouble and expense of importing your art supplies all the way from Mexico, Mr. Locke?' Walker asked politely.

'The bristles on Mexican brushes are finer and better secured than those on any other brushes and the paint is much smoother than paint from other countries. I like to stock the best, Chief Inspector.'

Walker instructed Locke to open all of the boxes. Locke removed a Stanley knife from his pocket, extended the blade and cheerfully obeyed. When the boxes were open, Walker took the knife from Locke and passed it to Broadhurst. He then proceeded to examine the boxes' contents.

The contents of all boxes were identical. Each contained an almost equal number of paint tubes and paint brushes; a large number. The smell of something resembling turpentine was quite strong.

Walker randomly selected a tube of paint from each box, removed each cap and, without hearing any protest from a smiling Locke, squeezed. From all of the tubes oozed only paint.

Walker was wondering what he would do next when an image entered his mind. He quickly walked to the door and asked Constable Braddock to bring him one of the paint brushes that was on display. Locke's smile diminished.

Braddock entered and handed Walker a brush. The constable then returned to the shop and Walker removed another brush from one of the boxes. Walker held the two brushes side by side and examined them. He didn't have to look too closely. The brush taken from the box had a handle that was noticeably fatter than the handle of the brush from the shop display.

Walker tightly held the handle of the fatter brush with one hand and, with the fingers of his other hand, grasped the bristles and pulled. When the bristles separated, Walker tossed them aside and up-ended the handle over his open palm. White powder poured from inside the handle. Locke's smile had by now completely vanished.

Walker crossed to the storeroom door and called out to Constable Braddock, 'Stewart, go out to the van please, and get me the portable lab.'

'Now for some "presumptive testing",' said Walker when Braddock had returned and handed him the kit.

After placing some of the white powder from the paint brush in a test tube, Walker mixed in some cobalt and covered the mixture with sulphuric acid. He then added hydrochloric acid, sealed the tube, and gave it a good shake. The contents of the tube turned a bright blue.

Handing the test tube to Braddock, Walker said, 'That will have to go to the lab for "confirmative testing" but there seems to be little doubt that the powder in these brushes is cocaine.'

Walker turned to Locke and said, 'David Locke, I'm arresting you for the illegal possession of a Class "A" drug.'

Locke was told to turn around and place his hands behind his back. As Walker attached handcuffs to Locke's wrists he said, 'You do not have to say anything but it may harm your defence if you do not mention, when questioned, something which you later rely on in court. Anything you do say can be given in evidence.'

Walker then addressed Broadhurst. 'Arrest Miss Richards for the same offence – and for assaulting a police officer. Then handcuff and caution her.'

Walker walked over to the doorway and summoned Johnson.

'You and Stewart can load these boxes into the van and take them to the police station, Sam,' he said when Johnson reached the storeroom. 'And please lock up the shop when you leave.'

Walker was about to say something to Broadhurst when his mobile phone rang. Pulling it from his inside pocket he held it to his ear. As he listened his expression became grim. Finally, he spoke. 'I'll be there in ten minutes.'

As Walker returned the phone to his pocket, he said to the two constables, 'A change of plan. After you men have loaded the van, one of you take it back to the police station. The other officer can accompany DS Broadhurst while she delivers Mr. Locke and Miss Richards to the station.' He paused and turned to face Broadhurst. 'When Locke and Richards have been processed, Sergeant, and the van has been emptied, I want you and the two constables to meet me at Cook's office. There's been another murder.'

CHAPTER TWENTY-SIX

The secretary was standing by her desk crying into a handkerchief when Walker entered the reception area.

'In there, Chief Inspector,' she sobbed, pointing to Cook's office.

Cook was laying on his back on the floor behind his desk. Walker, now wearing gloves and booties, forced himself to look at the body. He knew that he would soon be feeling extremely sad.

Walker began his survey with the face. Cook wore the same expression of amazement that Walker had seen on Anna's face. His eyes were wide open and so too was his mouth. His lips formed a perfect "O". His stabbing, like Anna's, had obviously come as a complete surprise.

Walker turned his eyes downward and looked at the torso. Cook's suit jacket was open and there was a small circle of blood on his shirt, just below the left side of his chest. In the centre of this circle was a small hole. Walker noted, upon very close inspection, that the edges of torn shirt surrounding this hole were pointing outwards.

Walker knelt and felt for a pulse. He didn't expect to find one. He knew Cook was dead.

Walker stood and looked around the office. He saw that Cook had a small safe. He and Broadhurst had not noticed it on their previous visit because it was low against the wall and concealed by the desk. The safe was the type that was opened with a key. The key was in the lock and the door of the safe was open.

There was noise coming from the reception area and Walker saw that the pathologist and scene of crime officers had arrived.

Doctor Simons and two men, all wearing white coats, blue gloves and blue booties, entered the room. Simons greeted Walker and knelt beside Cook's body. She placed a hand under Cook's jaw.

'I can tell you he hasn't been dead long, Chief Inspector. He's quite warm,' said Simons. 'I'd say he died no more than two hours ago.'

Walker looked at his watch. It was just after twelve.

After photographs had been taken, including close-ups of the hole in Cook's shirt, Simons unbuttoned the shirt and exposed Cook's chest.

'This looks almost identical to the wound on Anna,' said Simons. 'The post-mortem will determine if it was made by the same weapon.' She looked up at Walker. 'It's up to you, of course, to determine if it was made by the same person.'

Walker nodded, thanked Simons and walked out to the reception area. Broadhurst and Constables Braddock and Johnson had arrived. Walker instructed Johnson to place crime scene tape across the office doorway and told Braddock to return down the stairs and prevent media members from entering the building. Broadhurst was consoling the still weeping secretary.

'When did you find Mr. Cook's body, Ms. Sutton?' Walker asked.

'Oh, about an hour ago. I didn't come into work until about an hour ago. I placed my mother in a nursing home this morning.' She sobbed once loudly and then wiped her nose with her handkerchief before continuing. 'When I arrived, his office door was open and I could see his legs sticking out from behind his desk.'

'Did you go into the room?'

Sutton nodded and, sobbing softly, said, 'Yes.'

'Did you touch the body?'

'No.'

'Did you notice anybody leaving the building as you were arriving?' asked Walker.

Sutton stopped sobbing and stared up at Walker. 'As a matter of fact, I think I did!' she exclaimed. 'I had to park my car a fair way down the road and as I was walking here I thought I saw someone come out of this building and walk in the opposite direction.'

'Can you describe the person?'

'I'm afraid I'm very short-sighted. All I can say is that the person was wearing dark clothing.' Sutton paused before adding, 'Of course, he could have been coming out of the optometrist's office.'

'He?' said Broadhurst.

'Well, I think it was a man. This person was very tall.'

'Was this person carrying anything?' asked Walker.

'I'm sorry,' Sutton replied, 'I couldn't see.' She began sobbing again.

They were interrupted by the arrival of an imperious woman who belied Sutton's statement correlating height with gender. This woman was very tall. She was also wearing dark clothing; a black, tight-fitting trouser suit that accentuated her slimness. Her hair, which was also black, was straight and cut short. She had large dark eyes and high cheek bones, and Walker thought that he might have labelled her a "handsome woman" if not for what seemed like a permanent scowl on her face. She commanded the secretary to tell her what was happening.

Before Sutton could reply, Walker spoke. 'May I ask who you are, Madam?'

'I'm Mrs. Cook,' she said arrogantly. 'And who are you?' She apparently did not realise that Walker and Broadhurst were detectives.

Walker introduced himself and showed the woman his credentials.

'What are you doing here?' she asked demandingly.

'We have some bad news,' said Walker. 'Would you like to take a seat?' He gestured towards the chairs.

'No. I'd prefer to stand. And I'll ask again. What's happening?'

Walker gave a slight shrug of his shoulders and said quietly, 'I'm sorry to have to tell you this, but your husband is dead.'

'What?'

'Your husband is dead, Mrs. Cook. He's been murdered.'

The woman blinked once and then, in a steady voice, said, 'Where is he?' She then looked towards Cook's office for the first time and moved as if to enter.

Broadhurst immediately blocked her path and said, 'I'm sorry Mrs. Cook. You can't go in there. It's a crime scene.'

The woman suddenly lowered her head and began crying. Broadhurst took her arm and guided her over to the chairs.

'I'm terribly sorry for your loss, Mrs. Cook, but we must ask you some questions,' said Broadhurst.

The woman, who was now seated, nodded as she removed a handkerchief from her small handbag and wiped her eyes. She had stopped crying.

'When did you last see your husband, Mrs. Cook?' Broadhurst asked as she seated herself next to the woman.

'When he left the house for work this morning.'

'What time was that?'

'About a quarter to nine.'

'And why have you come to the office now?'

'Because my husband was going to take me to lunch.' She began crying again.

Broadhurst looked up at Walker and raised her eyebrows. He nodded. He had some questions.

'Did your husband have any enemies, Mrs. Cook?' Walker asked as he sat on the other side of the woman.

'Not that I know of.'

'What about his clients? Do you know if he was having problems with any of them?'

'He never spoke about work,' she said as she wiped her eyes again.

'Did your husband ever mention Anna Gruber?' asked Walker.

'The woman who was murdered? No, he never mentioned her.' Mrs. Cook suddenly turned her head and looked directly at Walker. 'Wait a moment! Do you think the person who killed her is the same person who killed my husband?'

Walker didn't reply. He stood and walked over to the secretary's desk. She had stopped sobbing but was looking very glum.

'What about you, Ms. Sutton? Did you know Anna?' Walker asked.

'I met her years ago when Mr. Cook drew up a pre-marriage contract for her and her husband.'

'Has Mr. Morris been back here since Mr. Cook drew up the marriage contract?'

'Yes. He's been here several times since then.'

'Oh? And why was that?'

'Mr. Cook handled Mr. Morris's divorce from Anna Gruber.'

'He represented Morris in his divorce from Anna?' Walker was surprised. Cook hadn't mentioned that.

'Yes.'

'And were there any problems?'

'Well they were always arguing,' said Sutton. 'But Mr. Cook argued with most of his clients and they all kept coming back.'

'What about phone calls and letters from other clients? Any angry ones? Anyone making a threat against Mr. Cook?'

Sutton shook her head. She then said, 'There were probably a lot of people who disliked him. He could be brusque and arrogant but I doubt anyone would kill him for that.'

You'd be surprised, thought Walker. He said, 'So you know of no-one who's troubled him lately?'

'Only you, Chief Inspector.' She tried to smile but failed.

Walker smiled and then asked her another question, 'Did you open or touch the safe after you found Mr. Cook's body?'

'No.'

'Were you surprised to see it was open, Ms. Sutton?'

'I didn't notice it was open,' Sutton replied. 'When I saw the blood on his shirt I came straight out. I didn't look at anything else.'

'When the pathologist and crime scene men have finished in there, I'd like you to go in with Constable Johnson here,' Walker paused and looked at Johnson who nodded, 'and see if anything is missing from the safe.'

'I wouldn't know what was missing,' said Sutton. 'I didn't know everything he kept in the safe.'

'Examine the contents anyway,' Walker said. 'Later on, you may realise something isn't there that should be.' He then thanked her for her help, nodded again to Johnson, and once more expressed his condolences to Mrs. Cook. Then, with a slight movement of his head, he indicated to Broadhurst that it was time to go.

As they were about to leave the room, two men from the mortuary emerged from the stairwell and headed for the doorway from which the crime scene tape now hung.

When Walker and Broadhurst entered the stairwell, Walker stopped. He thought for a moment and then spoke.

'Paige, why don't you get yourself some lunch and then take Peter's car to the hospital and drive Peter and his mum home. The hospital should release him into his mother's care. Then get a cab back to the station, pick up your car and go home yourself – and don't forget to get a docket off the cab driver so that the department can reimburse you.'

'What about you, sir?'

'I have to see someone and then I'll get one of the uniforms to join me while I interview Locke. He'll probably claim he knows nothing about the cocaine but hopefully we won't have too much trouble getting him sentenced for possession,' said Walker. 'What I'd like to be able to charge him with is distribution. We'll have to work on that.' Walker sighed. 'I'm also going to have to spend time doing the station's paperwork. There's a heap of it to get through and the superintendent is due back on Monday.'

'Sure you don't want to join me for a quick lunch first?' asked Broadhurst as, with Walker in the lead, they began their descent of the narrow stairs. 'Sounds like you're going to need some sustenance,' she said, before adding, 'My treat.'

'Thanks, but no,' replied Walker. 'I'll get something to eat from the person I'm going to see.'

'A woman, sir?' asked Paige, smiling down at him.

'Yes, a woman, Sergeant,' replied Walker, turning his head and smiling back at her. 'But it's not what you think. I'll explain later.'

Through the glass door at the bottom of the stairs, they could see some of the jostling news reporters awaiting them.

'What are you going to say to that mob, sir?' asked Broadhurst.

'I'm not going to say anything to them,' replied Walker. 'My speaking to them last time is the reason why I have so much paperwork on my desk.'

CHAPTER TWENTY-SEVEN

Sergeant Williamson accompanied Walker into the interview room. Locke, who had been formally charged, photographed, finger-printed and had provided a DNA sample, sat at the table with his arms folded and a defiant expression on his face. Next to him sat his solicitor, Ambrose Wittenberg, an elderly grey-haired man, who was wearing a navy pin-striped suit, a starched white shirt and a crimson necktie. Wittenberg also wore steel framed spectacles through which he was perusing a sheaf of papers that lay on the table in front of him. Although the lawyer knew both Walker and Williamson, he did not acknowledge the police officers' entry or presence.

While Williamson fiddled with the station's ancient recording machine, Walker took a seat directly opposite Locke. He then silently studied Locke, who only managed to return Walker's gaze for a few seconds before dropping his eyes to the table.

When Williamson eventually seated himself next to Walker, indicating the tape recorder was now operating, Walker began reciting the date, time, and names of those present.

'You have been advised of your rights, Mr. Locke. Is that correct?'

Locke nodded.

'Please speak for the benefit of the tape recording, Mr. Locke.'

'Yes,' said Locke. 'I've been advised of my rights.'

'And I understand you are prepared to answer my questions.'

'I am.' Locke cast a sideways glance at his solicitor who, by a slight shaking of his head, indicated he was not in agreement with Locke's decision.

'You have been charged with the possession of an illegal substance, Mr. Locke,' said Walker. 'Would you like to comment?'

'Yes, I would. I know nothing about the drugs that you found in my shop.'

Walker had expected this. Keeping his face expressionless, he said, 'Do you admit importing from Mexico the paint brushes in which the drugs were found?'

'Yes, but I did not know that they contained drugs.'

'Your shop's paperwork shows that all of the brushes containing drugs were imported at considerable expense and cost you far more than any of the other brushes you have in your shop. Why would you pay so much for them unless you were aware of their contents?'

Locke sighed. 'As I previously explained, the Mexican brushes have bristles that are finer and better secured than brushes from other countries.'

'Yes, you did tell me that,' said Walker. 'But if they are so good, and cost you so much, why didn't you have any of them on display in your shop?'

'Because they were for a special client. I ordered them especially for him and he purchased every brush that came from Mexico. He is a restorer and wants only the best. He is originally from Mexico and knows how good these brushes are.'

'A restorer? And he needs that many brushes? What is he restoring? The Sistine Chapel?'

Locke shrugged and said nothing.

'Why doesn't he import the brushes himself?' Walker asked.

'He doesn't have an importer's license.'

'Couldn't he get one?'

'He told me he couldn't, Chief Inspector. He said he had previously had some problems with officials in his home country. It now looks to me that these problems had to do with drugs.' Locke held out the palms of his hands. 'I've foolishly allowed myself to be used.'

'What is this special customer's name, Mr. Locke?'

'Sanchez. Miguel Sanchez.'

'And do you have an address for this Mr. Sanchez?'

'No, I don't,' said Locke. 'All I know is that he lives somewhere in London.'

'How did you communicate with him? By phone?'

'No. He would simply turn up at my shop. At least once every two months.'

Walker considered this to be both unusual and unlikely. He studied Locke's face carefully. 'What does Sanchez look like, Mr. Locke?'

Locke rubbed his chin and, with a thoughtful expression on his face, looked up at the ceiling. Slowly he said, 'He's short, and fat, with dark, greasy looking skin and has long black hair that he wears in a pony-tail. He also has very dark eyes and a thick, black moustache that goes down the sides of his mouth.'

Wittenberg gave his client an incredulous look. Then, remaining silent, he looked down once again at the papers in front of him.

Walker also said nothing. He stared at Locke for a few seconds and then abruptly terminated the interview.

Before Walker rose from his chair, Wittenberg looked at him and said, 'I will be applying for bail for my client, Chief Inspector.'

Walker smiled. 'Of course you will.' Then, to Williamson, he said, 'Escort Mr. Locke back to his cell please, Sergeant.'

Walker headed for the door. As he reached for the handle, he turned briefly and said, 'Goodbye, Mr. Wittenberg. You know the way out.'

'Oh, I'm not leaving yet, Chief Inspector,' said the solicitor, remaining in his seat as Williamson led Locke out of the room. 'I'd like to see Miss Richards. I'm representing her too.'

CHAPTER TWENTY-EIGHT

When Walker entered the incident room the following morning he was surprised to see Kent sitting at his desk tapping on his computer keyboard. He had a white bandage wrapped around his head.

'Peter! What are you doing here?'

'Oh, the headache's gone and I feel fine, sir,' Kent replied, looking up and smiling at the chief inspector.

'There's often delayed shock with injuries such as yours. You should be home resting.'

'If I was at home my mother would be fussing over me and I'd get no rest. I'd rather be here where it's more peaceful.'

Walker smiled. He was going to say something when Broadhurst entered the room.

'Superman!' she exclaimed. 'I didn't expect to see you again so soon.'

Kent grinned and watched Broadhurst as she placed her bag on her desk and sat down in her chair. Walker fondly watched both of them as he sat in the absent DC Osborne's chair. Then a serious expression appeared on his face. He stood and walked over to the white-board where he attached a photograph of Cook next to one of Anna. Both photos had been obtained from Facebook, a site that Walker found useful for finding out about others but would never consider using to reveal information about himself.

'Well, we now have two murders and the pathologist believes both victims were killed by the same murder weapon – the post-mortem should confirm this.' Walker stared at the photos. 'So, I think we might assume that they were both killed by the same person.'

'And unfortunately the number of suspects is growing,' said Broadhurst.

'Who else has been added to the list?' asked Kent.

'Mrs. Cook,' replied Broadhurst. 'She's tall and has short black hair. And when we saw her she was wearing trousers. She could certainly be mistaken for a man from behind. She would also have a strong motive for killing both victims if she knew about the affair.'

'And we haven't yet checked to see where she was at the time of both murders,' said Walker as he wrote "Elizabeth Cook" on the white-board. 'However,' he added, before pausing for a couple of seconds, 'our list of suspects is now shorter, not longer.'

'How is that, sir?' asked Broadhurst. Bewilderment was in her voice and on her face.

'The woman I went and saw yesterday, the one you were so curious about,' said Walker to Broadhurst, 'was Doris the loquacious lunch lady.' When Broadhurst looked confused, he said, 'You know her, the talkative woman who works in our canteen.' Walker went on to explain. 'She was leaving Locke's shop when I arrived there. She says she arrived at Locke's shop at nine o'clock when it opened yesterday morning and didn't leave until I got there. When I spoke to her in the canteen yesterday afternoon she assured me that both Locke and Richards had been in the shop the entire time she was there. So neither of them could have killed Cook who, according to the pathologist, died no earlier than ten yesterday morning.'

'So if the person who killed Cook also killed Anna, then that person can't be either Locke or Richards,' said Kent.

'Exactly,' said Walker as he erased the names "David Locke" and "Denise Richards" from the white-board. 'So now we focus on Mrs. Cook and Mr. Morris.'

'What's happened with Locke and Roberts, sir?' asked Broadhurst.

'Well, as expected, the powder found in the brush handles has been confirmed as being cocaine and, also as expected, Locke denies all knowledge of it. He blames the Mexicans. Says they were using him without him knowing about it.'

'So how were these Mexicans supposed to distribute it once it arrived here?'

'I asked him that. He says he had one customer who bought all of his fat handled brushes. Gave me a stereotypical description of a Mexican. Short, fat, dark haired and swarthy. And, of course, with the requisite handlebar moustache.' Walker laughed.

'And what about Richards, sir?' asked Kent.

'Well, she's admitted assaulting you but maintains that she thought you were a thief after Anna's car. And when I asked her about the drugs she denied all knowledge of their existence.'

'Will they be given bail?' asked Kent.

'Possibly,' said Walker. 'If we are going to succeed in sending that pair to prison we need to find out more about this mysterious "Mr. Sanchez".'

'Do you really think he exists?' said Broadhurst.

'Yes, I do – although I don't believe his name is Sanchez or that he is a Mexican,' replied Walker. 'Someone has to be handling the distribution. There's too much cocaine for Locke to be distributing it on his own from his shop.' Walker was thoughtful for a moment and then said, 'We're going to have to get onto the regional drug squad and find out all we can about cocaine distribution.'

'Would you like me to do that, sir?' asked Kent.

'Yes, please, Peter,' said Walker. 'I'd like you to ring the Colchester drug squad first, but if they're not aware of any large-scale cocaine distribution in Essex then call the London Met. Locke may be telling the truth when he says "Mr. Sanchez" comes from London.'

'Yes, sir,' said Kent.

'Also, find out what you can about Mrs. Cook. Particularly her background. I'd like to know a bit more about her before we speak to her again.' Walker paused. 'And see if you can find out if anyone sold or lost a stiletto recently. Call all of the antique dealers in the area.' Walker frowned and paused again before adding, 'And, Peter.'

'Yes, sir?'

'Don't go into dangerous situations unless you have back-up. Understood?'

'Yes, sir,' said Kent quietly, shamefaced.

Broadhurst smiled to herself. She had lost count of the number of times Walker had responded to calls without back-up. And, in spite of admonishment from Sheen on more than one occasion, she knew he would not change his ways.

Broadhurst's thoughts were interrupted by Walker's next words: 'How would you like to join me on a visit to Morris, Sergeant?'

'I'd love to, sir,' Broadhurst replied, 'but I think I should attend Cook's post-mortem.'

'What? It's on this morning?'

'Yes, sir. I received a call from Dr. Simons as I was driving here. She's bumped Cook's PM to the top of the queue,' said Broadhurst. 'She's giving this case top priority. I think she's quite concerned.'

'As am I, Sergeant,' said Walker. 'As am I.'

CHAPTER TWENTY-NINE

There was far more activity on the street than there had been the last time Walker visited the house with the bright yellow front door. There were a lot of cars on the road but the inspector was fortunate enough to find a parking space right outside the co-op. There were also many people on the footpaths. It was a warm day, but not as hot as the previous few days, and people were out enjoying the sunshine.

As Walker locked his car, he watched the people. Most of them were entering or emerging from the co-op. Among those coming out was a solid, well-dressed man who was carrying a newspaper and, not far behind him, an equally solid middle-aged woman struggling with two plastic bags full of groceries. A young couple, walking hand in hand, were about to enter the shop but politely stopped to allow a thin, white-haired lady to enter before them.

Coming down the hill towards the co-op was a young, casually dressed woman pushing a pram, while approaching from the other direction was a very tall man wearing a dark suit and hat. The man suddenly stopped and patted his coat pockets. He had apparently forgotten his wallet because he abruptly turned to retrace his steps. As he did so, he nearly collided with a female jogger who had been coming up the hill behind him. Walker saw her stop and smile at the man before continuing on her run.

As she approached, Walker recalled reading somewhere that what made women most attractive to men were the physical features that men did not have. This woman certainly had physical features that Walker did not have. She had long blonde hair pulled back into a pony tail, large eyes, a small straight nose, full lips, prominent breasts, and a tiny waist. She may not have had rounded hips but her athletic figure, only partly concealed by a tight pink tank top and high white shorts, was nevertheless most appealing to Walker. As she passed close by she smiled at him and Walker even found attractive the droplets of perspiration forming just above her upper lip.

Walker returned her smile and his eyes followed her as she continued running up the road. Eventually he looked away and began walking purposefully towards the yellow door.

When Morris responded to Walker's knock he followed the same procedure as before. Without saying a word, he gestured for Walker to enter, then locked the door and led Walker down the hallway. They seated themselves in the same chairs they had occupied on Walker's previous visit. Morris appeared to be even more nervous than he had been on that occasion.

'You know that Malcolm Cook is dead?' said Walker.

Morris nodded but said nothing. He was staring at the floor.

'Where were you yesterday morning – between 9 a.m. and 11 a.m.?'

Morris looked up and stared at Walker with his dark eyes. His facial expression was hostile. 'Here! Working!'

'I believe it was Mr. Cook who drew up your pre-marriage contract with Anna,' said Walker. 'Were you happy with that contract?'

'No, I was not,' Morris replied. 'But that wasn't Cook's fault. He was following my instructions. It was Anna's demands that I didn't like. If I didn't have Cook place them in the contract she wouldn't have married me.'

'Why did you use Cook to draw up the contract?'

Morris shrugged his shoulders and said, 'I needed a solicitor to draw up the contract and he was the closest.'

'You hadn't used him previously?'

'No,' said Morris.

'Did you like Mr. Cook?'

'No!' Morris snarled. 'I thought he was a pompous, thieving prick. But I didn't kill him.'

'Why do you call him a thief, Mr. Morris?' asked Walker.

'Because he charged me a small fortune to handle my divorce from Anna.'

Walker watched Morris's eyes closely. 'Did you know Cook had been having an affair with Anna while she was married to you and while she's been living with Locke?'

'What?!' Morris looked stunned. 'Are you sure?'

'That's what Cook told me, Mr. Morris.'

'That bastard!' swore Morris, sitting up straight and grabbing the armrests of his chair. 'He represents me against her in our divorce and at the same time he's screwing her! No wonder I did so badly in the settlement in spite of the pre-marriage agreement. What a slimy, unethical prick!'

'There does seem to have been a conflict of interests and if he was still alive I'm sure he would have to answer to a legal ethics committee,' said Walker. 'But he's not alive and my only concern is to find out who killed him.'

Morris slumped back in his chair and glared at Walker. 'Well, it wasn't me,' he said, 'but if I'd known what he was up to, I certainly might have.'

Walker stood up. He knew he didn't have enough to arrest Morris. Not yet. He said, 'I have to tell you, Mr. Morris, that you are a major suspect in both murder cases. Please make sure that you remain available to us as we may need to ask you some more questions.'

A fuming Morris followed Walker as the inspector headed down the hallway. Walker then waited patiently while Morris unlatched and opened the front door. As he began the walk towards his car, Walker could hear the door's bolt being secured.

On the drive back to the police station, Walker thought about Morris. The man was certainly volatile – and still very nervous. Walker wondered whether Morris had known about the relationship between Cook and Anna before Walker had told him.

As Walker entered the incident room, Kent rose from his chair, greeted him and held out a small piece of paper.

'A Detective Inspector Mowbray from Chelmsford rang asking for you, sir,' said Kent. 'He said to call him on this number. He said it was urgent.'

CHAPTER THIRTY

The Chrysler came to a halt outside a small cottage located just to the north of Chelmsford. Walker and Kent climbed out. Kent had not yet been involved with a dead body, so Walker had brought him along for the experience.

On the front doorstep of the cottage, enjoying the warmth of the sun, stood Detective Inspector Paul Mowbray. He was a big man, both in height and girth. He had made an unsuccessful attempt to conceal a predominantly bald head by utilising a few long strands of grey hair that originated just above his left ear. His face was pink and round, his nose was fleshy, and he had rolls of fat under his chin. His only attractive facial feature was the pair of pale blue eyes that seemed to continually express amusement. Like Kent, he wore an ill-fitting, dark blue suit.

'Hello, Julian,' he said, with a broad, friendly smile, as Walker and Kent entered the front yard. 'Who's your turbaned companion?'

Walker laughed and said, 'Hi, Paul. This is DC Peter Kent. He was the victim of a sneak attack by a drug dealer.' He turned to Kent and said, 'Peter, this is my old friend Detective Inspector Paul Mowbray.'

'Never you mind the "old",' chuckled Mowbray as he extended his hand to Kent. 'Pleased to meet you, Peter.' The pair shook hands and Mowbray's face then took on a serious expression. 'As I told you on the phone, Julian, I think the poor bugger inside was probably killed by the same person that did your two victims. He was found this morning but he's been dead for a few days. A neighbour who called in to ask if he'd feed her cat while she was away noticed the smell and called it in. The body's a bit of a mess, what with the heat and all, but our pathologist reckons he was stabbed once in the heart by a very sharp instrument. There's very little blood – only a small circle of it on the front of his shirt. And the small hole in the centre of that circle appears to be square shaped.' Mowbray coughed before continuing, 'I spoke to my boss and he said, if I'm happy with it, you're quite welcome to take over the case. And I am happy, so here you are.'

Mowbray removed some gloves, booties and a small jar from his pocket. 'As I said, the victim's been dead a few days so you might want to stick some of this up your nose.'

'Vicks?' said Walker. He watched Mowbray remove the familiar jar's cap and insert a fat finger.

'A little trick I learned from an American film I saw on the telly. It helps mask the smell,' said Mowbray as he applied a liberal amount of the grayish ointment to his nostrils.

Walker took some of the ointment from the jar now held out by Mowbray and dabbed it just below his nose. He indicated Kent should do the same. He was a little concerned for his sergeant but Kent didn't seem to be worried. Walker mentally shrugged. Maybe Kent would be less affected by viewing dead bodies than he was.

The detectives donned gloves and booties and, led by Mowbray, entered the cottage.

The pathologist, who was unknown to Walker, was kneeling and placing his instruments into a black leather bag. He was a large, grey-bearded man, wearing thick lensed spectacles. He looked up through these when he sensed Walker's approach.

Walker introduced himself and said, 'I realise you won't know when he was killed until you've examined the body back at the mortuary, but can you give me a guess?'

'I don't like to guess, Chief Inspector,' said the pathologist, 'but I can tell you that he was killed no later than last Sunday. The PM will allow me to be more precise.'

'Thank you, sir,' said Walker as the pathologist resumed packing his bag.

'So,' Walker said quietly to no-one in particular, 'this man was killed before Anna.'

The body, which was now being bagged, was in an advanced state of decomposition and the stench, even though lessened somewhat by the Vicks, was powerful. Walker wasn't bothered by the smell but he had made sure that his eyes avoided the body.

Walker need not have worried about his junior officer. When Kent looked at the body he studied it for a long time. Walker noted that not only was Kent unperturbed, he actually appeared to be fascinated.

Eventually Kent looked up at his surroundings. His eyes widened and his face revealed pleasure. From all of the walls hung dozens of framed drawings. And most of these drawings were related to comic strips with which Kent was familiar. The detective constable was enthralled. After giving each drawing a thorough examination, he decided to have a look at the other rooms in the cottage.

The body was now bagged and Walker and Mowbray were about to leave for some fresh air when Kent called to them. He took them into an adjoining room and pointed to an empty wooden picture frame that lay on the floor near one of the walls. Then he pointed to the empty picture hook attached to one of the few empty spaces on that wall.

Walker looked at the wall and then at the frame on the floor. He then walked to the doorway and disappeared into the room where the body had been found. Moments later he returned with one of the white-coated scene of crime officers. Walker pointed to the floor and said to him, 'When you've finished next door would you please check that picture frame for fingerprints?' The man nodded and Walker motioned to Kent and Mowbray to follow him.

After placing their gloves and booties in a bin standing near the front door, and removing most of the Vicks from their noses, the three detectives moved to the centre of the cottage's small front yard. There was no-one else around. Walker was a little surprised that no media representatives were lingering.

Walker said, 'What can you tell me about the victim, Paul?'

'Well,' said Mowbray. 'His name is Nigel Clement and he's forty-nine years of age. He worked as a clerk for the local council, had no family, and lived alone. According to his employers he's worked at the council since he left school. The neighbour who noticed the smell told me his parents died in a car accident about ten years ago and apparently he inherited the cottage which he'd lived in since he was born. He was quite well off it seems. The neighbour said his parents left him quite a few quid.' Mowbray paused. 'I asked the neighbour, who seems to know everything that goes on around here, whether he had had any visitors lately and she said he never had visitors. She also said that he had never had a girlfriend.' Mowbray chuckled. 'So that would also help explain why he was well off.'

Walker and Kent smiled and Mowbray reached into an inner pocket of his suit coat. 'I've got a good photo of him here. It was taken with his parents so it's over ten years old but it's good enough to stick on your crime wall.'

'Thanks,' said Walker, absently taking the photo and slowly placing it in his inside coat pocket.

Mowbray was watching Walker intently. After a few seconds had passed he said, 'I know that look in your eye, Walker. You're onto something, aren't you?'

'I could be,' said Walker. 'Thanks to Peter.' He paused. 'Before coming here, I thought this case was about drugs or jealousy. Now I'm wondering whether it might be about something else.'

'What?' asked Mowbray.

'Drawings,' said Walker and then went on to explain. 'Clement seems to have a drawing missing and I remember Locke telling me that a drawing belonging to Anna was missing. I thought it was a diversion at the time but now I'm wondering if he was telling the truth. Maybe there's a connection.'

'Drawings?' said Mowbray. 'Why would anyone kill for a drawing? It's not as if they're paintings. Surely they can't be that valuable.'

'Some of them are,' said Kent. His face reddened as the two senior detectives looked at him. He quickly continued, 'Most of the drawings in the house would be valued in the hundreds of pounds but, in the room where the empty frame was found, I saw a 1930's Hal Forster "Prince Valiant". That's worth thousands. And I also saw a Winsor McCay "Little Nemo". There's an example of that strip in the Louvre. They're rare and extremely valuable.'

Walker and Mowbray continued to stare at Kent. Mowbray had his mouth open but said nothing. Walker began to slowly nod his head.

Suddenly Walker appeared to have made a decision. He smiled, grabbed his friend's hand and shook it. 'Thanks, Paul,' he said. He then turned abruptly and hurried towards the gate.

'Where are you off to in such a hurry?' called Mowbray.

'We have to get back to our station,' Walker shouted over his shoulder. 'I have to talk to a drug dealer.'

CHAPTER THIRTY-ONE

Walker and Kent sat side by side at a heavily scratched table in the station's small interview room. The door opened and Locke, who had not been granted bail, entered. He was accompanied by Constable Johnson. Johnson quietly closed the door behind them and indicated to Locke that he should sit in the chair facing the two detectives. Locke sat and Johnson moved behind him, leaning against the wall.

'I'm not talking to you without my solicitor being present,' said Locke. He spoke without too much conviction. He looked tired, unhappy, and a little suspicious.

'Relax, Mr. Locke,' said Walker. 'We haven't brought you in here to talk about your drug charge.'

'And I'm not talking to you about Anna either. As I've already told you, I didn't kill her.'

'We know you didn't,' said Walker, 'but we do know that you hacked into Anna's computer and knew about her relationship with Cook.'

Locke's bushy eyebrows rose in surprise but Walker's bluff worked. 'Okay, I'll admit to that,' Locke quietly conceded and then, realising the implication, added in a loud voice, 'but I didn't kill Cook either!'

'Calm down, Mr. Locke. We know that also,' said Walker. 'We want to talk to you about something different. We want to ask you some questions about Anna's missing drawing.'

Again, Locke looked surprised. 'What about it?' he said.

'Can you describe the drawing?'

'It was a picture of two boys,' said Locke. 'It was more of a cartoon than a realistically drawn picture. It looked like it was drawn with a pen and there was no colour.' Locke paused and then added, 'It had some faded German writing on the back but Anna never told me what it meant. It also had a date on the back. Eighteen hundred and something.'

'Do you remember how big the drawing was?' asked Walker.

Locke thought for a moment before speaking. 'It was bigger than the cover of a hardback novel – but smaller than a sheet of computer printing paper.'

'Where did Anna get the drawing?'

'From Morris. She said that he gave her that drawing, and another one, as part of their divorce settlement,' said Locke. 'But from the way she spoke I suspect she took them without his permission.'

'There were two drawings?' said Walker.

'Yes.'

'What happened to the other one?'

'Anna took it to an art dealer to have it valued,' said Locke, 'but he made her such a good offer that she sold it to him.'

'Do you know how much he gave her for it, Mr. Locke?'

'No, but I know she bought a bottle of Bollinger. Anna usually drank red wine but she also liked good champagne. The champagne I sometimes bought her was good but not as good as this one.' Locke smiled. 'She was happy and I was happy that she was able to buy an expensive bottle of her own. She was so happy that she decided to sell the dealer the second drawing and buy another bottle.' Locke's smile vanished and he lowered his head. 'But she died before she could take it to him.'

'Do you remember when she sold the first drawing?' Walker asked.

'It would have been about two weeks ago, I think.'

'One last question, Mr. Locke,' said Walker. 'Do you know the name of the dealer?'

'No. All I know is that he has a shop in Colchester. Anna found him on the internet.'

Walker pushed his chair back and stood up. 'Well, you've been helpful, Mr. Locke. Thank you for your cooperation.' Walker nodded towards Johnson and said. 'The constable will now escort you back to your cell.'

When Walker and Kent entered the incident room they discovered that Broadhurst had returned from Cook's post-mortem.

'Hi, Paige,' said Walker. 'What did you learn?'

'The pathologist confirmed that Cook died no earlier than ten a.m. and that he had been stabbed by the same weapon that killed Anna. The forensics report also came through. Nothing useful. And only Cook's fingerprints were on the safe. There were dozens of other prints in the office but none of them belong to anyone we know.'

Walker then told Broadhurst about the Chelmsford murder. 'It looks like the victim was killed by the same weapon that was used on Anna and Cook. So that's another post-mortem for you to attend,' he added.

'Isn't that out of our jurisdiction?' she asked.

'The case has been passed on to us.'

'It does seem that the best way for us to solve these murders is to find that weapon,' said Broadhurst, 'or at least where it originated.' She turned to Kent. 'How much have you found out about it, Peter?'

'Nothing,' replied Kent. 'I haven't had a chance to search yet. I started with Locke's case and called both the Essex and London drug squads but they weren't able to help. Essex haven't got a big problem with cocaine and London, which does have a problem, knew nothing about any drugs coming out of Essex. I then started checking up on Mrs. Cook and was just finishing when Inspector Mowbray called.'

'What did you find out about her?' Broadhurst asked.

'Only that she was once an actress. Mainly on the stage but she has done a little television work.'

'I thought she looked vaguely familiar,' said Broadhurst who was an avid television watcher. 'I think I've seen her in an episode of one of the crime shows.'

'If her reaction to her husband's death was an act, then she's certainly an accomplished actress,' said Walker. 'Anyway, I think we can forget about her for the moment. I think we should now focus on the drawings.'

'What drawings?' Broadhurst asked.

Walker told her about Locke's earlier mention of Anna's missing drawing and the drawing Peter had noticed was missing from Clement's cottage. 'There is a link there,' he said. He then went on to tell Broadhurst what he and Kent had just learned from Locke in the interview room.

'I think we should talk to this art dealer,' said Walker.

'But we don't know his name,' said Kent.

'No, we don't,' said Walker. 'But we do know that his business is in Colchester. He shouldn't be too hard to find. How many art dealers do you think there are in Colchester?'

Broadhurst had already begun tapping on her computer keyboard and in less than a minute was jotting down numbers on a piece of paper.

She handed the paper to Walker and said, 'There's only a few, sir. Here are their phone numbers.'

'Thanks,' said Walker. 'I'll give them a call and see which one remembers Anna.'

'If you find him are you going to go and see him?' asked Broadhurst.

'Oh, I'll find him,' said Walker, 'and I'll make an appointment to see him tomorrow.'

As he walked towards his office and his telephone, Walker added with a smile, 'So go home now and get an early night. I want you both here by eight in the morning for our visit to Colchester.'

CHAPTER THIRTY-TWO

At nine the following morning, the three detectives were sitting in the office of Ronald Stone, the art dealer who had purchased the drawing from Anna. He had fussed over them when they arrived, locating, arranging and dusting extra chairs, and offering the detectives cups of tea and biscuits.

Stone was a short man of medium build. He had a neatly trimmed grey beard and moustache, bushy grey eyebrows, and hazel eyes that were partly obscured by tinted spectacles. His hair, which was also grey, was thick and fairly long, resting on the collar of his tweed jacket. Attached to the collar of the dark olive shirt he wore under the jacket was a pale yellow bow tie.

Stone was not only very affable, he was also extremely talkative. And he spoke with the same accent as the one used by the Queen when making her Christmas Day broadcast.

For the first five minutes of their visit, the detectives were regaled with the history of Stone's business. Walker, fascinated by Stone's bow tie, politely feigned interest, Broadhurst stared at the ceiling, and Kent, totally absorbed in his surroundings, allowed his eyes to dart from one to another of the many works of art hanging on the walls. He had discarded the head bandage which Walker suspected had been worn the previous day simply to keep his mother happy.

'When you rang and identified yourself, Chief Inspector,' said Stone, finally turning to the purpose of their visit, 'I thought it may have been about the break-in I had here on the Friday a week ago. But of course when you said you were from Wivenhoe, I knew it couldn't be about that. Anyway, I'd already rung the local police station and told them nothing had been stolen. And if you hadn't told me what it was about, or where you were from, I would have thought it very strange to have three detectives turn up about a break-in when nothing was stolen wouldn't I?' He paused for breath and Walker spoke before he could continue.

'You told me on the phone that you had purchased a drawing from Anna Gruber,' Walker said.

'Oh yes. A pretty woman. Long blonde hair and blue eyes. Very pretty. So sad that she was murdered. I saw her photo on the telly and recognised her straight away. I only recently bought the drawing from her.'

'Do you remember when you bought the drawing, Mr. Stone?'

'When? Let me see.' Stone reached behind his chair and grabbed a thick leather bound book that was sitting on the top of a low filing cabinet. He placed the book on the desk in front of him and began riffling through the pages. 'Ah yes. Here we are. A nineteenth century German original drawing. A pen and ink cartoon featuring two young boys. Purchased for one hundred pounds from A. Gruber.' He looked up at the detectives and said, 'After the seller's name I always write their address and date of purchase.' His eyes returned to the page and he said, 'It was purchased from Miss Gruber on the thirteenth and today's the twenty-third so,' he paused again while he counted the days marked in his book, then exclaimed with a smile, 'ten days ago!'

Walker was about to ask another question but he was too slow.

'She only came in for a valuation but, to be honest, I didn't have a clue as to what it was worth. I don't normally deal in German art, but I did know someone who would buy it and I knew what he would pay. So I took the opportunity to make a quick, small profit. Miss Gruber was so pleased by what I offered she sold it to me right then and there. She told me that she had another one that she would sell to me if I would pay the same price. I told her I would and she left. I then immediately put the drawing on the internet asking for offers above one hundred and fifty pounds. I knew of course, that my client would see it, rush in here, and make an offer higher than all others. There's nothing better than a quick sale.' Stone winked, and smiling broadly, finally paused.

Walker took the opportunity to ask a question. He had an idea that he already knew the answer but asked it anyway. 'Who bought the drawing, Mr. Stone?'

'Nigel Clement. Poor man. You know the one who was murdered down near Chelmsford – oh, how silly of me. Of course you would know! Lovely man. Quietly spoken and very polite. And a very good client. He saw the drawing on the internet a couple of hours after I put it on and immediately rang me. I told him I had already received some calls from interested parties and he said he would more than match any offer. So I said I would hold it for him and he rushed here early the next morning. He made me a very good offer as I knew he would so I sold it to him. As I said, a lovely man. And when I told him I might be able to get hold of another, similar, drawing he became quite excited. He did ask the drawing's provenance but I told him I didn't know. I wasn't familiar with the artist because, as I've already told you, I rarely deal in German works. I specialise in British art. And I certainly wasn't going to tell him what Miss Gruber told me!'

Walker jumped in with another question. 'What did she tell you about the origin of the drawings, Mr. Stone?'

'She said she had found the drawings in an old abandoned farmhouse just outside Hanover. That they were in an old, rotting, leather briefcase that bore the letters "H. G.".' Stone laughed. 'I think she concocted the story to enhance the value of the drawings. Herman Goering was certainly an infamous Nazi art collector, as we know, but I doubt that he would have been interested in this drawing. And it's very unlikely that Goering was ever in Hanover.'

'I think it's likely that he was, Mr. Stone,' said Walker. 'The first German attacks on Allied bombers using Japanese style "kamikaze" planes took place over Hanover and it's probable that Goering, as head of the Luftwaffe, was on the ground to observe and encourage his suicide pilots.'

'Oh,' was all Stone said in reply.

Broadhurst, familiar with Walker's occasional vocalising of his almost obsessive interest in European history, permitted herself a little smile.

'You said that when you put the drawing on the internet you received some calls from interested parties. Were there many, Mr. Stone?' Walker asked.

'Only a couple. An American collector made an offer of one hundred and fifty-five pounds and there was also interest from someone in France. But his offer was less than I had paid for the drawing so I'm afraid I was a little rude to him. Surprisingly there were no inquiries from Germany. The Germans of course would be the ones most familiar with its value and maybe the price I put on it was too high.' Stone paused briefly. 'They were the only phone calls but later there was someone who came in here and asked to see the drawing. But it was too late. I had already sold it to Mr. Clement the day before. He seemed annoyed and asked me who had purchased it. He became quite angry when I refused to give him Mr. Clement's name. I told him that I might soon have another one and he asked where I was getting it from. When I refused to give him that information he became very angry and stormed out.'

'What did this man look like, Mr. Stone?' Walker asked.

'Let me see if I can remember,' said Stone, looking up at the ceiling and stroking his beard. 'Ah, yes. He was very tall and had black hair and very dark eyes.'

'And he visited you on the Friday?'

'Yes. Friday was a most upsetting day. First his unpleasant visit in the afternoon and then the equally unpleasant break-in that night. Very upsetting. Yes, it was on the Friday. The day after I sold the drawing to poor Mr. Clement and two days after I purchased the drawing from poor Miss Gruber. Yes, he visited me on the Friday a week ago yesterday.'

'Do you have a security camera, Mr. Stone?' Walker asked.

'No, I've never been concerned about theft. But now that my office has been broken into I will give the purchase of a camera some careful consideration. I really should safeguard my property.'

Walker, who was far more interested in the visitor than in property, said, 'We'll speak with the detectives who investigated your break-in. They may have seen something useful on CCTV.'

'Oh, I overheard one of the detectives say that we no longer have CCTV on our little street, Chief Inspector. Our council removed it. Anyway, most of the businesses in this street have their own cameras.' Stone smiled. 'And I've just decided that I will have one installed as well.'

Silently cursing, Walker forced a smile and stood up. He thanked the dealer for his help and shook his hand. The other two detectives rose from their chairs, nodded at Stone – who looked as though he was disappointed that they were leaving – and followed Walker to the doorway. When he reached the doorway Walker halted and turned. He stepped back to allow Broadhurst and Kent to pass him and said, 'One last question, Mr. Stone. Do you take your purchase book home with you at night or do you leave it here in the office?'

'Oh, I always leave it here on this cabinet.' Stone smiled. 'If I took it home I might misplace it or forget to bring it back.'

Walker again thanked the dealer and exited the office, closing the door behind him.

When Walker reached the top of the stairwell, where Broadhurst and Kent were waiting for him, Broadhurst said quietly, 'What a windbag! And what a phoney accent!'

Walker refrained from responding to Broadhurst's comments. Instead he said, 'The description of Stone's angry visitor fits Morris. Locke's suspicion about Anna stealing the drawings from Morris may have been right and Morris wanted them back. He could have recognised his drawing when it was put on the internet and came here determined to retrieve it.'

'I can understand Morris asking Stone for the address of the purchaser,' said Broadhurst, 'but why would he ask Stone the name of the seller when he knew it was Anna?'

'Maybe he wasn't sure that it was Anna,' said Kent. 'Maybe he thought Anna had sold both drawings to someone else and that that person had sold one of them to Stone. He asked Stone about the seller because he wanted to know for certain.'

'It's a possibility, Peter,' said Walker who had begun descending the stairs. 'But we can't prove any of it. Although Stone apparently didn't make the connection, I think we can reasonably assume that the person who visited Stone was the person who later broke into his office to obtain the address of the purchaser from Stone's book. But was it Morris? The description fits him but it also fits thousands of other men. It's too vague.'

'If it was Morris, why would he want the drawings so badly that he was prepared to kill for them?' said Broadhurst as she began following Walker down the stairs. 'And,' she added, 'if he was killing for drawings why would he kill Cook?'

'Cook must have some connection to the drawings,' said Walker. 'I think we should talk to his wife and his secretary and see if they know anything about them.'

'When do you want to see them, sir?' asked Broadhurst.

'As soon as possible,' said Walker. 'We'll start with the secretary. Call her and ask if she can meet us outside Cook's office within the next hour.'

They exited the building and stood on the footpath while Broadhurst made the call.

'Miss Sutton's agreed to meet with us, sir,' said Broadhurst, closing her phone.

Walker was about to respond when they were suddenly distracted by a loud scream.

CHAPTER THIRTY-THREE

A long-haired, bearded man, dressed in a red-checked flannel shirt and baggy blue jeans, burst from a shop entrance further up the road, swerved and came running towards the three detectives. The man was huge. He was at least four inches taller than Walker. Nearly seven foot. And he was much, much heavier.

A well-dressed young woman, the one who had apparently emitted the scream, emerged from the same shop yelling, 'Thief! Thief!' and ran after him. The man was big but he certainly wasn't slow. She had no chance of catching him.

As the big man ran, long hair flowing behind him, pedestrians who saw him coming stepped, or jumped, out of his way. Those who were slow, or didn't see him, were swatted aside as if they were annoying insects. He certainly did not allow anyone to reduce his speed. Those who had moved out of his way, or had made contact with him and were now sitting or lying on the ground, were yelling or screaming according to their gender.

Broadhurst and Kent instinctively stepped on to the narrow road but Walker stayed where he was in the middle of the footpath. The giant was almost upon him.

As the giant began raising an arm to brush Walker aside, the detective suddenly crouched and launched himself forward and upward.

Walker's right shoulder slammed into the man just below his rib cage. The sound of impact, like a loud slap, and an accompanying loud exhalation of air, reverberated up and down the street. The giant, who had come to an abrupt halt, rose into the air and then began falling backwards. Walker swiftly reached out and grabbed the big man's shirt, slowing his descent and preventing his head from smashing into the stone footpath. Walker had quickly concluded that he did not want any more problems with the police complaints department. The giant now lay flat on his back, gasping for air, with pained eyes staring upwards at a sky that, for him, was filled with constellations.

Walker stood upright and, with a frown on his face, began carefully examining his grey suit coat. Satisfied there were no rips in the fabric, and without looking down at the man who was now groaning, he calmly spoke to Broadhurst and Kent. 'Make sure he stays still and call the local police. Then call Miss Sutton and tell her we have been delayed but to please wait for us.'

While Broadhurst was pressing numbers on her phone, Walker went over to speak to a blonde, wide-eyed young woman dressed in a white blouse, a black mini-skirt, and low heeled black shoes. It was the woman who had chased the big man from the shop.

When Broadhurst had finished making the phone calls, Kent moved closer to her and spoke softly, 'I thought you said the chief inspector didn't like violence.'

Broadhurst replied with a smile. 'Oh, he wouldn't have enjoyed that.' Then she added, 'But I did, didn't you?'

The big man lifted his head. He then slowly raised his upper body until he was leaning on one elbow.

'Chief Inspector Walker said you're to stay still,' said Broadhurst, gently placing the sole of her shoe on the centre of his chest and forcing him to return to a horizontal position.

The big man quickly lifted his head again. With wide-opened eyes he stared at Broadhurst and whispered, 'Chief Inspector Walker?'

When Broadhurst nodded, the big man emitted a loud groan and dropped his head to the footpath. 'The "Grey Man",' he wheezed. He then closed his eyes, and muttered, 'Just my luck.' These words were followed by a softly uttered four letter expletive.

CHAPTER THIRTY-FOUR

The three detectives were in Colchester police station. Broadhurst and Kent sat patiently in uncomfortable hallway chairs; chairs usually occupied by members of the public, and watched Walker. He was standing at the station's front counter answering questions and signing papers. One uniformed officer, an overweight sergeant, was asking the questions and writing down Walker's answers while another, a thin constable, was nervously pointing out where, on various sheets of paper, Walker should place his signature.

'Chief Inspector Walker?'

Walker finished signing the last piece of paper and looked up. A large, brown-suited man with a round face and prominent, slightly protruding front teeth, had silently appeared at Walker's side. He closely resembled the beaver Walker had recently seen on a television wildlife documentary.

'I'm DI Matthew McDonald. I'm sorry about all this.'

'That's alright,' said Walker, gripping McDonald's extended hand. 'I know certain procedures have to be followed.'

'Francis Haynes, the gentleman you just apprehended,' said McDonald, 'is anxious to see you. He claims to have information that will help you with one of your current cases.'

'Does he?' said Walker. 'I suppose I had better see him then.'

Walker nodded to the two uniformed men behind the counter and, accompanied by Broadhurst and Kent, followed McDonald along the narrow hallway.

Haynes was seated behind a table in the interview room, flanked by two burly, uniformed officers. Walker and McDonald sat in the two chairs facing him and Broadhurst and Kent leant against the wall.

'What do you want to tell me, Mr. Haynes?' asked Walker, leaning forward so that his elbows rested on the table.

'I know you don't do deals, Chief Inspector, but if what I tell you is useful will you put in a good word for me with the judge?' Haynes spoke with a squeaky voice.

'There are no guarantees of course,' said Walker who tried not to show his surprise at hearing such a big, intimidating man speaking with such a high-pitched, non-threatening voice, 'but if whatever you tell me proves beneficial to me then I will do my best to help you.'

'Fair enough,' said Haynes. 'I want to tell you what I know about Locke and his drugs. I know it's your case because I saw in the paper that you were the one who arrested him.'

Walker made sure his face didn't reveal his reaction to this statement. He'd come to Colchester and received useful information about one of two of his major cases and now someone he'd literally bumped into in the street was going to give him information on the other? What were the odds of that happening? Walker was extremely sceptical. He studied the big man's eyes. Finally, he said, 'Go on.'

'I worked for Locke but I didn't do any drug selling. I acted as a sort of bodyguard when these men came up from London to buy coke from him. That usually happened once a month. I'd just stand there, see that they didn't threaten him, and also make sure they handed over the money without any trouble.'

'Do you know the names of these men?' asked Walker.

'Locke called the main man "Jimmy",' said Haynes. 'He's very thin and has a real long nose. I don't know his last name. I never seen him before he came to visit Locke.'

'That doesn't help much,' said Walker.

'No, but I know one of the men who was with him. I'd been inside with him. A real little weasel named Warren Daniels. He's only a small-time crim. He's been done a couple of times for burglary. You'll have no problem with him.'

Walker withdrew a pen and notebook from the inside of his coat pocket and wrote down the man's name. He shouldn't be hard to find and, given the right incentive, would talk. Walker then asked Haynes, 'What about Denise Richards? Was she involved?'

'Yes. She was the one who counted the money.'

Walker smiled. So, he thought, we'll be able to charge you with more than assault on a police officer, Miss Richards.

'Tell me Mr. Haynes,' Walker said. 'Was Anna Gruber also involved?'

'I think so. I didn't see her in the shop but I'm pretty sure she knew what was going on. She went with Locke when he went to see his suppliers in Mexico. Locke was in love with her. He wouldn't have cared that she didn't help out. But Miss Richards did. She hated Miss Gruber.'

'Where were the drugs usually kept?'

'In the back room of his shop. When the drugs were there I slept in the shop at night to keep them safe until they were picked up by the men from London. Locke usually had the boxes delivered to his garage and then he would move them up to the shop's back room as soon as he could. He figured it was best not to keep them in the garage for too long in case it was broken into. He was always worried when stock was in there – especially after he bought Anna that red car. He thought that she would forget to lock the door when she took the car out.'

'If you were working for Locke why did you rob that shop today?' asked Walker. 'Surely he paid you well.'

Haynes looked down at his hands and exhaled. 'He sacked me a couple of months ago and I've run out of money.'

'Why did Locke sack you?' asked Walker.

'A load of boxes arrived just before Locke went on his last trip to Mexico. "Jimmy" and his mates weren't due to visit until he returned. Anyway, one night while he was away I decided to sample the merchandise. When Locke got back he must have noticed some of his coke was missing but he didn't say anything. The next day he said he wouldn't need me any longer and gave me quite a large amount of money,' he paused, 'and some coke.'

'He gave you cocaine? To sell?'

'No, Chief Inspector.' Haynes raised his eyes and looked at Walker's face. 'I'm a user. You don't get hooked on the stuff like you do with heroin. You don't need the stuff but you want it, if you know what I mean. It keeps you happy so I love it. I was buying it off Locke while I was working for him and I continued to buy it from him after he let me go – I'm still buying it when I can get down to London. But it's pricey and I quickly used up the money Locke gave me. That's why I robbed that jewellery shop this morning.' Haynes paused. 'I don't mind going to prison. In fact, it will probably do me good. Help me to forget about coke. But I don't want to spend a long time inside. That's why I'm talking to you. Hopefully you'll help me get a reduced sentence.' He folded his huge arms. 'So, Chief Inspector. Is what I told you useful?'

'Yes, it is, Mr. Haynes.' Walker opened a folder that lay on the table and began scanning the pages. 'I see that you have quite a record. Theft, extortion, assault. You've spent quite a lot of time in prison.' Walker locked eyes with the big man. 'As long as you are prepared to testify in court I will do my best to help you. A word in the right ear might ensure that your sentence is not as long as it should be.'

'Thank you, Chief Inspector. I have no problem with going to court. Locke and "Jimmy" and his mates are afraid of me, I'm not afraid of them.' Haynes coughed and then spoke hesitantly. 'Can I ask you something?'

'What?' said Walker as he pushed back his chair and stood.

'Where did you learn to do what you did to me in the street?'

Walker smiled. 'When I played Rugby we had a special defence coach who taught us how to tackle properly. He was good. He'd played Rugby League in Australia.'

CHAPTER THIRTY-FIVE

As a result of their sojourn in Colchester, Walker had little doubt that Locke would be found guilty of drug distribution as well as importation. And that both he and Richards would end up spending many years in prison. Now, Walker thought as he finally departed from the city, he could focus on the murders.

They were not long out of Colchester when Walker noticed in the rear vision mirror that Kent was looking particularly pale.

'What's wrong, Peter?' Walker asked. 'You don't look well.'

'I'm okay, sir,' replied Kent, grimacing as he spoke.

Walker saw the grimace and brought the car to an immediate halt at the side of the road. He turned off the ignition and moved his upper body so that he faced the rear seat.

'What is it, Peter?' asked Broadhurst who had also turned to face Kent. 'Your face has gone very white.'

'It's just a headache. But I've never had one like this before and it seems to be getting worse.' Kent tightly closed his eyes and gritted his teeth.

'We're taking you to the hospital, Peter,' said Walker, turning and reaching for the ignition key. 'It's probably a delayed reaction to that blow you took to the head.'

'No hospital please, sir,' said Kent firmly. 'But I think you'd better drop me home if you don't mind. My mother will call in the local doctor. He'll fix me up.' Kent began a fumbling search for his mobile phone. 'I'd better call my mum and let her know we're coming. Otherwise she'll fly into a panic when we arrive.' The pain he was suffering was made obvious by the way in which his words were uttered.

'I'll ring her, Peter,' said Broadhurst. 'You lay back and try to relax.'

'And ring the secretary again, please Paige,' said Walker. 'Ask her to wait a little while longer.' Walker was watching for a break in the flow of traffic.

'I'm sorry about this, sir,' said Kent, sounding more than a little embarrassed.

'Don't worry about it, Peter,' said Walker as the Chrysler moved to join the other cars on the busy road. 'But I still think you should be going to hospital.'

Walker expected to find Mrs. Kent upset and flustered. But when they arrived at Kent's home in Thorrington, she was surprisingly calm and efficient. She had already called the doctor, who was on his way, and she now insisted that Walker and Broadhurst come into the house and wait while she ushered her son into a darkened bedroom.

When she emerged, and had quietly closed the door behind her, she led Walker and Broadhurst into a sitting room.

'I know you are in a hurry but this won't take long,' she said, indicating to the two detectives that they should be seated.

They sat. Walker was expecting a lecture about taking better care of her son so was quite surprised by the words she now spoke.

'I know you are trying to find out where this stiletto knife may have come from.' She sat up straight in a chair facing them. 'Peter has been spending a lot of time on his computer and on his phone finding and calling antique dealers, auction houses and museums. He's even been contacting those stately homes that are open to the public to see if they owned an old knife which had been stolen. But he has had no luck.' She reached across to a small table and picked up a sheet of paper.

Walker and Broadhurst watched and waited. They remained silent.

'I think there was one thing that Peter may have overlooked. The knife originated in Italy and may have been taken from there by a soldier from one of the occupying armies during the Second World War. That means it may have been kept by the soldier's family who later sold it. And a possible purchaser of such an item could have been a dealer in militaria.' Mrs. Kent passed over the sheet of paper. 'I got onto the internet and made this list of British militaria dealers.'

Seeing the expressions on Walker's and Broadhurst's faces, Mrs. Kent said, 'There's no need to look so surprised. I spent fifteen years working for a computer programming company after Peter's father walked out. Right up until two years ago when I retired – early retirement I might add.' She smiled. 'I'm not in Peter's class but my skills are above average. And this was a very simple task.'

Walker stared at the paper for a moment before looking up and saying, 'Thank you very much, Mrs. Kent. This will be very useful.'

'That's not all, Chief Inspector. The British weren't the only foreigners in Italy during the war, as you no doubt know.' She reached over and took another sheet of paper from the table. As she handed it to Walker she said, 'Apart from the other Allies, there were also the Germans. And there are a lot of militaria dealers in Germany. Here is a list of those whom you might wish to contact. I hope you can speak German.'

CHAPTER THIRTY-SIX

Walker reversed the Chrysler into a space not more than fifty metres from the grey brick building once occupied by Cook. He looked at the clock on the dashboard. It was just after one p.m. The drive to Kent's home, and the time spent obtaining the surprising, but very welcome, information from Mrs. Kent, had considerably delayed their arrival in Wivenhoe.

The secretary, dressed casually in pale brown cotton trousers and a white, long-sleeved blouse, was standing patiently on the footpath outside the building. She greeted Walker and Broadhurst pleasantly, graciously accepted their apology for being late and, at Walker's suggestion, accompanied them to a nearby coffee shop.

After Walker had ordered a large plate of sandwiches and three cups of tea, he asked the secretary whether Cook was interested in art.

'I don't know, Chief Inspector,' she replied, looking up at him through the thick lenses of her glasses. 'He never mentioned anything about paintings to me. You would have to ask Mrs. Cook.'

'What about drawings?' asked Walker, 'Did you ever see him with any drawings in his office?'

Sutton thought for a moment and then said, 'I do remember Mr. Morris taking a bright red folder into Mr. Cook's office once, and I heard them having one of their very loud discussions. That particular discussion was about drawings. It ended in a row, as their discussions often did, and when Mr. Morris left he was very angry, which was also not uncommon.'

'Mr. Morris had drawings with him when he saw Cook?'

'He had a folder,' replied Sutton. 'I never actually saw the drawings.'

'Did Morris have the folder with him when he left?'

'No, I don't think he did. In fact, I'm sure he didn't. He must have left it with Mr. Cook. But I never saw the red folder again. Mr. Cook must have put it in his safe.'

'When you looked in Mr. Cook's safe on the day he died you didn't see the folder?' Walker asked.

'No. And I looked through the contents of the safe thoroughly, as you told me to. There were folders in there but not that red one.'

At that moment their order arrived. Although he was famished and the sandwiches looked appetising, Walker realised that the luncheon was over. He needed to make yet another visit to Morris's house. And make it as soon as possible.

CHAPTER THIRTY-SEVEN

Constables Johnson and Braddock, summoned by Walker to assist in the search of Morris's house, arrived at the same time as Walker and Broadhurst. They found the yellow door standing open, the area around the handle splintered, and a broken chain and bent iron bolt laying on the tiled floor at the entrance to the hallway. The door had been kicked open.

'Mr. Morris?' called Walker.

Morris's head appeared around a corner at the end of the hall. When he saw who it was, he uttered an exasperated groan and his head disappeared.

Without waiting for an invitation, Walker and his companions entered the house. As they made their way down the hallway, Walker quietly said to the two constables, 'We're looking for a square bladed knife and for an old black and white drawing with German writing on the back.'

The living room, once so neat and devoid of clutter, was a mess. Furniture was upturned and books and paper were strewn everywhere. Even the painting that had been hanging on the wall on Walker's previous visits, was laying on the floor.

Morris had obviously returned one of the chairs to its original position and was now sitting slouched in it, glaring at the police intruders.

'What happened, Mr. Morris?'

Morris remained silent for a few seconds and then said, 'Someone's broken in, haven't they? That should be obvious even to you lot.'

'When did this happen?' Walker asked.

'While I was down at the "Rose and Crown". I was only away for a couple of hours.' He looked despairingly around the room.

'Why didn't you call the police?'

'Looks like I didn't have to. You're here aren't you?' He glared at Walker again and then said, 'What do you want this time?'

'I want to ask you some more questions and I'd like your permission for these officers to search your house,' said Walker.

'Why not?' Morris waved his arms and added, 'they can't mess the place up any more than it is now, can they?'

Walker nodded to the constables, indicating that they should begin their search. He then up-righted two of the overturned chairs. After positioning them so that they faced Morris, he and Broadhurst sat down.

'I want to ask you questions about some drawings, Mr. Morris.'

'What drawings?' said Morris who had been glaring at Walker but now suddenly turned his eyes away to focus on the wall.

'Drawings that were in the possession of your ex-wife, a Chelmsford art collector and, I suspect, your solicitor. All of these people have been murdered and all of the drawings are missing. I believe that these drawings came from you, Mr. Morris.'

Morris looked back at Walker who thought he saw something like fear in Morris's dark eyes. 'If you're talking about the old drawings that came from Germany,' said Morris, 'what can I tell you that you don't already seem to know? I gave two to Anna as part of our divorce settlement and two to Cook as payment for handling the divorce. And,' he added, 'I don't know anything about an art collector from Chelmsford.'

'There were four drawings?'

'Yes.'

'Where exactly did they come from?' Walker asked

'I found them in an old farm house in Germany.'

'Were they in an old briefcase that had the initials, "H. G." on it?'

Morris looked surprised. 'Where did you hear that?'

'Never mind,' said Walker. 'Is it true?'

'No, of course not.' Morris tried to laugh. 'That's what I told Anna to make her think they were more valuable than they really were.'

'Why would you want Anna to think that?' asked Walker.

'Because,' said Morris, 'if she didn't think drawings, books, or papers were valuable, she was likely to rest a glass of wine on them.'

Walker realised he wasn't going to learn anything more about the drawings from Morris. He stood up and said, 'Do you mind if I have a wander around, Mr. Morris?'

Morris shrugged and said, 'Do what you have to do.'

Walker began his tour of the house on the top floor. He noted that, as was the case with the downstairs living room, and as with the rooms in Locke's house, there was a consistent two-colour décor. The bathroom was decorated in pale blue and white while the bedroom was decorated in white and various shades of green. A small study had white walls and black furnishings.

When Walker returned to the ground floor, Morris was still sitting in his chair. He was watching, without apparent interest, as the constables, assisted by Broadhurst, searched through the papers and books scattered on the floor.

Walker wandered into the kitchen. This, he noted, had the same colour scheme as the living room. Brown and white. The white floor tiles had been extended into this smaller room and the table, chairs and bench tops were all dark brown.

Walker was about to re-enter the living room when he realised that something was not quite right. It suddenly registered with him that although most things in the kitchen were coloured either brown or white, a mat under the white refrigerator was dark green. Why dark green? Walker wondered. Maybe, he thought, because it was the only mat handy when needed? But why, he further asked himself, was a mat needed under a fridge

Walker called Braddock and Johnson into the room and asked them to help him lift the refrigerator off the mat. When they had done so he turned the mat over. Attached to its underside with sticky tape was a clear plastic bag and in the bag was a piece of thick, yellowing paper. On the paper, clearly visible, was an ink drawing of two boys.

CHAPTER THIRTY-EIGHT

Morris had been arrested and escorted to the police station by Johnson and Braddock. Walker had attempted, with limited success, to secure Morris's front door, while Broadhurst called Kent to see how he was faring and to let him know about Morris's arrest. Walker and Broadhurst were now entering the police station parking lot in Walker's old Chrysler.

'You may as well go home and enjoy what's left of the weekend, Paige,' said Walker. He frowned. 'The superintendent will be back on Monday so I'll have to come in tomorrow to finish off my paperwork.' Then he smiled. 'But tonight, I'm off to a friend's house for a nice home-cooked meal.' He climbed out of the car and added, 'I just have to pop upstairs and get the nice bottle of wine I've got stashed in my desk drawer.'

Broadhurst smiled as she got out of the car and said, 'Good for you. I hope I get to meet this friend of yours one day.'

'You will. I'll have you and your latest boyfriend over to my place for dinner soon so that you can meet her,' said Walker. 'Very soon, I promise.'

Broadhurst's smile faded as Walker hurried towards the station entrance. What latest boyfriend? It had been months since she'd last been out with a man. She spent her free evenings not socialising but watching movies on television and reading her beloved crime novels, a passion she unknowingly shared with Walker's "friend". Still, when she went to Walker's house to meet his girlfriend she supposed she could take Kent along. Walker wouldn't mind. She quite liked Peter

157

and knew that he fancied her. She started to smile again as she opened the door of her car.

Constable Braddock was leaning against the counter talking to Sergeant Williamson when Walker entered the station. When he saw Walker, he straightened up and said, 'Morris says he needs to speak to you, sir. Urgently.'

'Is a solicitor with him?'

'No, sir. He says he doesn't want a solicitor.'

Walker looked at his watch and sighed. 'I suppose I better see what he wants. Do you mind coming down with me, Stewart? Best I have a witness in case he later accuses me of police brutality.'

Braddock smiled broadly and eagerly followed Walker along the corridor towards the stairs.

Once they had entered the small, white-walled cell, Walker said to Morris, 'Make this quick please, Mr. Morris. I don't have much time.'

Morris, who was sitting on a thin, narrow bunk, said, 'I want to tell you the real story about the drawings, Chief Inspector.'

'Go on then. I'm listening.' Walker noted that all of the man's previous hostility had vanished.

Morris looked into Walker's eyes. 'Firstly,' he said, 'I didn't find those drawings in a farmhouse. I bought them from Anna's brother about eighteen months ago when Anna and I went over to Germany for Anna's father's seventieth birthday celebration. I guessed that they had been stolen because he sold them to me so cheaply – and because he told me not to tell Anna where I got them.' Morris began speaking more earnestly. 'Anna had told me previously that he'd been in prison for theft when he was younger. Anna hated him. She wouldn't tell him our address in England for fear he'd come and visit. She wouldn't even give her parents our address in case they gave it to him. They corresponded via a post office box Anna had in Colchester.' Morris looked down and shrugged. 'Anyway, when Anna eventually saw the drawings, I told her I'd found them in a deserted farmhouse while I'd been cycling just outside Hanover.'

'And you gave two of these drawings to Anna as part of your divorce settlement,' said Walker.

'Yes, and one to Cook as part of his fee for handling my divorce.'

'You now say you gave him only one,' said Walker. He looked intently at Morris. 'Why didn't you give him both?'

Morris looked at the floor. 'I took only one of them with me when I went to see him. He was so reluctant to take it I knew he wouldn't have wanted another one.' Morris looked up again at Walker. 'And when he finally accepted the one I took in, he allowed me so little off my bill that I was disgusted. We had a huge row.'

'Then why did you let him keep it?'

'I had to. I had no choice. I had very little money at that time.'

'Is that it?' said Walker. He glanced at his watch. He was in a hurry but he sensed that Morris had more to tell him.

'No. There's more.' Morris shifted position on his bunk and again looked down at the floor. Walker noted that the nervousness Morris had exhibited during Walker's first two visits to Morris's house had returned.

'On the night before Anna was killed,' Morris began, 'I was visited by a man wanting to speak to Anna. He said she had something that belonged to him. When I said she didn't live at my address, he didn't believe me and became quite angry. Then when I told him we were divorced, and gave him her new address, he calmed down and left. The next day, the day Anna was killed, he returned and said that Anna had told him I had two drawings that belonged to him. He demanded that I give them to him and threatened me.' Morris looked up. He was becoming agitated. 'But then I got angry. I didn't believe they belonged to him and I certainly wasn't going to simply hand over the drawings to a stranger. So I told him I'd given both of them to my solicitor as payment for a debt. He got furious then and asked for Cook's address. After I gave it to him, he stormed out of the house.' Morris paused and rubbed his cheeks with his hands. 'When I heard that Anna had been killed, I thought it may have been him. Then when

Cook was murdered, I was sure of it. I knew Cook would have told him that I still had a drawing so I knew he'd come back. I'm sure that he was the one who broke in when I finally left the house to go to the pub.'

'Why didn't you call the police station or tell me about the man and your suspicions when I came to see you?' Walker asked.

'Because I knew you wouldn't believe me. You probably don't believe me now!'

'Why did you tell me that you'd given Cook two drawings and not show me the one you had hidden?' Walker asked calmly.

'Because if I told you that I had one of the drawings you might have taken it and I couldn't risk that. I had to keep it. As I said, I knew he'd come back and when he did, he would have killed me if I didn't have the drawing.'

'Why did you go to so much trouble to hide it?' Walker stared hard at Morris.

Morris sighed and looked down. Walker's stare seemed to be penetrating his brain. 'I didn't want him to find it before I'd had a chance to bargain with him. For my life.' Morris's shoulders slumped. 'And now you've got it and when he finds out he'll kill me.' His face now became haggard. He looked up at Walker and there was pleading in his eyes. 'That's why I'm telling you this. When you let me out of here you're going to have to give me protection.'

'Why would we let you out?'

'Because I didn't kill anybody.'

Walker was sceptical. He stared at Morris for a few seconds before speaking. 'Tell me, Mr. Morris. What did this man who visited you look like?'

'He was tall, dark-haired, and had very dark eyes.'

'That doesn't help much,' said Walker. 'That description fits many people. Including you.'

'Oh, I'm not as tall as him, Chief Inspector. He was even taller than you. What are you – six foot five?' When Walker nodded, Morris continued. 'This bloke was at least two inches taller than you.' Morris paused. He was becoming confident and some of his old arrogance was returning. He then said, 'And I don't look like him in other ways, Chief Inspector. I've got dark olive skin. This man's skin was pale. Very pale. It was probably the reason why he wore a hat. To protect his skin from the sun. He always took his hat off after he entered my house but would put it on again before he left. The first time he arrived, he was wearing a wide brimmed felt hat and the second time a straw one.'

Walker had a flashback; a sudden mental image of the tall man who had nearly collided with the pretty jogger. That man had been wearing a wide brimmed hat.

Walker had a sudden thought. What if the man had been headed not for the co-op but for Morris's house? And what if he had turned back not because he had forgotten his wallet but because he had seen Walker and recognised him as a policeman?

Walker had another thought. The man who had visited the art dealer in Colchester. Did he have pale skin? If so, perhaps Morris was telling the truth. Walker resolved to telephone Stone. He would also ask him about the address Anna had given him.

Walker looked at his watch and realised that if he didn't leave now he would be late getting to Jenny's house. He still had to go upstairs and get that bottle of wine.

'I'm sorry, Mr. Morris, but I have to go.' Walker was about to exit the cell when yet another thought struck him. 'I'll come and talk to you again. I'll need the name and address of Anna's brother. If this pale-skinned man does exist, perhaps Anna's brother knows who he is.'

Morris said, 'Anna's brother, whose name was Matthius, died three months ago, Chief Inspector. He was stabbed.'

CHAPTER THIRTY-NINE

It was a quarter to eight on Monday morning. Sheen had returned from Brighton and had arrived at the police station early. He was now at his desk and Walker was sitting facing him. Walker was there to explain why some reports hadn't been completed but Sheen wasn't interested in discussing unfinished paperwork. He was interested in the arrest of Morris.

'Congratulations on solving this case, Julian.' Sheen smiled briefly at the chief inspector and then became serious. 'I must say, I didn't like receiving the news of another murder occurring on my patch while I was in the company of such high-ranking officers.' He paused, looked downwards and flicked his finger at an imaginary speck of dust on his uniform. He then looked up again and continued speaking. 'The chief constable even said to me that perhaps the next series of that popular television murder show – I forget what it's called – should be set in Essex instead of the Cotswolds!' He looked momentarily embarrassed by the memory but quickly recovered and gave Walker another brief smile.

Walker returned the smile but before he could reply, Sheen spoke again.

'Well, we now have the guilty party in custody. That's all that matters.' Sheen folded his arms, leaned back in his plush office chair and smiled again. He then said, 'I've arranged to give a press conference at eleven o'clock.'

Walker emitted a slight cough. He hesitated for a moment and then said, 'You might want to hold off on that, sir. I think we might have the wrong man.'

'What?!' The superintendent's face registered disbelief and he sat up straight. 'What are you talking about?'

Walker sighed. Then, keeping his eyes on Sheen's face; a face that was now successively expressing surprise, curiosity, and anxiety, Walker began relating Morris's story of the pale skinned man. When Walker had finished telling the story, Sheen sat back in his chair with a relieved look on his face and laughed dismissively. 'Sounds like poppycock to me, Chief Inspector.'

Walker remained silent.

When he saw the serious expression on Walker's face, Sheen said, 'Surely you don't believe Morris's story?' There was now some concern in his voice.

'I'm afraid I do, sir.'

'Why?'

Walker sat up straight and spoke earnestly. 'Morris's description fits the man I saw outside his house. And I've just spoken to the art dealer in Colchester. He wears tinted glasses so he didn't know whether the tall, dark-eyed man who visited him had very pale skin or not, but he did say that the man he saw was carrying a hat. The dealer also said that the address Anna Gruber gave him was Morris's, not her own. It all fits in with Morris's story.' Walker took a breath and continued quickly before Sheen could respond, 'And I've just received the forensics report from Chelmsford. There were several fingerprints found on the empty frame in Clement's house but none of them belong to Morris.'

The superintendent remained silent for a moment. He then exhaled loudly and said, 'None of that means Morris didn't kill those people. He had that drawing in his possession, didn't he?'

'He had only one drawing in his possession, sir. We've searched his house thoroughly and didn't find the others. And we also didn't find the stiletto.'

'So he's hidden them somewhere else. He'll tell us eventually.' Sheen's thin lips curved into a smug smile. 'He's guilty and we have him locked up. Case closed!'

Walker was about to argue when Broadhurst appeared in the doorway. 'I'm sorry for interrupting, sir,' she said, 'but we have a problem.'

'What?!' snapped the superintendent, glaring at her.

'Sergeant Williamson rang through asking me to tell Chief Inspector Walker that a woman has just come into the station and given Morris an alibi for the time Cook was killed. The sergeant's put her in one of the interview rooms.'

Walker stared at Broadhurst without speaking.

'A woman?' said Sheen. His annoyance at Broadhurst's intrusion was replaced by bewilderment at hearing her words.

'Yes, sir,' said Broadhurst. 'She told Sergeant Williamson she was at Morris's house the morning Mr. Cook was killed.'

Sheen's face hardened. 'She's lying! She's probably a close friend or relative and just wants to save him,' he said. 'Or,' he added shrewdly, 'she could be Morris's accomplice. By coming in and making this claim she's providing an alibi for both of them.'

'Sergeant Williamson says she's a married woman who claims to be Morris's lover, sir,' said Broadhurst, 'and apparently she can prove she was there with Morris. It seems there was a reliable witness.'

'There doesn't seem to be much respect for the Ten Commandments from anyone involved in this case,' muttered Walker. 'Murders, theft, adultery, lies, and now more adultery. What next? Someone coveting someone else's donkey?'

Broadhurst smiled.

'I'm glad to see that you find this funny, Sergeant,' the superintendent said sarcastically. He turned to Walker. 'This means you'll have to release Morris.' He then looked up at the ceiling and said despairingly, 'What a catastrophe! I'm supposed to hold a press conference in a couple of hours! It's too late to cancel. What am I going to say?'

'May I make a suggestion, sir?' said Walker.

The superintendent stared at Walker for a few seconds with an expression of suspicion on his face. Finally he said, 'Go ahead.'

'Why not use the press conference to appeal to the public for information about the weapon? We can supply a picture of a square bladed stiletto.'

The superintendent placed a thumb and forefinger on his chin and stared thoughtfully at the surface of his desk. Eventually he made a decision. 'Yes,' he said slowly. 'That's actually not a bad idea. That should grab the press's attention.' He looked at Walker and said, 'And hopefully stop them asking why you arrested someone for three murders he didn't commit.'

'Yes, sir,' Walker said quietly, 'but actually there may have been four murders.'

'What?!' the superintendent's eyes widened in surprise.

'Yes, sir,' said Walker. 'It's possible that whoever killed Anna, Cook and Clement, also killed Anna's brother.'

'Where? When?' the superintendent spluttered. He had a horrified expression on his face.

'Don't worry, sir,' said Walker. 'It didn't happen on your patch. He was killed in Germany three months ago.'

The superintendent glared at Walker for a long moment and then said, 'I think we'll let the German police look after that one, Chief Inspector.'

CHAPTER FORTY

When Walker and Broadhurst entered the interview room they were stunned. Even Walker could not prevent the amazement from showing on his face. Standing in the centre of the room, calmly smoking a cigarette, was Mrs. Cook.

Walker finally found his voice. 'Good morning, Mrs. Cook. I'm sorry to have kept you waiting.' Walker gestured towards an empty chair.

'Good morning Chief Inspector. Sergeant.' Cook, dressed in the same dark trouser suit she had been wearing when the detectives had first met her, seated herself behind the battered table.

'I'm sorry, but you can't smoke in here, Mrs. Cook,' said Walker. 'Would you like a cup of tea or coffee?'

'No thank you.' Cook extinguished her cigarette by grinding it against the end of the table. 'Let's just get on with this, shall we?'

Walker and Broadhurst seated themselves in the chairs opposite Cook and Walker said, 'Is it true that you were with Richard Morris on the morning that your husband was killed?'

'Yes. We are – for want of a better word – "lovers", and have been for some time. Since soon after my husband began fooling around with that slut, Anna Gruber. When she was married to Richard.'

'So you did know that Anna and your husband were having an affair,' said Walker.

'I'd hardly call it an affair but, yes, I did know he was having sex with her. It wasn't hard to find out. When he started behaving like a love-sick teenager and leaving for work extra early, I followed him. I saw Gruber enter his building soon after he arrived so I waited a while and then I went in. I went upstairs and could hear them in his office.'

'You didn't confront them?' asked Broadhurst.

'No.' Cook examined her nails. 'I nearly did but then I realised that if he became aware I knew, there would be a divorce. And I couldn't afford that.'

'So you decided to get even by having an affair with Anna's husband,' said Walker.

Cook locked eyes with Walker. 'My relationship with Richard started out as an act of revenge but it soon developed into something we both enjoyed. Richard was still in love with Anna and I was in love with nobody.' Cook shrugged. 'But it was convenient and satisfying.'

'Did you tell Morris that your husband was having an affair with his wife?' asked Walker.

'No, I didn't. And I don't think he ever found out. If he did know he certainly never said anything to me.'

'Why would Morris have an affair with you if he was in love with his wife, Mrs. Cook?' asked Broadhurst.

Cook gave Broadhurst a sardonic smile and said, 'Because he's a man, Sergeant. And I'm sure you know how weak men can be.'

Broadhurst stared at Cook but said nothing more.

'Can it be confirmed that you were with Morris on the morning of your husband's murder, Mrs. Cook?' asked Walker. He watched the woman's eyes closely.

'Yes. The postman was delivering mail when I entered Richard's front yard and he saw Richard opening the front door. The postman knows both of us.'

CHAPTER FORTY-ONE

'Well,' said Walker, 'I may not like Mrs. Cook, but I believe her. And I'm sure the postman will confirm her story.'

'And that eliminates Morris from our list of suspects,' said Broadhurst.

'Yes, it does,' Walker said. Then he smiled.

'What's funny?'

'I was just thinking about the expression on the superintendent's face when you told him Morris had an alibi. I thought he was going to have a stroke.'

'And I thought he was going to have another stroke when you led him to believe that we'd had four murders here in Essex,' said Broadhurst, trying unsuccessfully not to smile. 'That was very unkind of you, Chief Inspector.'

Walker laughed. He and Broadhurst were seated in the police cafeteria. Walker had again missed breakfast so had ordered his usual eggs, sausages, bacon and cup of tea. Broadhurst hadn't missed breakfast so had purchased only a cup of tea.

Broadhurst waited until Walker had swallowed the last piece of sausage before speaking again. 'Do you really think Anna's brother was killed by the same man?'

'It's a possibility,' said Walker, wiping his lips with a paper serviette and reaching for his tea, 'but if he was, he was killed before our victims. That, plus the fact that he was killed in Germany, would possibly mean that the stiletto originated in Germany and not here in England.'

'If you think that,' said Broadhurst, 'why suggest to the Super-intendent that he use the press conference to appeal to the English public for help in tracing its origin?'

'I suggested it simply because it gave the superintendent a reason not to cancel his press conference,' said Walker. 'If he had nothing to tell the press and had to cancel, you can be sure we would have been the ones to receive the brunt of his anger.'

'We won't know for sure that Anna's brother was killed by the stiletto unless we contact the German police,' said Broadhurst, 'and I don't think the superintendent would be very happy about us getting involved in the German murder.'

'He'll come around,' said Walker. 'He'll agree to anything if he thinks it will help the "Grey Man" catch the "Pale Man".'

Broadhurst said nothing. She appeared to have been surprised by his words.

'What?' said Walker. 'I know you think it annoys me but allow me to let you in on a little secret. I'm actually quite pleased with my nickname.' He winked, but Broadhurst wasn't fully convinced.

'If the stiletto originated in Germany,' said Broadhurst, returning to the more comfortable subject, 'then maybe the killer is German.' A thought suddenly came to her. 'Did you ask Morris whether the pale-skinned man had an accent?'

'No,' said Walker, 'and I should have.' He looked at his watch and then reached inside his coat pocket for his mobile phone. 'He should be back in his house by now. I'll give him a call.'

'DCI Walker here, Mr. Morris,' said Walker after Morris had picked up his phone and identified himself. Walker turned on his phone's speaker so that Broadhurst could hear what Morris had to say.

'Yes, Chief Inspector?' Broadhurst noticed that Morris, under-standably, spoke warily.

'Did the pale-skinned man have a foreign accent?'

'No, he was English. He did have a slight accent but it sounded like he came from the East End,' said Morris. 'That's why I didn't think the drawings belonged to him as he claimed. Anna's brother had never been to England so he couldn't have stolen it from this chap.' Morris was quiet for a moment and then said, 'I never thought of it before, Chief Inspector, but I suppose the light-skinned man could have visited Germany, maybe purchased the drawings in that country, and Matthius stole them from him there.'

'A good point, Mr. Morris. Thank you,' said Walker.

'Are you keeping a close watch on my house, Chief Inspector?' Morris suddenly sounded nervous.

'Yes, we are, Mr. Morris. There's a car there twenty-four hours a day.'

'It's just that I can't see it.' Morris sounded a little sceptical.

'Well, that's good, isn't it? If you can't see it, neither will the pale-skinned man.'

'I suppose so. Was there anything else you wanted to ask me?'

'No, that's it for now thank you. Goodbye, Mr. Morris.'

Walker was about to close his phone when a thought occurred to him. He would ring Stone and ask him the question he had just put to Morris.

Walker pressed Stone's number, which, like Morris's, he had stored on his mobile, and waited for the art dealer to answer. Stone's sudden loud response drew the attention of two uniformed, female constables sitting at the next table. Two frowning faces turned towards Walker but the frowns quickly vanished when they recognised him. Two blushing faces quickly turned away as Walker turned off his phone's speaker.

His introductory query about accent were the last words Walker uttered for what seemed, to Broadhurst, to be a very long time. Finally Walker, sounding a little exasperated, offered his thanks and farewell and ended the call.

'Fortunately, one of his clients just turned up,' said an obviously relieved Walker as he returned the phone to his pocket. 'He said much the same as Morris – but of course in a much longer-winded way.

He is positive the "Pale Man" is English. He said, and I quote, "Just between you and me, Chief Inspector, my visitor's accent was one that I once had, and one which I've spent most of my adult life trying to eradicate. That man is a Cockney".'

Broadhurst laughed and said, 'I told you that windbag had a phoney accent!'

'Yes, you did,' replied Walker. 'I accept your assertion that Stone is a phoney, but, more importantly, do we accept his assertion that our killer is English?'

CHAPTER FORTY-TWO

Walker and Broadhurst entered the incident room to find Kent, looking healthy and cheerful, eagerly waiting for them. Walker and Broadhurst performed their usual routine of moving chairs over to Kent's desk and sat down. Broadhurst then proceeded to relay to Kent, in great detail, the events that had occurred in the relatively short time since Morris's arrest. Walker leaned back in his chair and, without interrupting, patiently waited for her to finish.

When Broadhurst finally ended her lengthy narration, Kent asked, 'What's happening with Morris?'

'He's been released and I told Bob Williamson to keep an eye on him,' Walker replied. 'Bob's having a car sit out the front of Morris's house twenty-four hours a day for the next few days. The "Pale Man" doesn't know we've got the drawing so I think he'll be back to confront Morris. Morris thinks so too. He's scared.'

'May I have a look at the drawing?' asked Kent.

'Of course,' said Walker, standing and heading for his office. 'It's in my desk.'

When he returned he handed the drawing to Kent and walked over to the white-board. As he erased the names "Richard Morris" and "Elizabeth Cook", Walker said, 'I must remember to take that drawing down to the evidence room later.'

'That's Max and Moritz!' said Kent, staring at the drawing.

'Who are they?' Broadhurst asked.

'They were the main comic strip characters in nineteenth century Germany,' said Kent. 'In fact, some historians say they were the world's first regular comic strip characters.'

'Never heard of them,' said Broadhurst.

'No, you probably haven't. But I'll bet you've heard of the "Katzenjammer Kids", the world's longest running newspaper comic strip,' said Kent. 'That was an American strip created in imitation of "Max and Moritz" at the end of the nineteenth century. William Hearst used it to sell his newspapers to the thousands of newly arrived German immigrants.'

'Fascinating,' said Broadhurst, rolling her eyes at a smiling Walker.

Kent was too focused on the drawing to notice his fellow detectives' amused reaction to his enthusiastic narration. He continued to study the drawing, but silently now. Suddenly he frowned and quietly said, 'I've seen this drawing before.'

Broadhurst smiled and said, 'Where, Superman? In a comic book?'

'No,' replied Kent. 'Max and Moritz have been reprinted in English language publications,' he paused for a few seconds, 'but I've seen this one somewhere else.'

Something about the way Kent spoke caught Walker's attention. He looked closely at Kent. 'What is it, Peter?'

'I've seen this drawing in a museum.' He looked up at Walker with both surprise and consternation on his face. 'This drawing has been stolen from the Wilhelm Busch Museum.'

'Willum what museum?' said Broadhurst.

'Wilhelm Busch. He was the creator of "Max and Moritz". He lived in Hanover and they built a museum there to honour him,' said Kent. 'They also exhibit the work of other comic strip artists.'

'You've been there?' Walker asked.

'Yes,' replied Kent. 'I went there several years ago to see a Carl Barks exhibition.'

'Who?' asked Broadhurst.

'Carl Barks. The American artist who created Donald Duck's Uncle Scrooge for Walt Disney's comic books.'

'And you definitely saw this drawing in the museum, Peter?' asked Walker, sitting himself in Osborne's chair.

'Oh yes, sir. It was on the wall with three others. Together they tell a story. This is the first in the set. The two boys, Max and Moritz, are planning some mischief. The second drawing shows them carrying out the mischief and the third shows them being caught. The final picture has them being punished. The four drawings first appeared in the German magazine, "Münchener Bilderbogen".'

'So, if the drawings Morris had were stolen by Anna's brother from a museum,' said Broadhurst, 'who would want to kill him?'

'Maybe the killer stole the drawings from the museum and Anna's brother stole them from him,' said Kent.

'In order to determine who the killer is,' said Walker, 'perhaps we should be asking why he is prepared to go to such extreme measures to obtain these drawings.'

The three detectives remained silent for a moment, all apparently deep in thought. Then Broadhurst spoke.

'Is this drawing very valuable, Peter?'

'It could sell at auction for as little as one hundred pounds,' replied Kent. 'But this is a single panel of a four panel sequence. If all four panels were sold together, they would bring much more than four hundred pounds.'

'So Stone gave Anna a good price,' said Broadhurst.

'Yes,' said Walker. 'But only because he was guaranteed a quick profit.'

'Being worth around one hundred pounds does not make this drawing particularly valuable, does it?' said Broadhurst.

'People have killed for less,' said Walker. 'But our killer is taking plenty of risks and seems to be acting obsessively. He's obviously killing for a reason other than financial gain. But what other reason could there be?'

'Maybe the killer is someone like Clement,' said Kent. 'A collector.'

Walker thought about that for a while and then said, 'You may be right, Peter, many collectors are obsessive. I think however, that our killer's obsession is about more than simply adding something to a collection.'

Walker stood up. 'I think we should contact the museum as well as the police in Hanover. I think that's the only way we are going to learn something useful about the killer and maybe why he is going to such extreme lengths to obtain the drawings.' He looked at his watch and said, 'I'll do that later. Right now, it's time to face the media.'

'You're attending the press conference, sir?' said Broadhurst. She was surprised. Sheen was renowned for making solo appearances whenever he had the opportunity to be in the limelight.

'Yes, I think the superintendent wants me there to answer unwanted questions; specifically questions that might arise about police competency in handling this case.'

CHAPTER FORTY-THREE

A few years ago, Superintendent Sheen had set aside one of the police station's smaller rooms specifically for press conferences. The room contained a table and a single chair at one end and about twenty other chairs, lined up in rows, facing the table. When the room had been set up, Walker had figured that twenty chairs was an optimistic number for press conferences conducted by the superintendent. And in the past he had been proven right. Today however, he was surprised. All of the chairs were occupied and several people were standing at the rear and sides of the room. And making the room even more cramped was the large amount of television equipment. Obviously, several reporters of the news had come from beyond Essex.

In such a small room, the noise was deafening. Questions were being hurled at Walker even before he had seated himself next to Sheen, on a chair only recently placed at the table. Walker smiled when he realised that this chair was much lower than the one occupied by Sheen.

Eventually the noise subsided so that the words of the superintendent could be heard. He introduced Walker, knowing full well that the chief inspector needed no introduction, and then quickly brought up the subject of the murder weapon. He spoke of the stiletto's history, of the various blades, and the importance of locating one with a particular blade. As he spoke, he held aloft a picture of the stiletto.

To Sheen's relief, when he finished speaking, the questions immediately asked of him by the media members related only to the picture of the stiletto.

Sheen's relief, however, was relatively short-lived. Sarah, the blonde television reporter who had, one week earlier, provided Walker with the opportunity to appeal for bus travelling witnesses, rose to her feet. Ignoring Sheen, she asked Walker why Morris had been released.

Walker glanced sideways at Sheen who, with obvious resignation, simply shrugged and looked for dust on his uniform.

'Mr. Morris was arrested,' said Walker, 'because the evidence pointed to him. And it pointed to him because he had given us false information. Once in the police station however, he realised the need to cooperate and gave us truthful answers to our questions. His answers have been of enormous benefit to our investigation and because we no longer have any reason to believe he was involved in the murders, he has been released.' Walker paused and a barrage of questions were directed at him. Walker ignored them and said, 'All I am prepared to say from this point is to ask that you please respond to Superintendent Sheen's request and assist us in our public appeal for information about the murder weapon. Thank you.'

Walker turned his head and looked directly at Sheen, thus indicating to the assembly that he no longer considered himself to be part of the conference.

The superintendent, taking his cue, quickly stood up and gestured towards a pile of papers on the table. They were photocopies of the printed computer drawing he had previously displayed. He said, 'I would greatly appreciate it if you each took one of these photographs of the murder weapon and used it in an appeal for information to your respective readers or viewers.' Sheen then said, 'Thank you all for coming,' and gave Walker a quick, gentle nudge. Walker immediately rose and followed his boss towards the room's exit. They ignored the dozens of noisy questions that pursued them.

CHAPTER FORTY-FOUR

Walker returned the phone receiver to its cradle rather forcefully and walked out of his office into the incident room feeling quite frustrated. Broadhurst, standing next to Kent's desk, was watching him. She could see that he was irritated.

'Language problem, sir?' she asked.

'No, everyone I spoke to was fluent in English. It just took ages to find someone who knew anything about the thefts. And then, when I did find someone, we kept getting interrupted.' Walker once again moved Osborne's chair over to the desk where Kent was sitting. 'It seems the museum is very busy at the moment. It's the middle of their tourist season.'

'Did you learn anything useful, sir?' asked Kent as Broadhurst dragged her chair over.

Walker removed his jacket and sat down. He realised that, since this case had begun, he had spent more time sitting on DC Osborne's chair than on his own. 'Yes,' he said, cheering up slightly, 'I guess I did.' Then he frowned and said, 'There were still questions I wanted to ask but the curator had to hang up.'

Walker proceeded to tell the others what he had managed to learn from the museum's head curator. 'The theft of the four Busch drawings occurred almost two years ago and the main suspect was a man named Johannes Radke. The theft coincided with Radke losing his job as a guard at the museum. He was dismissed because he consistently turned up for work late and intoxicated. The police interviewed him but nothing could be proven.'

'Do you think this Radke might be the killer, sir?' asked Kent.

'I don't think so. I asked the curator, Frau Schmidt, if he was tall with dark hair, dark eyes and pale skin and she said he was short, fat, had brown hair and blue eyes and that his skin was no whiter than anyone else's.'

'If he's not the killer then he might also have been murdered,' said Kent.

'No, he's still alive,' said Walker. 'Frau Schmidt saw him on Friday. She told me she often sees him from the train on her way home from work.'

'Did she say where, sir?' asked Kent.

Walker looked at the piece of paper he had brought from his office and said, 'She said a place called "Schünemannplatz".'

'Is that where he lives?' asked Broadhurst.

'I don't know. I was about to ask her whether she had his home address when she told me she had to go and hung up.'

'I know where Schünemannplatz is,' said Kent. 'When I was in Hanover I used to go by train to the Kaiser Centre most mornings and the station I'd get off was one station after Schünemannplatz station.'

'What's the "Kaiser Centre"?' asked Broadhurst.

'A gym. A very good one.'

'You went to a gym?' said Broadhurst. There was disbelief in her voice.

'I used to exercise all the time,' said Kent, defensively. 'As a matter of fact, I'm thinking of taking classes again next week at the university's gym.'

Broadhurst uttered a single 'Ha!' but before Kent could respond, Walker interrupted. As much as he enjoyed the somewhat affectionate bantering in which his junior officers sometimes engaged, he needed them to get back to thinking about the case.

'What would Radke be doing that would allow him to be observed so frequently by Frau Schmidt from a train?' Walker said.

'I think I can guess,' said Kent. 'The curator implied that Radke had a drinking problem. He may also be unemployed. Anyway, next to the train line, near the station, is a large plaza where dozens of drunk and unemployed males and females congregate every day.'

'So Radke shouldn't be difficult to find,' said Walker.

Broadhurst looked at Walker with suspicion in her eyes. She said, 'You're not thinking of going there are you, sir?'

'We might have to eventually. But first we'll see what the Hanoverian polizei can tell us.'

Their discussion was interrupted by the brief ringing of Walker's office phone. It was followed soon after by the buzzing of his mobile. Walker pulled his mobile from his pocket and held it to his ear for a few seconds without speaking. Then he leapt to his feet.

'Come on!' he said as he grabbed his coat and moved swiftly towards the doorway. 'The "Pale Man's" returned to Morris's house.'

CHAPTER FORTY-FIVE

Morris was laying on his back on the kitchen floor. Broadhurst knelt beside him and sought a pulse. She slowly shook her head. Walker made sure that he didn't look directly at the body. He focused on the pale-faced, barely conscious Constable Braddock who was on the floor alongside Morris. Braddock was sitting in a huge pool of blood, leaning back against a dishwasher. Constable Johnson was kneeling next to Braddock, using a towel to try and stop the blood that was coming out of Braddock's neck. From the amount of blood on the towel and on the floor, it was obvious to Walker that the young constable had been stabbed in an artery.

'He went out there,' said Johnson, nodding with his head toward the rear of the kitchen.

Walker moved over to the doorway and made a quick survey of the yard and laneway. He could see no-one. But then he didn't expect to. He knew the "Pale Man" was long gone.

'How long ago did you call for an ambulance?' Walker asked as he turned back to face the scene of carnage.

'Before I called you!' said a panicking Johnson. 'And it'd better hurry up!'

Walker looked around. Kent was standing nearby, staring down at Morris's body. Broadhurst was on her phone. She had organised a search of the nearby streets and was now setting in motion an All Ports Warning.

Walker placed his hand on Johnson's shoulder and quietly asked him what had happened.

'Start at the beginning, Sam,' said Walker before Johnson could reply to his question.

'We were sitting in the car across the road out front and I decided to get us some lunch from the co-op,' said Johnson, trying to put more pressure on Braddock's wound with a new towel that was fast becoming blood-soaked. 'When I came out I heard a whistle and saw Stewart about to enter the front yard. He beckoned to me, pointed at the open front door, and then disappeared inside. By the time I got in here both Morris and Stewart were on the floor. A tall, pale-skinned man with very dark eyes, and wearing a dark suit and hat, was standing over Stewart. He had a very skinny knife in his hand. When he saw me he turned and ran out the back door. I couldn't chase the bastard because I knew I had to help Stewart. Blood was squirting out of him like a fountain!'

Broadhurst had finished making her calls and had left the room. Kent was still silently studying Morris's body. He had noted a wound in Morris's hand. It was surrounded by blood. A defensive wound. Unlike Anna and Cook, Morris had not been surprised by the attack. He had been ready but had been unable to ward off the fatal lunge. The killer was not only extremely accurate with his thrusts – as indicated by this killing and by the killings of Anna and Cook – he was also very forceful with his blows. The knife had passed entirely through Morris's hand.

Kent's musings were interrupted by the distant sound of an approaching ambulance and by the sound of Walker's voice.

'Peter,' said Walker, to whom Kent's appraisal of Morris's body seemed almost ghoulish. 'Sam will be accompanying Stewart so I want you to follow the ambulance in their car and then take Sam from the hospital to the station. Use Sam's fresh memory to make a facial composite of the killer and email it to all the main television stations. I want it on the evening news.'

Walker then spoke to Johnson. 'I'm sorry that you won't be able to stay at the hospital with Stewart, Sam, but we have to get the composite made as soon as possible.'

Johnson nodded and Walker asked him for the keys to the station car. Johnson replied that he thought they were in Braddock's pocket. Walker knelt, apologised unnecessarily to the now unconscious Braddock, and felt for the keys. When they were finally located, Walker passed them to Kent.

'Don't forget to add a note to the email, Peter, advising that the killer has albino-like skin.'

'You can't say that, sir,' said Broadhurst, who had returned with more towels. 'You'll be in trouble for offending albinos.'

'Alright,' said Walker testily, silently cursing. He longed for the days of pre-political correctness. 'Put "very pale skinned". You'd better not use the word "white" or you'll upset some other group.'

At that moment two ambulance medics, carrying a large medical bag and a stretcher, burst into the room. They were closely followed by the pathologist and three scene of crime officers. Walker indicated to Broadhurst that they should retreat to the back yard.

They stood on the small patio at the top of the steps leading down into the yard. Broadhurst was watching a police car speed down the lane. She said, 'I doubt he's still around, sir.'

'No, and I doubt that he'll be back. Morris probably told him we had the last drawing. I'd say that's why the "Pale Man" killed him.'

'The killer is very good at getting away,' said Broadhurst. 'I've been wondering about how he travels. After you told us you saw him walking up from the docks, I thought that perhaps he'd come by boat.'

'No, he would've had to rely too much on the tide,' said Walker. He was quiet for a moment and then spoke again. 'There's also a train station down there but it's unlikely that he's using trains. Certainly not now. He wouldn't be standing on the station platform while the police are hunting him. No, he's driving.'

'He was at Stone's office very quickly after Stone put the drawing on the internet,' said Broadhurst. 'So if he did come from another country he most likely came by plane and then drove from an airport. And as Stansted is the closest to Colchester maybe we should check his description with that airport's rental car companies?'

'A good idea, Paige,' said Walker, 'but it would probably be best to contact rental car agencies at all the major airports.' Walker was again silent for a moment before continuing. 'If we had the car's registration number as well as his description, we'd have more chance of catching him. Especially if he tried to leave the country via the tunnel.'

'Of course if he lives in England,' said Broadhurst, 'then he could have his own car, and may have no intention of leaving the country.'

'Yes,' said Walker. 'And if he does live here, he will probably have gone into hiding. Especially now that he's certain we know what he looks like.'

'Well, if he lives here, and has gone into hiding,' said Broadhurst, 'let's hope that his likeness appearing on all the television screens tonight will help us find his hiding place.'

'Yes, let's hope so,' said Walker, making for the doorway leading back into the house. 'After you've made your calls to airport rental car companies check the cameras on the roads out of Wivenhoe. Although we don't know what kind of car he's driving, it might be an idea to record the registration plates and check out the owners of any cars that are speeding. Our killer is probably too smart to travel over the speed limit but you never know. Having stabbed a policeman, he may be panicking.'

'Yes, sir.'

'And while you're doing that I'm going to telephone the German police.'

CHAPTER FORTY-SIX

When Walker and Broadhurst reached the incident room they found Kent and Johnson, sitting side by side at Kent's desk, staring at Kent's computer screen. Johnson was making comments while Kent deftly manipulated images.

Without looking away from the screen, Johnson replied, 'Not too good,' when asked by Broadhurst how Braddock was faring. Broadhurst shook her head, sat down at her desk, opened her computer and began searching for phone numbers.

Walker saw that Kent was using the recently adopted and highly sophisticated EvoFIT system to create a facial composite. Progress, Walker marvelled, and went into his office to make his phone call.

It took a long time for Walker to find a police officer who could assist him. As with his previous call to Germany, the problem was not one of language but of finding someone familiar with the subject he wanted to discuss.

'Inspector Dietering here. How may I help you?'

'I'm Detective Chief Inspector Walker from Essex Police in England, Inspector Dietering. I'd like to talk to you about one of your murders.'

'Ah! Essex! I hear you have plenty of murders of your own, Chief Inspector Walker.'

'Yes,' laughed Walker. He then became serious and said, 'I think that our murderer may also be responsible for a murder in Hanover.'

'Which murder is that, Chief Inspector?'

'The victim's name was Matthius Gruber. I believe he was killed about three months ago.'

'Yes, I remember the case. A moment please while I bring it up on my computer.'

There was a short silence and then Dietering spoke again. 'Matthius Gruber. A minor thief. He was stabbed. Case unsolved.' Dietering then asked, 'What makes you think he was killed by your man, Chief Inspector?'

'Our victims were stabbed by a square-bladed stiletto. Was your victim also killed by such a weapon?'

'It does not say so here in my report, Chief Inspector Walker, but it should say in the pathology report whether he was killed by such a weapon. I don't have that report with me but I can get it and send you a copy. What is your email address?'

Walker recited his email address and thanked the German inspector. Then he said, 'One other thing, Inspector Dietering. Do you know a man named Johannes Radke?'

'That name is mentioned here in this report. He was a close friend of Matthius Gruber. He was questioned about the murder but told us nothing. Why do you ask about him, Chief Inspector?'

'All of our victims were killed because of drawings stolen from the Wilhelm Busch Museum, Inspector Dietering,' said Walker. 'I recently spoke to the museum's head curator, Frau Schmidt, and she told me Radke was believed to be responsible for the theft.'

'Just a moment, please.' There was silence for several seconds before Dietering spoke again. 'Yes, Radke was our chief suspect in that case, which has also not been solved. Radke was interviewed but refused to speak to us. We searched his apartment but found nothing.'

'He wouldn't speak to you?'

'He would not say a single word. He has been arrested many times, usually for misbehaving while drunk, and he never says a word. He hates us,' said Dietering. He then added in a different, rather amused tone, 'Although he won't talk to us, Chief Inspector Walker, he might, given the right incentive, talk to you. Why don't you come and visit us?'

'I might just do that, Inspector Dietering,' replied Walker, who then thanked the German and said 'Auf Weidersehn', thus ending the conversation.

When Walker looked out into the incident room, he saw that Johnson had departed, presumably returning to the hospital. Kent was typing on his computer keyboard and Broadhurst was speaking into her telephone. Walker watched them while he thought of his conversation with the German police inspector. He wondered how he could convince Superintendent Sheen to authorise a trip to Germany.

Walker's thoughts were interrupted by the ringing of his phone. He picked up the receiver and listened without speaking. Seconds later, stunned and pale-faced, he lowered the receiver. Braddock hadn't made it.

CHAPTER FORTY-SEVEN

Braddock had been well-liked. The next morning, throughout the police station, officers were experiencing both extreme sadness and extreme anger. Walker was also experiencing extreme guilt. Since taking control of the case, following the murder of Anna Gruber, he had failed to prevent another three deaths, including, most tragically, the death of one of their own. This brought the total of murders committed by the "Pale Man" to six, for Walker had just received the German pathologist's report confirming that Matthius Gruber had been killed by the square-bladed stiletto.

Superintendent Sheen was especially angry. That one of his own men had been murdered was outrageous. Walker had been summoned to his office.

'What are you doing about this, Chief Inspector?' Sheen demanded. He sat stiffly behind his desk.

'Everything that can be done, Superintendent. The killer's description has been sent all over Britain. Every police officer in the United Kingdom, all air and sea ports, the Tunnel, and all the major railway stations are on alert. The composite picture of the killer, which according to Johnson, is a very good likeness, was sent to all the major newspapers and television stations. Calls of sightings have been pouring in ever since it was first shown on the news programs last evening.' Walker did not mention that several of these calls had come from as far afield as the Orkneys and involved UFOs.

Slightly mollified, Sheen said, 'Yes, I saw the picture on the news.' He looked down and flicked dust before saying, 'Very realistic. Was that made by Kent?'

'Yes sir.'

'Tell him I said, "good work".'

'I will, sir.'

'Alright then. Off you go on and catch this bastard.'

A relieved Walker made a hasty exit and headed for the incident room. He was glad that he had not mentioned to the superintendent the German pathologist's report. Now was not the time. News that the murderer had begun his spree in Germany, that he was possibly a German, and that therefore a trip by Walker to Germany would probably be necessary, was best kept for later.

As he entered the incident room, Walker saw that all the phones were in use. Kent was at his desk, listening to his phone and making notes, Broadhurst was talking into her phone, and DC Osborne's desk and phone were currently being used by Probationary Police Constable Isobel Dakarta.

Dakarta was a short, slim girl with dark skin, large brown eyes, and long, black hair that was braided and tied up at the back of her head. She was fresh out of the police academy and Walker had heard that she was enthusiastic and extremely clever.

'Sir!'

The excitement in Broadhurst's voice immediately took Walker's attention away from Dakarta and he walked quickly to her desk. 'What is it, Paige?' he asked.

'It looks like we might have something,' Broadhurst said. 'A woman named Arlene Curtis just rang. She operates a small business in Frinton and says the pale-skinned man has come into her shop several times. She says that he lives nearby.' She handed Walker a sheet of paper. 'Here's her address.'

Walker took the piece of paper and said, 'I'll head out there now. I'll take Kent with me and leave you ladies to man the phones.'

Broadhurst narrowed her eyes and looked at Walker as though she suspected him of being provocatively sexist.

Walker smiled at her and said innocently, 'We'll keep in touch using our mobiles.'

CHAPTER FORTY-EIGHT

When Walker and Kent entered the shop and introduced themselves, they received a very friendly greeting from a tall, solid woman with short, spikey, black hair. She was probably in her mid-thirties and wore a tight, black t-shirt and equally tight, black jeans. Despite her somewhat masculine appearance, Ms. Arlene Curtis had a soft, very feminine voice.

'I'm pleased to meet you, gentlemen. It's gratifying to receive such a prompt response to my call.' Arlene Curtis's manner of speaking made it evident to Walker that she was well-educated and rational. He now felt more confident that he wasn't on a wild goose chase.

'What can you tell us about your pale-skinned customer, Ms. Curtis?' Walker asked. He studied the enquiring eyes in the woman's make-up free face while Kent surveyed the small shop's tightly compact, enormous range of stock. As well as groceries, dairy products, frozen goods, bread and newspapers, there were rubber sandals, sunglasses, t-shirts, paperback novels, stationery, postcards, confectionary, cosmetics, cheap jewellery, toys and even shoe laces. From this tiny shop, Ms. Curtis sold just about every item that someone on holiday might need.

'Firstly, I must tell you that I recognised him immediately when I saw the photo in this morning's newspaper. It's an excellent likeness. Anyway, he first came into my shop just over a week ago and has been in about three times since then. He speaks only when spoken to and is soft-spoken, with a London accent. He is very serious and polite, and well-dressed in his suit and hat. He always takes the hat off when entering the shop. As I said, he's very polite.' Curtis paused to sneeze, covering her mouth and nose with her hand. 'Sorry, gentlemen,' she said, removing her hand and smiling. 'Spring fever in the summer.'

'On the phone, you told my sergeant that he lives nearby,' said Walker.

'Yes. I believe he rents a room from Mrs. Dorrington who has a residence across from the park, on the Esplanade – the road that runs parallel to the beach. I saw him entering her house one evening as I was walking home. I don't know the road number but the house can usually be identified by the "Room to Rent" sign Mrs. Dorrington hangs in the window.' Curtis paused, shook her head, and then said, 'The sign is not there at the moment so the directions I'm giving you are useless. It would be far easier for you if I was to simply take you there.'

Before Walker could respond, Curtis had rotated the "Open/ Closed" sign on the shop's front door and was ushering the two detectives outside onto the footpath.

Walker had insisted that they travel to Mrs. Dorrington's by car even though the house was not too far away. They drove to the end of the shop-filled street and, with an expanse of grass preventing them from continuing any further in that direction, turned to the right. In a matter of seconds, Curtis had instructed Walker to brake, shrewdly selecting a stopping point well before they had reached their actual objective.

'That's the house, Chief Inspector.' She leaned forward and pointed. 'The fully detached, three-storey dwelling with the red-brick fence and the driveway.'

Knowing that the detectives would not require her presence any longer, Curtis opened the car door and told them she was returning to her shop. Walker said that he would drive her and then return but Curtis smiled and shook her head.

'Thank you, Chief Inspector, but no, I'll walk. It will provide a much needed benefit to my cardio-vascular system.'

As she departed, Walker called out his thanks and Kent returned her wave.

Kent was pleased to be so close to the sea. He loved the smell of salt and the cries of the gulls. However, although he was thoroughly enjoying the blinding reflection of the sun's rays on the water's surface to his left, he was nevertheless far more excited by what he imagined was about to happen in one of the houses on his right. 'Shouldn't we contact the Colchester police, sir?' he asked Walker.

Walker, who was studying the house pointed out to them by Curtis, replied, 'No. They'd likely arrive with sirens blaring and cause him to scarper – if he's still in there.'

'You don't think he's in there, sir?'

'No, I don't,' said Walker. 'I think he's long gone. So calling the Colchester police would be a waste of their time.'

CHAPTER FORTY-NINE

Convinced that the "Pale Man" was no longer in the house, Walker decided to forgo stealth and simply march up to the front door and knock.

The woman who opened the door was very different from Ms. Curtis. She was older, shorter and considerably heavier. She had bluish-grey hair, currently in rollers, and wore a white apron over a yellow and red, polka-dot dress. She was similar to Ms. Curtis however, in that she greeted them with pleasant words and a wide smile.

'Mrs. Dorrington?' said Walker, reaching for his identification.

The woman nodded and said, 'I'm so sorry, gentlemen, but all of my rooms are taken. There is a nice place further down the road that may have a vacancy.'

'We're police, Mrs. Dorrington,' said Walker showing her his card. 'I'm Detective Chief Inspector Walker and this is Detective Constable Kent. We'd like to ask you about one of your guests.'

For a moment the woman seemed alarmed but she quickly recovered and asked, 'Which one? I have three at the moment.'

'We are interested in a guest who has very pale skin.'

'Pale skin? Oh! You mean Mr. Simpson.' Mrs. Dorrington leaned sideways so that she could see past Walker into the front yard. 'He must not be in at the moment. His car's gone.'

'When did you last see him, Mrs. Dorrington?'

Mrs. Dorrington thought for a while and then said, 'It would have been two, maybe three, days ago. He was going up the stairs. I rarely see him. He keeps to himself. Doesn't even join us for breakfast – even though it's paid for. The only time I know he's in is when his car's in the driveway.'

'When did he move in here, Mrs. Dorrington?' asked Walker.

'Nearly two weeks ago. A Friday morning I think it was.'

Friday, thought Walker. The day he visited Stone. He said, 'Do you mind if we come in and have a look at his room, ma'am?'

The woman hesitated for a moment and then said, 'I suppose it will be alright.' She stepped back to allow the detectives to enter.

"Simpson's" room was on the second floor. Mrs. Dorrington knocked to be sure the room was vacant, then removed a key from her pocket and unlocked the door.

The room was tidy. The bed was neatly made and there was no sign of recent occupation. Walker opened the doors of a small wardrobe while Kent pulled out the drawers of a small, bedside cabinet. Both the wardrobe and cabinet were empty. Walker was checking under the bed when Kent announced that he had found something. Walker's disturbance of the bedspread, which Mrs. Dorrington was now straightening, had revealed a small piece of cardboard laying on the floor between the cabinet and bed.

Walker removed nitrile gloves and a small evidence bag from a larger bag in his coat pocket and, after donning the gloves, carefully picked up and placed the piece of cardboard in the bag. He examined it closely through the plastic. It appeared to be a part of the end flap from a small box; a box that had probably contained a commercial product. What that product was Walker did not know, but he thought it might be helpful to find out.

The piece of cardboard might also provide a fingerprint, but for Walker this was not a major concern. This room, the bathroom, and the stairs would most likely all supply prints that could be compared with those found on the frame in Clement's house. Walker would call the crime laboratory when they were back in his car.

'Did you watch television last night, Mrs. Dorrington?' asked Walker.

'Oh yes. Mr. Beale and I watch it together every night.'

'Mr. Beale?'

'Yes, he's one of my guests, Chief Inspector. My other guest, Miss Cummings, usually watches it with us but she's away in Italy at the moment. She's a teacher at the local school.'

'And you didn't see the picture of Mr. "Simpson" on the news?' asked Walker, pulling from his pocket, and showing the woman, a photo of the composite.

'Oh, was that him? I've never seen Mr. Simpson wearing a hat. He certainly doesn't wear one indoors and, as I said, I've never seen him outdoors.'

'Didn't you hear about the pale skin?'

'No, I had the sound turned down. Mr. Beale had fallen asleep in his chair, as he usually does, and I didn't want him disturbed. He's quite elderly you know.'

Walker quietly sighed and said, 'Do you know the type of car Mr. "Simpson" drives, Mrs. Dorrington?'

'All I can tell you is that it's white and looks fairly new. I don't know much about cars.'

'Alright,' said a slightly exasperated Walker. 'Thank you anyway.'

Walker was about to leave the room when the woman said, 'Mr. Beale will know. He knows a lot about cars. He used to be an automobile salesman.'

Walker brightened and asked, 'Where will we find Mr. Beale? Is he in his room?'

'Oh no,' she laughed. 'He's sitting out in the back garden enjoying the fresh air.'

On the ground floor of the house, the windows were small and the thick curtains were drawn, keeping this area cool and in semi-darkness. It was in sharp contrast to the back yard where it was hot and extremely bright. Walker and Kent found themselves squinting when they emerged from the house but their eyes quickly adjusted to take in a well-mown lawn and several trees that, while not high, carried plenty of lush foliage. Under one of these trees had been placed a striped deck-chair and in it reclined a white-haired man, wearing a dark, checked coat, light-brown trousers, a white shirt and a dark-brown tie. On his feet were brown, laced-up shoes.

Mr. Beale appeared to be asleep, but, as Mrs. Dorrington led the detectives to his chair, his hazel eyes opened. Through a pair of thick-lensed spectacles he curiously scrutinised Walker and Kent.

'What can I do for you, gentlemen?' asked Beale after Mrs. Dorrington had made the introductions. He had a surprisingly strong voice which emerged from a mouth largely concealed by a thick, grey moustache.

'Mrs. Dorrington says you may be able to tell us the type of car driven by Mr. Simpson.'

'If the car parked out the front was Mr. Simpson's then I certainly can. It's a Ford Fiesta and I'd say it was no more than three years old.'

'Would you happen to know its registration number, sir?' Walker asked.

'No. I'm sorry, but my memory is no longer as good as it once was.'

Walker cursed silently. White Ford Fiestas were the most common cars in the entire United Kingdom. He said, 'Well thanks anyway, Mr. Beale. We won't disturb you any longer.'

As Walker turned to leave, Beale said, 'Why do you want to know about that chap's car, Chief Inspector?'

'It was on the news last night, Mr. Beale. Apparently you were asleep and missed it.' Walker glanced at his watch. 'I'm afraid we have to hurry now but Mrs. Dorrington will give you all the details. Goodbye, sir.'

When they were back in Walker's car, Walker said, 'You call for the forensic team to come and go over "Mr. Simpson's" bedroom and the bathroom, Peter. I'll call Paige and ask her to check and see if any white Ford Fiestas stolen two to three weeks ago have not yet been recovered.'

When Kent had finished making his call, Walker was still speaking to Broadhurst.

'You will also have to call airport car-rental agencies again, Paige. We need to know the names and addresses of those who have returned a white Fiesta since yesterday afternoon. We also require details of white Fiestas still on loan.' Walker paused. 'And have all the road cameras for this area checked out. We might get lucky and learn the car's plate number.'

When Walker had finally closed his phone, he said to Kent, 'I had forgotten about Clement's post-mortem. Paige has to go down to Colchester this afternoon.'

'You don't think anything useful will be learnt from the PM do you, sir?'

'No, I don't,' replied Walker. 'It's just a formality.'

Kent nodded and then asked, 'Where to now, sir?'

'Back to Ms. Curtis's shop, Peter. Let's see if she can identify your little find from "Simpson's" bedroom. I have a good feeling about it.'

CHAPTER FIFTY

Arlene Curtis was sitting on an upturned box, sorting out newspapers. She looked up and revealed surprise when she saw the detectives entering her shop.

'Chief Inspector Walker! Constable Kent! I didn't expect to see you again so soon. Am I to assume you did not capture the pale-skinned man?'

'He was gone, unfortunately,' said Walker.

'That's not good news,' said Curtis with a frown, placing on the ground the papers she had been holding and standing up to face the detectives. 'I'm sorry I was not able to provide my information much sooner.'

'Never mind, Ms. Curtis. Your information was very helpful,' said Walker, smiling at the woman before adding, 'and we're hoping that you may be able to help us some more.'

'Certainly, Chief Inspector. If I can. What is it you want to know?'

Walker removed the small plastic bag from his pocket and handed it to Curtis.

'Can you identify this piece of cardboard? We found it in the "Pale Man's" bedroom and are hoping it's from something he purchased here.'

Curtis carefully examined the cardboard through the plastic. Eventually she shook her head and said, 'I'm sorry, Chief Inspector, but it's not from any product I sell in my shop.'

'That's alright, Ms. Curtis,' said Walker, attempting to hide his disappointment as the shopkeeper handed the small bag back to him.

'It was worth a try. I thought if it was torn off a product sold from a local shop, then you would be the one most likely to recognise it.' Walker stared at the cardboard for a moment before replacing it in his pocket. 'Thanks anyway for all of your help and perhaps we shall see you again sometime.'

Walker and Kent both nodded courteously at Curtis and were about to turn and leave when she said, 'Wait a moment, Chief Inspector. As it doesn't come from any product I sell, it may come from something sold at a pharmacy. There are a few in this street but why don't you try Boots? Their shop is almost directly across the road.'

'Of course!' said Walker, giving Curtis a smile so broad that it caused her cheeks to flush. He then grasped her hand, shook it, and was about to leave when Curtis spoke again.

'If the product wasn't sold at Boots you might want to check the street's CCTV cameras. They should help you determine your "Pale Man's" movements.' Curtis hesitated and she lowered her eyes contritely before quickly adding, 'Please forgive me, Chief Inspector. Naturally you would have thought of that.'

Walker laughed and said, 'Please don't apologise, Ms. Curtis. Our recent bad luck with non-functioning CCTV has caused me to ignore them. But if the ones in your street are operational they may prove to be very useful. I thank you again.'

CHAPTER FIFTY-ONE

When they entered the pharmacy, the detectives headed directly for the prescription counter. An elderly man, with thinning white hair and wearing the customary white coat, watched their approach.

'May I assist you gentlemen?' asked the man, who was obviously the pharmacist on duty.

'I'm Detective Chief Inspector Walker and this is Detective Constable Kent,' said Walker, showing the man his credentials and then handing him the small plastic bag. 'Can you identify the product box from which this piece of cardboard was torn?'

The pharmacist brought the bag close to his silver framed glasses and slowly examined its content. He then shook his head. 'I'm sorry, but I don't know what it is.'

A slightly despondent Walker was about to say, 'Thanks anyway,' when the pharmacist suddenly yelled out: 'Pamela!'

With the name reverberating in his ear-drums, Walker watched as the pharmacist beckoned to a slender, white-coated young woman who was standing sentinel at the front of the shop.

'Pamela may be able to help you, Chief Inspector,' said the pharmacist. 'She's the one who re-orders stock.'

As she casually approached, Walker observed that the brown colour of the woman's shoulder-length hair seemed natural and that her rather pretty face was completely devoid of make-up. She was also not wearing earrings or any other jewellery.

When the woman finally reached the counter, the pharmacist handed her the plastic bag and said, 'These men are detectives,

Pamela, and want to know if that piece of cardboard is off the box of a product we sell.'

Without acknowledging the detectives' presence, the woman merely glanced at the piece of cardboard, before turning and walking up the shop's middle aisle.

A slightly bemused Walker and Kent followed her progress with their eyes. Half way up the aisle she stopped, half-turned, and pointed at a shelf. She then moved almost robotically towards the front of the shop.

Walker and Kent raised their eye-brows at each other before starting up the aisle to examine the shelf pointed at by Pamela.

'Fake tan!' exclaimed Walker when he saw the many self-tanning sprays and gels on the shelf. 'He's camouflaged his skin!'

Walker looked around for Pamela. He saw that she was now standing rigidly behind a counter at the shop's entrance. Removing the photo of the "Pale Man's" likeness from the inside pocket of his jacket, Walker strode towards the counter.

Holding the photo close to Pamela's face, Walker curtly said, 'Did you sell a synthetic tanning agent to this man?'

The woman glanced at the photo and then stared at Walker's face. Walker felt slightly uncomfortable. Her large eyes, an unusual emerald green in colour, were blank. Like the rest of her face, they were totally devoid of expression.

'Yes,' she said, very calmly.

'When?'

'Yesterday.'

'Didn't you recognise his picture on television last night or in this morning's newspaper?'

'I don't watch television and I don't read newspapers.' She spoke in a very even, unemotional tone.

Walker wondered if this young woman might be suffering from Asperger's Syndrome. He stared at her for a moment, half-regretting his brusque manner. Then, turning to Kent, he indicated it was time for them to leave.

CHAPTER FIFTY-TWO

Superintendent Sheen was a little preoccupied when Walker entered his office the following morning. Sheen intended to speak at Braddock's funeral service the next day and didn't know what he was going to say. He knew nothing about the young constable. He could not recall ever having spoken to him.

The superintendent raised his eyes from the page on which he was attempting to write and said, 'What can I do for you, Chief Inspector?'

'I just wanted to report on our progress – or rather lack of progress – in catching the killer, sir.'

Sheen sat up straight and stared hard at Walker. 'I heard that you located where he was living but that he was gone by the time you got there.'

'Yes, sir,' said Walker. 'He's done a runner and I doubt very much that we'll see him around here again. He's managed to obtain three of the four drawings and knows we have the fourth. He'd be very foolish to attempt to get that one, and I don't think he's a foolish man.'

'No, he certainly seems to be smarter than my detectives.' Sheen glanced down at his sleeve and flicked away an imaginary piece of dust before looking up again at the inspector. 'What are you going to do now?'

'There's not a lot we can do, sir. He's almost certainly changed his appearance. We know he purchased a self-tanning gel and he's probably no longer wearing a wide brimmed hat.'

'Tanning gel won't protect his skin from the sun, will it?'

'Not the one he bought, sir, but he'll most likely stay indoors during the day. If he does have to go out he'd have to wear some sort of protective head covering but I don't think it will be the type of hat he's been wearing so far. Maybe a cap with a long peak.' Walker paused and then said, 'One thing in our favour is his height. He may tan his skin and change his headwear, but he can't disguise his height.' Walker paused again. 'With the amount of publicity he's received I think he's gone into hiding and that he'll stay where he is until things quieten down.' Walker paused again. 'As far as his car is concerned, we've checked the rental car companies, and the stolen car list, but no luck. It's probably his own car and he's now keeping it hidden.'

'You checked the cameras on the roads out of Frinton, I presume?'

'Sergeant Broadhurst did, sir, and it looks as though she may have found the car he's driving.'

'And?' Excitement entered Sheen's voice.

'There were three white Fiestas captured on film leaving the area at the appropriate time. Two have been identified and cleared but the third had its plate numbers concealed by mud.'

'Damn!' said Sheen, closing his eyes and sinking into his chair. 'He is a clever bastard.'

'Yes, sir. He is.'

'Are the calls from the public still coming in?' asked Sheen, sitting up straight again in his chair.

'Yes, sir, but the ones we've received so far have been about recent sightings. We're going to spend the afternoon checking out calls. Hopefully we'll find a reliable sighting of him prior to his visit to the art dealer two weeks ago. I'd like to know where he was living before Mrs. Dorrington's boarding house.' Walker went silent for a few seconds and then said, 'Of course he may have been living in Germany when he saw the dealer's advert on the internet.'

Sheen leaned back in his chair and stared hard again at Walker. 'Germany? The other day when you were in here you said you thought this pale-skinned man had committed his first murder in Germany when he killed Anna's brother. Why did you think our killer was responsible for the brother's death?'

'Because the drawings were purchased by Morris from Anna's brother and, like our victims, Anna's brother was stabbed.'

'Might that not be a coincidence?'

'It could have been, sir, except that the German pathologist's report confirms that Matthius Gruber was killed by the same weapon used on our victims.'

Sheen sat up very straight and said, 'You've been in contact with Germany?'

'Yes, sir. A German police inspector sent me the pathologist's report,' said Walker. 'And I've been in contact with the German Museum from which, we've discovered, the drawings were stolen. The German police officer who sent me the report also told me that the chief suspect in the museum theft was an associate of Matthius Gruber.'

'You have been busy,' said Sheen quietly. His narrow eyes narrowed even more and he stood up. He crossed to his window and looked out. A couple with a young child were slowly walking along the narrow path that diagonally crossed the grassy playing field behind the police station. Sheen silently watched them without really seeing them.

Walker was silent.

Eventually the superintendent turned and faced Walker. He said, 'So you believe the killer is German, that he has now fled back to Germany, and you want to go to Germany to help the German police apprehend him?'

'No sir,' said Walker. 'I believe the killer is English and I also believe that he is still in England. I would however, like to have your permission to visit Germany.'

'Why?'

'Because I think that by going to Germany, and talking to the suspected museum thief, we'll have the best chance of learning the identity of the killer.'

'Well I doubt very much that the German police would appreciate your roaming around their patch, Chief Inspector,' said Sheen. 'Why don't you telephone and ask your friend in the German police to put your questions to the suspected museum thief?' Sheen returned to his seat and watched Walker's face closely.

'My German police friend informed me that the suspected thief, whose name is Johannes Radke, refuses to talk to them. He did say, however, that Radke might talk to me. Inspector Dietering invited me to Germany, sir, and I wouldn't ask for your permission to go there if I didn't think it was absolutely necessary.'

Sheen rested his elbows on his desk and stayed silent for a moment. Finally, he said, 'Let me think about it.'

'Thank you, sir, and if you do give your permission for a visit I'd like to have DC Kent accompany me.'

'Kent? Why?'

'Because,' said Walker, 'he knows Hanover and will make it unnecessary for me to require a German police guide. If I have a German policeman with me then Radke will refuse to talk.'

'I'll let you know after tomorrow's funeral for young Braddock,' said Sheen, picking up his pen. 'Speaking of which, what can you tell me about him? I'm speaking at his funeral and haven't yet decided what to say.'

Walker was quiet for a moment. He had been very surprised to learn that the funeral was to be held so soon after Braddock's death. He had also been surprised that there had been no post-mortem. Someone in authority had obviously intervened.

'All I can tell you is what I told Stewart on the day Anna was murdered,' Walker eventually replied. 'I said that he had a good memory and an organised mind. I told him that those traits were valuable assets for a policeman and that I was sure he would go far in the force.'

'Excellent, Julian, excellent,' said Sheen, as he reached for a sheet of paper. 'Would you remind repeating that?'

CHAPTER FIFTY-THREE

The church was packed. Not only were people crammed into the pews, they were also standing in both side aisles and at the rear of the church. In the front row were Braddock's mother, father, and close family members. Other relatives, family friends, and neighbours, were scattered about the church, inter-mixed with uniformed and plain-clothed friends and colleagues from the police force.

Walker, who was standing just inside the front entrance, observed that most, if not all, of the police officers from his station were in attendance. He recognised many by the backs of their heads; a recognition aided by the fact they were wearing uniforms. He saw Dakarta and Johnson sitting about half way down and Broadhurst and Kent, both dressed in their "Sunday best", standing against a wall to his right. He could see Bob Williamson, who was also standing against a wall, wearing a uniform coat he had actually buttoned up. So far, it was managing to stay that way. Walker wondered who was on the front desk at the station. Maybe the place had closed down for the day.

He was not displeased that he had to stand. The length of Walker's legs did not allow him to sit comfortably in most church pews. Not that he had sat in many churches. And, when he had, it was usually for a funeral.

Walker looked at the stained-glass windows. They may have been garishly coloured, contrasting sharply with the grey stone walls and floor, the dull brown wooden ceiling rafters and the subdued colours of the mourner's clothes, but here Walker's distaste for bright colours was outweighed by his fondness for the past; a past revealed by both the construction and pictorial content of these windows.

He looked up at the ceiling. Its height was such that it seemed to diminish Walker's own stature, momentarily making him feel insignificant. The ceiling's height also amplified and reverberated the many whispered conversations, making it seem to Walker as if they were in a very large cavern.

Finally, Walker turned his gaze towards the coffin. Although most people are usually discomforted at a funeral by being reminded of their own mortality – despite the attending clergyman's praise of life after death – Walker realised, as he looked at the polished brown casket, that he was feeling only anguish; an anguish far stronger than any he had previously experienced.

His parents' funeral services, like many funeral services nowadays, had focused on a celebration of the life of the deceased. This helped ease the anguish. But how, thought Walker, can you celebrate a life that had only just begun?

Walker's melancholic musings were interrupted by a sudden reduction in sound, soon to be replaced by complete silence. A white-garbed figure had risen in front of the congregation and all eyes turned towards him. The service was about to begin.

It was a short service, made memorable by a touching eulogy given by Stewart's brother, John. Sheen's tribute, which followed, was thankfully brief.

In the churchyard, once the coffin had been lowered and words spoken over it by the clergyman, the mourners started to disperse. Walker approached Stewart's father, took his hand and offered his condolences.

The tall, thin, grey-haired man placed his other hand on Walker's arm and said, 'Thank you for being here, Chief Inspector. It would have meant a lot to Stewart. He idolised you.' Tears began to form in his pale blue eyes and he waited a moment to regain his composure. Increasing the pressure of the grip on Walker's arm, he said, 'And thank you for those kind words.'

'Words?' Walker was puzzled.

'Yes. Those words spoken in the church by Superintendent Sheen. I know that they were borrowed from you. The superintendent had never spoken to Stewart, but you had, and those were the exact words you said to him. He told me when he came home that day when the young woman's body was found. He was so happy and proud.'

'I only spoke the truth, Mr. Braddock.'

'That doesn't matter. What is important is that you said it.' He released his hold on Walker and looked deeply into his eyes. 'I hope you catch this man, Chief Inspector. But if you don't, I know that you will have done your very best.'

CHAPTER FIFTY-FOUR

'That's the last of the calls finished with, Chief Inspector.' Broadhurst was leaning against the door's frame and gazing into Walker's office.

Walker looked up from his desk where he had been busy completing a progress report and other long-overdue paperwork. He looked out into the incident room and saw that Dakarta had departed, presumably to resume normal duties. Kent was typing away on his computer keyboard.

'Nothing useful, Paige?'

'No, sir. There have been no reliable sightings of the killer prior to his visit to the art dealer. It's as though he never existed before that day.' She paused as she remembered something. 'Oh – and the lab called. Prints taken from Mrs. Dorrington's house match one of the prints found on the picture frame in Clement's house.'

Walker stood and followed Broadhurst into the outer room. Kent stopped what he was doing and turned to face the other detectives as they took their customary seating positions. He said, 'Not one of the calls I've received has proved useful, sir.' He then added, 'Much the same as with the calls we received in response to the requests for information on the stiletto.'

'How did you go with the list of militaria dealers provided by your mother?' Walker asked.

'I've contacted all of the militaria dealers in England but none of them know anything about a square bladed stiletto.'

'What about the German dealers?'

'No luck there either, sir. But I haven't been able to contact many of them. It seems there's a big militaria collectors' fair in Frankfurt at the moment and most of the dealers are there.'

'What else can we do, sir?' Broadhurst asked.

'Nothing here. At least not for the moment. I'm still convinced the answer lies in Germany.'

'Do you think the Superintendent will let you go, sir?' asked Broadhurst.

'I asked him and he said he'd think about it. I expect to hear from him today.' Walker stretched his arms and tilted back his head. 'I'm optimistic. The Superintendent will have much more pressure placed on him by his superiors now that a policeman's been murdered.'

Walker turned his head so that he faced Broadhurst. He said, 'I hope you don't mind, Paige, but I asked the Superintendent if Peter might join me on the trip because of his familiarity with Hanover.'

'I don't mind, sir,' Broadhurst said. 'In fact, I'm pleased. My passport has expired. I remembered last week when I picked up Anna's from Locke but haven't done anything about it yet. Besides,' she added with a smile, 'you know I hate flying.'

'How about you, Peter?' said Walker, turning his head again. 'Is your passport up to date?'

'Yes, sir.' Kent had a wide grin on his face. 'And thank you, sir.'

'You're very welcome, Peter.'

Kent watched Walker as he stood and made his way towards his office. When he was certain that the inspector was far enough away not to be able to hear him, Kent turned his eyes to Broadhurst and spoke softly.

'Are you sure you don't mind not going to Germany, Sarge?'

'Of course I don't mind,' Broadhurst replied. 'It'll be like a comic book adventure. The "Grey Man" and "Superman" hunting the "Pale Man".' She smiled. 'And like in a comic book, all of the characters have "man" in their names. No place for a woman.'

'There are female characters in comic books – and some of them are the main characters.' Kent tried to look serious. 'You'd fit in, Sarge. I think of you as "Wonder Woman".'

Broadhurst laughed and was about to lean across and thump Kent on the arm when she heard Walker call their names.

Standing in his office doorway, Walker said, 'Have either of you made plans for tomorrow night?'

Broadhurst's face expressed suspicion and Kent simply looked puzzled.

'No, sir,' Broadhurst said slowly.

'No, sir,' echoed Kent.

'Good,' said Walker, 'because I'm inviting you and your partners to dinner at my place to meet my friend, Jenny.'

'Thank you very much, sir,' said Broadhurst, 'but I'm between partners at the moment.'

'Yes, thank you very much, sir,' said Kent, 'but I don't have a partner at the moment either.'

'That's a shame,' said Walker. And then, with a slight smile, he added, 'Looks like you'll have to come with each other.'

CHAPTER FIFTY-FIVE

As she drove her Audi towards Walker's house, Broadhurst realised she was feeling nervous. It was a feeling with which she was not familiar. She was pleased to have been invited to dinner at her boss's home but she was not sure whether she was pleased at having Walker organise Peter as her "dinner date". She recalled that she had thought about asking Peter to accompany her when Walker had first mentioned dinner at his place. The thought had really pleased her then. But that was then. This was now. And she hadn't asked Peter. Walker had arranged it. She really liked Peter and she had even thought about what it would be like to have a relationship with him. But that had been fantasising. Apart from the fact that she was slightly older, and had a higher rank, it was a well-known fact that relationships with workmates did not work out. Or so she had heard. Such relationships were also frowned upon by higher ranking officers. Usually. She suspected that Walker didn't care. Perhaps he would even encourage them? No, she reprimanded herself for her thoughts. This is simply dinner. And it's not a date. We are just "dinner companions". She brought her car to a halt outside Walker's front gate.

Kent was already there. But he hadn't gone up to Walker's front door. He was sitting in his car, nervously awaiting Paige's arrival. He would have liked to have driven her here but, before he had had the chance to ask her, she had made it clear that they would each take their own car. He was determined however, that they would enter Walker's house together.

Broadhurst was surprised, but admittedly very pleased, to find Kent, with a broad smile on his face, opening her car door for her after she had turned off the ignition. He looked quite handsome in a navy polo shirt and pressed pale blue jeans. Like her, he had followed Walker's explicit command that they dress casually for the occasion.

The dinner party was very enjoyable. The food, prepared by Walker with Jenny's more than capable assistance, had been delicious and the four of them now sat at Walker's table sipping the wine which was available in copious amounts. Both Kent and Broadhurst had brought bottles and these were consumed along with those provided by Walker. Kent, unnoticed – he thought – by the others, drank little, but he was still very much aware of the warmth of pleasant companionship.

Walker had suggested that they all use first names for the evening, even though he guessed that this would be beyond Broadhurst and Kent's capabilities. He was right. Regardless of how much wine Broadhurst was consuming, she continued to address Walker as "sir". And Walker began to wonder whether Kent could be persuaded to address him as anything other than "sir" even when under hypnosis.

'Now that we've finished eating,' said Walker, 'I have something to tell you. Our beloved chief has given his approval for Peter and myself to travel to Hanover. I fixed up the tickets on-line this morning and we depart on Monday morning.'

They all smiled and Broadhurst and Jenny spontaneously clapped their hands.

Kent was almost overcome by excitement. 'How long are we going for, sir?' he asked.

'Five days,' replied Walker.

'Five days!' exclaimed Kent. 'Once we've finished our work we may have some time to see the sights!'

Broadhurst smiled at Kent's exuberance and said, 'What sights, Peter? I thought Hanover was visited only for its trade fairs and conventions.'

'Oh, not at all. There's plenty to see. Apart from the Wilhelm Busch museum, there's the artificial lake with all of its restaurants – great food by the way.'

'What? Pig's knuckle and sauerkraut?' Broadhurst always enjoyed baiting Kent.

'No, that's popular in the south of Germany, not in the north,' Kent patiently explained. 'In Hanover, I love the asparagus, the potato pancakes, the sausages, and of course the bread rolls and cakes.'

'You sound like you're still hungry, Peter,' said a smiling Walker. 'Would you like some more dessert?'

'No thank you, sir. I've had sufficient. It was a wonderful meal.'

'Tell us more about Hanover, Peter,' said Jenny who appeared to be genuinely interested.

'Well, there's the Herrenhausen gardens. They have a maze there,' said Kent before adding, 'but it's not as good as the one at Blenheim Palace.'

'So that's it?' said Broadhurst. 'A museum, a lake, and some gardens?'

'No, of course not. They have an inner-city forest, which is the largest in Europe, and they have a wonderful zoo.'

'Don't most cities have a zoo?' asked Broadhurst, taking another sip of wine.

Walker topped up their wine glasses as Kent replied, 'Yes, but this one has some special features. It has a large enclosure with a pool which is shared by a brown bear and a polar bear. Most unusual. And!' exclaimed Kent as he suddenly remembered. 'It's one of the few zoos in the world to have a walrus!'

'Did you know,' said Jenny, 'that the walrus has a longer baculum than any other animal? According to some sources it can be as long as seventy-five centimetres. That's thirty inches!'

'What's a baculum?' asked Walker.

'A penile bone.'

The three detectives stared at Jenny. Her face reddened and she looked down at the contents of her glass.

'Where did you learn that?' asked Walker.

'I first read about it in a crime novel written by Kathy Reichs.'

'I've heard of her,' said Broadhurst. 'I haven't yet read any of her books but I intend to. She's very popular. They've even got a television series called "Bones" based on her books.

'"Bones"?' said Walker with a smile. 'You mean to tell me there's a TV show about animal penises?'

The others laughed and Jenny said, 'No. The main character is a forensic anthropologist. She solves crimes by studying the bones of victims.'

'So the walrus has the longest penile bone,' said Walker. 'Well it seems my long-held belief has been proven wrong. Apparently you *can* learn facts from reading modern crime fiction.'

'Yes, Julian, you can,' said Jenny. 'So perhaps you should start reading some. You might even enjoy it.'

'I did read plenty of fiction as a child. But only literary classics – including "Alice in Wonderland". I didn't think much of that book at the time, but I can now see a possible reason why the Carpenter was fascinated by the Walrus.'

CHAPTER FIFTY-SIX

It was after midnight. Broadhurst and Kent knew it was time to leave. As they thanked their hosts and said their farewells, Broadhurst noticed the look of concern on Walker's face. She said, 'Don't worry, sir. I have no intention of driving. I'm going to call for a taxi from my car.'

'I'll drive you home, Sarge,' said Kent. 'I'm under the limit.'

'Then you're the only one who is,' said Walker, laughing. His concern was gone.

'Thanks, Peter,' said Broadhurst with a smile. She then turned to Walker. 'I'll leave my car here and pick it up in the morning if that's alright with you, sir?'

'Of course it is,' Walker replied.

Outside it was completely silent. The sounds normally made by traffic and by nocturnal animals were absent. There were no street-lights but it was still possible to see. Some light came from behind the silhouetted figures of Walker and Jenny who stood arm in arm in the doorway of Walker's house but most light came from above. As Kent opened the passenger door of his car Broadhurst looked upwards. There were no clouds and no pollution to obscure the full moon and the millions of stars scattered across the black sky.

For the first part of the journey they didn't speak. Broadhurst lay her head back and closed her eyes. It had been a very enjoyable night. And it was not yet over.

As the car neared her home Broadhurst said, 'the chief inspector and Jenny seem really happy.'

'Yes, they do. They make a nice couple.'

'It's nice to have someone, don't you think?'

'Yes, I do.'

'Do you get lonely, Peter?'

'No. I've got my mum,' said a smiling Kent.

Broadhurst laughed. 'You know what I mean.'

'I know what you mean,' said Kent. 'Of course I get lonely. That's why I enjoy coming to work. I then get to enjoy the company of women younger than my mum. You and Isobel.'

'Oh? Do you fancy Constable Dakarta?'

'No, Sarge. She's too young. I prefer slightly older women.'

Broadhurst smiled and they both returned to silence.

Broadhurst lived in a small cottage just outside the village of Little Bromleigh. It was almost completely obscured by trees and shrubbery. Kent doubted he would have found it if he had not been guided by Broadhurst.

Kent turned off the Saab's engine and climbed out. As he walked around to open the passenger door, Broadhurst decided to cast aside her feminist principles and wait for him. For once she would act like a lady.

When they reached the front door, Kent leaned forward to give Braoadhurst a friendly kiss on the cheek. At that moment Broadhurst did the same and their lips unintentionally met. Surprisingly for both of them, there was no embarrassment or urgency to detach. Broadhurst moved easily into Kent's welcoming arms and they locked in a gentle embrace.

When the kiss finally ended they moved apart and Broadhurst said, 'Why don't you stay the night? You can drive me back to my car in the morning and save me the cost of a taxi.'

'If you want me to, Sarge.'

'Of course I want you to. I wouldn't have asked you otherwise. Don't you want to?'

'Yes, Sarge. I'd be pleased to be able to drive you back to your car in the morning.'

Broadhurst laughed. 'I'm not talking about driving me back to my car, you idiot. I'm talking about you staying the night. And for Heaven's sake, stop calling me "Sarge".'

'Sorry, Paige.' Kent smiled sheepishly.

'Do you mind if I ask you a personal question, Peter?' Broadhurst said as she searched her handbag for her front door key.

'No,' Kent said with some trepidation.

'Have you ever stayed overnight at a single woman's place before?'

Kent looked down at his shoes and paused before replying. 'No, I haven't.'

'Well, there's always a first time for everything, Peter,' said Broadhurst as she opened the door.

As they entered the house, Broadhurst turned her head to look at him. 'I suppose you think you'll be sleeping on the couch?'

Kent raised his eyes to hers. He could feel his face reddening. 'I don't know,' he said quietly.

'Well let me tell you, Constable,' said Broadhurst as she locked the door behind them. 'You won't be.'

CHAPTER FIFTY-SEVEN

It was three a.m. Moonlight was coming through the window, giving visibility but no colour. Kent and Broadhurst were laying naked on her bed. Kent was on his back gazing up at the dimly illuminated ceiling. Broadhurst had raised herself on one elbow and was watching him.

'I'm sorry, Paige,' said Kent, without looking at her.

Broadhurst reached out and touched his shoulder. 'Don't worry about it, Peter. I'm even a bit flattered that I should excite you so much.'

'I suppose there is always extra excitement when you are with someone you really like. Especially the first time.'

Broadhurst moved towards him. She slid her leg over his body and was soon sitting astride him. 'So let's try a second time,' she said, looking down at him with a cheeky grin.

Kent groaned with pleasure as she drew him inside her. As her large breasts began to undulate above him, he screwed up his eyes and sent his mind elsewhere. He tried concentrating on numbers, silently reciting multiplication tables. This helped, but his concentration was weakening, and weakening rapidly.

Just as Kent lost control, Broadhurst stiffened. She emitted a shrill, drawn-out cry of pleasure and then fell forward, crushing his lips with hers.

Kent placed his arms around her and smiled happily. Although physically tired, he was mentally exhilarated. He gave Broadhurst a squeeze in lieu of pinching himself. He couldn't believe this was happening.

Broadhurst rolled off him and lay close by his side. Once again she raised herself on an elbow and looked at his face.

'Any more of that and I'll believe you really are Superman,' she said in a mock-serious tone.

'Will there be more?' asked Kent, still unable to believe what had occurred.

'Of course! I don't believe in "one-night stands". However,' she said, laying back on her pillow and speaking in a tone that was now genuinely serious, 'we must be very discreet. No-one must know. Not even Walker – although you can bet he will guess.'

'Does this mean we're in a "relationship", Paige?'

Broadhurst turned a serious face towards his. 'We'll have to see about that,' she said thoughtfully.

Kent smiled and said, 'I must confess it's something I've fantasised about since this case began.'

'Me too,' said Broadhurst, as she moved her face towards his. 'Me too,' she repeated softly as she kissed him gently on the lips.

CHAPTER FIFTY-EIGHT

It was ten a.m. Walker and Jenny were sitting on the back verandah of Walker's house. They were just finishing breakfast.

'It looks like it's going to rain.' Jenny was gazing up at the few cloud-covered pieces of sky visible through the trees in Walker's back yard. She raised a cup of tea to her lips.

'It certainly does,' said Walker, leaning back in his chair and stretching. He yawned. 'Excuse me.'

Jenny laughed. 'I hope you're not starting to find my company boring.'

'Of course not. It's just that I didn't get much sleep last night.' He winked at Jenny.

Jenny smiled. 'Well, maybe we'll have to go back to bed.'

'Fine by me,' said Walker with a grin. 'It doesn't look like it's going to be a good day to go driving anywhere.' He took a sip of his tea.

'No, but I don't mind. I'm quite happy to spend the day here – catching up on lost sleep.' She smiled coquettishly.

Walker laughed. 'Great idea. I probably won't get much sleep tonight either. Apart from having you snoring next to me, I'm also going to have to get up early tomorrow to catch a plane.'

Jenny playfully leaned across the small table and punched Walker on the arm. 'I don't have to stay,' she said with a grin. Then, in a more serious tone, she asked, 'Did you want me to drive you and Peter to the airport?'

'That's very kind of you to offer, my darling, but I don't want you to miss work. Paige will drive us.'

'Okay then. If you prefer Paige. At least I offered.' She pretended to be offended.

Walker placed his cup back on the table and laughed. Then he said, 'I just remembered. She'll probably be here soon to pick up her car. We'd better wait until she's gone before we return to bed.'

'I suppose so,' said Jenny, speaking with mock sadness. Then, with a thoughtful expression on her face, she added, 'I like Paige very much. She's very friendly. But she has an air of loneliness about her.'

'Yes. I think she is lonely,' said Walker. 'She doesn't say much about herself but I don't think she's ever been in a long-term romantic relationship.'

'She's never been married?'

'No. And she's lived alone for as long as I've known her. She told me once that both her parents were drowned in a boating accident when she was a child and she went to live with a spinster aunt.' Walker took another sip of his tea before continuing. 'The year after she left school – the year she joined the police force – the aunt died and left Paige her house.' Walker returned his cup to its saucer. 'When she was appointed to Essex she sold the house and bought a small cottage in Little Bromleigh. She's lived there, on her own, ever since.'

'You've never considered having a relationship with her?' Jenny studied Walker's face intently.

'No. I think she's very attractive, and I enjoy her company, but we're workmates. And in the police force you are not supposed to get romantically involved with workmates.'

'I don't think that's going to stop her.'

'What do you mean?' Walker was puzzled.

'Peter.'

'Kent?'

'Yes. She likes him and he adores her. It's not like you not to have noticed.'

'I know they like each other and enjoy working together. But I don't know if Paige would allow herself to get romantically involved with him. Besides, he's younger than she is.'

'Only by a couple of years. Anyway, we'll know whether they're "involved" when she comes to pick up her car this morning.'

'How? What do you mean?'

Jenny grinned. 'We'll know once we see who drives her here. A taxi driver or Peter.' She wrinkled her brow and playfully wagged a finger at him. 'For a brilliant detective you can be a little dense sometimes, my darling.'

CHAPTER FIFTY-NINE

As soon as Walker entered the aircraft's aisle, a repressed memory surfaced; a memory of the limited leg space in economy class seating. At the end of every flight he had taken as an adult, Walker had vowed to never fly economy again. However, a few days after returning home, the vow had always been forgotten. So here he was again. The only good thing about the flight from Stansted to Hanover was that its duration was less than two hours.

Standing in a half crouch, Walker waited while Kent placed his carry-on bag in the overhead locker. As Kent moved into the window seat, Walker placed his bag next to Kent's. He then lowered himself into the aisle seat.

As expected, Walker's legs didn't fit in the space available. This time however, there seemed to be even less space than on previous flights. Was he growing?

Because it was physically impossible to position his legs directly in front, Walker placed his right leg in the aisle. This meant he would have to move his right knee up to his chest whenever other passengers or flight attendants passed along the aisle. His left leg was positioned so that it was in front of the empty seat separating him from Kent. He knew that this could cause a problem if someone claimed this middle seat but fortunately it now seemed unlikely. Walker and Kent had been among the last to board.

After fastening his seat belt, Kent closed his eyes and smiled. His legs were also pressed tightly against the seat in front but apparently any discomfort was offset by the excitement of their journey – or, thought Walker, by images of Broadhurst.

Walker fastened his seatbelt and half-listened to a flight attendant as she recited the safety procedure. Kent obviously wasn't listening. His eyes were still closed and he was still smiling.

Once the plane was in the air, Walker removed a map of Hanover from the inside pocket of his suit coat and began unfolding it. Kent was now emitting the same soft sounds that Walker had heard when he'd found Kent in the lane near Locke's garage. The sounds of gentle snoring.

It was then that the bald-headed man in front of Walker decided to fully recline his seat. The top of the man's seat forced Walker's map hard against his chest and Walker suddenly found himself unable to move. He was trapped in a leather vice.

Walker yelled, but the hairless scalp, which Walker was now forced to inspect at close range, was traversed by a narrow, black, plastic band. The man was wearing headphones and couldn't hear Walker's voice.

A flight attendant, who had apparently heard Walker call out and realised his predicament, suddenly appeared in the aisle alongside the bald man. The woman smiled at Walker and tapped the bald man on the shoulder. The man removed his earphones and the attendant knelt and briefly whispered in his ear. She then rose and smiled again at Walker before turning and moving swiftly down the aisle.

The bald man had quickly raised his seat to the upright position, unbuckled his seat belt, and turned to face Walker. He had a round, pleasant face and dark eyes. When he realised what had happened, he stood up, revealing that he was short and stout. He was dressed in an expensive looking, dark grey suit, white shirt and dark blue tie. He said, 'Please accept my sincere apologies, sir. It was most inconsiderate of me.' There was genuine concern on his face as he asked, with a slight accent, 'Are you hurt?'

Walker said, 'I'm fine now, thank you.' He smiled and said, 'I was trapped there for a while. I'm afraid my body was not designed for economy class seating.'

The man's eyes wandered over Walker's huge frame but he politely made no comment. Instead he held out his hand and said, 'I'm Alfred Kruger. And again, I am sorry for thoughtlessly causing you discomfort.'

Walker shook the proffered hand and said, 'My name is Julian Walker and your apologies are accepted.'

The amiable man smiled and then took a small card from his top pocket. He handed it to Walker. It was a business card that read, "Herr Alfred Kruger. Numismatics. Dealer in old coins and medals". These words were followed by a German address and a mobile phone number.

Kruger turned and sat down and Walker placed the card in the side pocket of his coat. Walker was about to study his map when a thought struck him. Medals.

Walker unbuckled his seat belt, stood up, placed his map on his seat, and moved into the aisle. He took a step forward so that he was standing, stooped, next to the seated Herr Kruger. Walker tapped the man on the shoulder and when Kruger looked up enquiringly, Walker politely asked him if he would mind answering a question about medals.

'Certainly, Mr. Walker. What would you like to know?'

Walker crouched down so that their eyes were level. He said, 'Are the medals you sell military medals?'

'Mainly. Military medals are the most popular. They are also the most valuable. The British Victoria Cross, the American Medal of Honour, the French Legion of Honour and one of the German Iron Cross medals are extremely valuable. But their value puts them beyond my reach and beyond the reach of most collectors. I specialise in the less valuable military medals. That's why I have been in England. I purchased a collection including a DSO and a DFC. They are easy to sell.'

'Do you deal in any other forms of militaria?'

'You mean flags, uniforms and weaponry? No I don't. I leave that to dealers who specialise in that area of collecting. I occasionally come across such items but I usually refer the owner to other dealers I know. And those dealers usually refer people with medals or coins to me. Why do you ask, Mr. Walker? Is there something you have you wish to sell?' Kruger smiled.

'I'm a policeman, Herr Kruger, and I'm investigating a series of murders committed using a very old and unusual dagger. It's possible that this dagger originated in Germany and, if it did, I am trying to find out where.'

'What type of dagger, Mr. Walker?' Kruger was now serious.

'A fifteenth century Italian stiletto with a square blade.'

Kruger became excited. 'I may be able to help you, Mr. Walker. A colleague of mine, who has a militaria shop in Hanover, had an old stiletto with a square blade. It must be the one you are looking for. Weapons of that age are rare so it is unlikely there are two of them.'

Now Walker became excited. 'Do you know what happened to this stiletto?'

At that moment they were interrupted by a flight attendant pushing a drinks' trolley. Walker had to take a step back and squeeze into the space between his and Krugers' seats. As soon as the trolley had passed he returned to Kruger's side.

'You asked me, Mr. Walker, if I knew what happened to the stiletto,' said Kruger. 'My colleague believes it was taken by someone who worked in his shop.'

'Did he report it to the police?' Walker hoped that he had because then there would be a record of the theft.

'No. He couldn't prove it and why would the police concern themselves about an old knife? It may have been rare but my colleague said that because of its poor condition it wasn't valuable. And nothing else was taken. He thought he would have a better chance of recovering his property if he alerted his fellow dealers. I was one of those he asked to watch out for it.'

'If it isn't valuable, why is he interested in recovering it?'

'Purely for sentimental reasons. He said it belonged to his father.'

CHAPTER FIFTY-NINE

'Do you mind giving me this dealer's name and address, Herr Kruger?'

'Of course I don't mind, Mr. Walker. It is my pleasure to help you. The man's name is Gunther Koppe. He mainly buys and sells Nazi military paraphernalia. His shop is near Empelde in Hanover. It is easy to find. You take a number nine tram from the city centre and alight at Bernhard-Caspar Strasse. The shop is in the small shopping centre next to the tram stop. It is easy to find,' he repeated before adding, 'He has been attending a big fair in Frankfurt but that ended yesterday so he should be back in Hanover by now.'

Walker stood up and removed a scrap of paper from his pocket. After writing down the information Kruger had provided, Walker thanked him and vigorously shook hands with the man. He then returned to his seat and fastened his seat belt. The aircraft would soon be preparing for landing.

CHAPTER SIXTY

B ecause they had only carry-on luggage, and therefore didn't need to wait at the carousel, Walker and Kent were out of the airport quickly. They were soon in a taxi heading towards the centre of Hanover. Walker suspected the driver was taking a scenic rather than a direct route but he didn't mind. He sat back and enjoyed the view. As always when in a foreign country, Walker could not help feeling a little excited.

There were no sky-scrapers and so far, Walker had seen no ancient buildings. He knew Hanover had been heavily bombed during the war so assumed that if they were to see any old looking constructions it was likely that they would be restorations. Nevertheless, the city was impressive. It was spacious and had wide main streets, bisected by tracks that carried slowly moving green and yellow trams.

Walker had made reservations at a hotel in the centre of the city, not far from the Kröpcke underground tram station. From here, Kent had informed Walker, they would have easy access to all of their intended destinations.

As soon as they had checked in and stored their bags in their rooms, the two detectives left the hotel and walked briskly along the broad pedestrian thoroughfare leading towards the city square. There were people everywhere, walking in all directions. Some were tourists but most were shoppers and office workers out to purchase food or simply to enjoy the fresh air and sunshine during their lunch break. Along either side of the thoroughfare stood window shoppers, some tourists checking maps, and several talented buskers. Seated on the ground, leaning against walls and shop windows were a few drunks and a couple of beggars. Kent suggested to Walker that he keep his hand on his wallet, for amongst this crowd there were also a few pickpockets.

When they reached the square, they found a tourist centre and, once again at Kent's suggestion, purchased two Hanover travel cards for the five days they would be in the city. They then crossed to the Kröpcke's metro entrance and took the escalators down to the tram platforms.

Walker had decided that their first objective should be police headquarters. To inform Inspector Dietering of their presence in his city and to obtain the address of Johannes Radke.

They did not have far to travel by tram, alighting at Markthalle and then proceeding on foot to the Calenberger Neustadt Quarter police building where Dietering was stationed.

The counter attendant to whom Walker introduced himself was a young, brown-uniformed woman who wore her hair in a pony-tail and spoke perfect English. She asked them to wait while she informed Inspector Dietering that they were there to see him.

When Dietering finally emerged through a rear doorway, Walker was surprised. As always, the image conjured up by the mind, while speaking to an unknown person on a telephone, differed markedly from that person's true appearance. Walker had pictured a tall, solid, blue-eyed, blonde-haired man. But of course, he realised, he had been stereotyping. Dietering was of medium height, slim, and had short, greying brown hair. He had a pleasant face, accented by friendly green eyes and a broad smile. He wore the same coloured shirt and trousers as the young policewoman.

'Good afternoon, Detective Chief Inspector Walker,' Dietering said and held out his hand. He was probably as surprised by Walker's appearance as Walker was by his.

'Good afternoon, Inspector Dietering,' said Walker, who shook hands and then introduced Kent. Dietering then offered his hand to Kent and the shaking procedure was repeated.

Once the formalities were concluded, Dietering took Walker and Kent into his office. He explained that, because the German Chancellor was in Hanover for the next few days, most of the station's staff were involved with security. Therefore he would be unable to supply them with a guide. He apologised for what he obviously considered to be a lack of hospitality. His concern however, was replaced by relief once Walker informed him that Kent was familiar with the city and that a guide would be unnecessary.

'Do you mind us going and speaking with Radke without being accompanied by a local officer?' Walker asked.

'Of course not. As I explained on the telephone he won't speak to us and he probably wouldn't speak to you if one of my men was with you,' said Dietering. Then he looked at Walker's broken nose and added, 'Of course, I do hope you will follow the correct procedures of interrogation and not use violence on the man.' He was smiling but Walker knew he was serious.

Walker laughed and said, 'I'm a peaceful man.'

For a moment, Dietering stared into Walker's eyes as if seeking the veracity of that statement. Then he winked and laughed. 'Good. And I hope you will offer me the same friendly cooperation when I come to your country seeking information from a criminal.' He opened a desk drawer and said, 'Let me get you Herr Radke's photograph and home address.'

CHAPTER SIXTY-ONE

As the tram slowed, Kent leaned down so that he could see the name of the station through the window. 'Nieschlagstrasse,' he said. 'The next station is ours.'

When the tram had come to a complete halt at Nieschlagstrasse and the doors opened, a scruffy looking man climbed aboard and positioned himself near the steps across from where Walker and Kent were standing. He had unkempt, longish hair that obviously needed washing and wore a short-sleeved un-pressed olive shirt, low-hanging baggy blue jeans, and a pair of dirty trainers. He did not look at Walker or Kent. He stared at the floor with an expressionless face.

When the doors had closed and the tram began to move forward, the man stepped forward. He stood close to, and directly facing, Walker and Kent. He spread his feet to help maintain his balance and reached into a back pocket of his jeans.

'Tickets please,' the man said, looking at Walker and Kent for the first time as he showed them an identification card. He was a transport inspector.

Walker and Kent showed the man their travel cards and, after a brief examination, he moved on to the next passenger.

The man had looked only briefly at Walker and Kent, yet, like everyone else they had so far come in contact with in Germany, he had addressed them in English. What, wondered Walker, made it obvious that they were not German?

When Walker and Kent alighted from the tram at the next stop, they saw that the shopping centre they were seeking was directly in front of them. After leaving Inspector Dietering and the police station – and acceding to Kent's proposal that they have lunch in the large Market Hall – Walker had decided that they would visit the militaria shop.

The shop, as Kruger had assured Walker, was easy to find. Illustrated war books, military uniforms, and military banners were prominently displayed in its front window. Not displayed however, were any items featuring a swastika.

When they entered the shop, Walker and Kent's senses were bombarded. Items seen in the window were replicated, not only in far greater number, but in more brilliant colours. Those in the window had obviously been left there too long and had been faded by the sun. But the colours from the flags hanging inside the shop so dominated his vision that Walker found it necessary to momentarily close his eyes. When he opened them, he observed that in the shop, as in the window, there were no swastikas on display. Not even on the buttons, badges and medals that were exhibited in the long, low, glass-topped cabinet that served as a counter.

Equally imposing was the smell and sound. The detectives' nasal passages were infiltrated by the strong, musty odour emanating from the flags and uniforms, causing Kent to wrinkle his nose. And the loud, thumping sounds of 1930's marching music threatened their eardrums.

Standing behind the counter, and closely watching them, was a man whom Walker assumed was the owner, Gunther Koppe. Once again, the actual appearance did not match Walker's preconceived image.

Koppe was a man of medium height with a large stomach. Although completely bald on top, he had long, thin, grey hair hanging from the back and sides of his round head. He also had a grey beard that reached his chest. His clothing, unlike that of Kruger, was very casual. He wore a loose, white t-shirt, baggy blue jeans, and, as Walker noted when the man stepped from behind the counter to greet them, brown open-toed sandals over white socks.

Kruger had telephoned Koppe to inform him that Walker was going to pay him a visit so, after introductions, the man was friendly and cooperative. He invited Walker and Kent to join him in a back room where, amongst boxes of stock and hanging uniforms, there was comfortable seating. Here there was also a large swastika. It formed the centrepiece of a huge red flag that was draped over a curtain rod.

'Ah, the swastika,' said Koppe, noticing Walker and Kent's interest. 'I have no sympathies for Nazism but most of my customers collect Nazi memorabilia. As you probably know, the public display of this particular insignia is prohibited in Germany, so I don't hang flags like that one in the shop. I keep my swastika decorated items in those boxes.' He pointed to three large cardboard boxes stacked against one wall. They took up much of the space in the room. 'I sell these items mainly through the internet to customers who live in other countries. There are some German collectors, but not many. And if someone wants to purchase from me in person they simply have to ask and I will take the item from here into the shop.'

'Couldn't you display them in your shop as part of an historical exhibition?' Walker asked.

'Legally I could but it's not worth the bother. People would still complain and I'd grow tired of explaining.' Koppe shrugged and clasped his hands on his stomach.

'Your shop is fascinating, Herr Koppe,' said Walker with a smile. 'It just takes a while for the eyes – and the ears – to get used to it.'

Koppe laughed. 'I love all this, Chief Inspector.' He waved his arms around. 'Apart from the swastikas – which, like most Germans, I despise – I love the banners and the uniforms.' Koppe grew serious. 'Do you know that, along with beer, there are three things that Germans most love? Marching, marching bands and uniforms. If I had not been at the collectors' fair in Frankfurt yesterday,' he said sadly, 'I would have been here in Hanover at the Schützenfest enjoying all three – and the beer too, of course.'

'Shootzenwhat?' said Walker.

'Schützenfest. A shooters' festival,' said Koppe.

'It's a marksman's parade and fair,' said Kent to Walker. 'In Germany there are a lot of shooting clubs and they all come to Hanover once a year with their uniforms, flags and brass bands for a special parade. The shooters march along with carriages, wagons and decorated carts. It is the longest parade in Europe. Eventually they all reach a large fairground where there are beer tents, food stalls and fun rides, including a huge Ferris wheel.'

Koppe laughed and said, 'You have described it well, Constable.'

Walker simply stared at Kent.

'Germans have always loved pageantry, Gentlemen,' said Koppe. 'Did you know that Hitler was the one responsible for introducing the torch marathon, the parade of nations, and the lighting of the cauldron, to the modern Olympic Games?'

'No, I didn't,' admitted Walker before turning to Kent and saying, 'but I'll bet you did, Peter.'

Kent reddened and smiled but said nothing

'So, Gentlemen' said Koppe, sitting up straighter in his chair and presenting a more serious facial expression. 'I don't believe you are here to discuss German culture. Alfred tells me you are looking for my stiletto.'

'Yes, we are,' replied Walker. 'We believe it was used in the murder of several people.'

'I am innocent,' said Koppe, smiling and raising his hands in the air. Then he quickly dropped them and the smile disappeared. 'Forgive me for my little joke. It was in bad taste. I realise this is a serious matter.'

Walker smiled. 'No apologies necessary, Herr Koppe. But tell me. This stiletto. It was stolen from your shop?'

'Yes. It was more than a year ago. I can't prove it but I believe an assistant took it after I dismissed him from my employ.'

'And Herr Kruger says you never reported this to the police.'

'No, Chief Inspector. It would have been pointless. It was always kept in this room and I didn't realise it was missing until a long time after the assistant had left. Also, it was not valuable as its condition was poor. I was attached to it because it was the only thing I had that belonged to my father. The police would not have wanted to waste their time looking for such an item.'

'Do you know where I might find this ex-assistant of yours?' Walker asked.

'No, I don't, Chief Inspector. He worked here for only a couple of weeks so I learned very little about him. He might even be dead by now. He drank too much. He was usually drunk when he arrived at work. That is why I dismissed him.'

'What was this assistant's name, Herr Koppe?'

'His name was Johannes Radke.'

CHAPTER SIXTY-TWO

The following morning, after enjoying a large breakfast in the hotel's dining room, Walker and Kent took a number three tram from Kröpcke to Schünemannplatz.

The building in which Radke lived was old and very much in need of maintenance. The lift was broken and the wooden staircase that the two detectives had to use, to reach the third floor and Radke's flat, was littered with rubbish and creaked threateningly. The walls were also in need of repair, with some areas revealing bare bricks underneath peeling paint and others featuring crude graffiti. Over all hung a stench that seemed to be part rotting food and part cat urine.

There was no answer when Walker thumped his fist on Radke's door. Radke was either not at home or ignoring them.

Kent tried to turn a rusted door handle and said, 'It's locked, sir.'

Walker raised his leg and slammed the sole of his shoe against the wood just below the handle. The door burst open.

'No it's not, Peter,' was Walker's reply.

Radke's flat consisted of two rooms; a bathroom and a combined kitchen, bedroom and living room. It was filthy and extremely untidy. An unpleasant odour came from the bathroom, from the unwashed dishes in the sink, from the food scraps and containers that covered a small table and littered the floor, and from the soiled sheets on a small, unmade bed. And there were empty beer cans and wine bottles everywhere. Radke was not at home.

'Let's try the plaza,' said Walker, wrinkling his face in disgust.

Both detectives took deep, pleasant breaths of fresh air when they exited the building. A short walk around a nearby corner took them into a partly tree-sheltered, concrete-covered square that was bordered on one side by the tram line.

Walker and Kent walked towards the largest of the numerous chattering, laughing, and alcohol swilling groups of men and women that stood under the trees on the far side of the square. One member of this group apparently noticed the approach of the two detectives and notified the others. There was immediate silence and several pairs of hostile eyes turned towards them.

Walker recognised Radke from the photograph given to him by Dietering. He also matched the description provided by Frau Schmidt.

'Herr Radke,' said Walker when he was close to the man. 'May I speak with you, please?'

'No!' said the short, stout man. He turned his back to Walker, raised a bottle to his lips, then tilted back his head and began swallowing the bottle's contents.

A much taller and stouter man with a long black beard and long, oily, black hair, stepped in front of Walker, placed the palm of his hand on the inspector's chest, and snarled, 'He said he doesn't want to talk to you. *Raus, Englander*!'

In one swift movement, Walker grabbed the man's fingers and forced them backwards. The sound of snapping bones was distinctly audible and the man dropped to his knees, screaming in pain. Kent took a step back, his eyes wide in astonishment.

Walker was about to speak again to Radke when another tall, but very thin, man, who was standing behind Walker and to Kent's left, suddenly moved forward. He raised a bottle with the obvious intention of bringing it down on Walker's skull.

'Look out, sir!' yelled Kent as he kicked out, his shoe connecting with the man's leg just behind the knee. This threw the would-be assailant off balance, causing a slight change to the trajectory of the bottle. It was not Kent's kick however, but his shout of warning that saved Walker. The inspector swiftly leant to the right, half-turned, and throwing up his left arm, deftly deflected the bottle with the palm of his hand. He then drove the point of his elbow into the thin man's throat. This time there was no scream as the injured man lurched backward. There was only a strangled, gurgling sound.

'Thanks, Peter,' said Walker, glaring at the man who, gasping and holding his throat, had now joined his companion on the ground. Walker then turned to face those of the group who were still standing.

'Are we all done?' Walker asked quietly.

Those unharmed were silent. There was still resentment on their faces but there was also fear. Walker moved closer to Radke who took a half-step backwards and raised his arms in a protective manner. Walker reached into his pocket and removed a folded bundle of bank notes. Each note was fifty euros

'Are you ready to talk to me now, Herr Radke?' Walker asked as he offered the man one of the notes and held up the others meaning-fully.

Radke grabbed the note, fearful that the offer would be withdrawn. 'Yes,' he said sullenly, as he avidly eyed the other notes in Walker's hand. 'I will talk to you.'

'Good. Then let me buy you a proper breakfast.' Walker indicated that Radke should follow him to a nearby outdoor café.

When the three men were seated at a table, a thin, obsequious young waiter, who had apparently witnessed the confrontation, hurried over to take their order. Other patrons had obviously also seen what happened, for there was much whispering and many furtive glances cast in the direction of Walker's table. But apparently no-one had bothered to call the police.

'Order whatever you like, Herr Radke,' said Walker, ignoring the attention being paid to his table by those seated around them. He also tried, unsuccessfully, to ignore the smell emanating from Radke.

Once the waiter had taken their order and hurried away, Radke said, 'What do you want to know?'

Walker, watching the man closely, said, 'We know you took drawings from the Wilhelm Busch museum and a stiletto from Herr Koppe's militaria shop –'

Before he could continue, Radke said, 'You can't prove that!' and, placing the palms of his hands on the table's surface, he began to rise.

'Relax,' said Walker, leaning across and grabbing the man's arm in a strong grip. He forced Radke back on to his chair. 'I couldn't care less about that. I want to know about the man who bought the drawings and knife from you. We believe that he is the man who killed not only your friend Gruber but also several other people in England, including a policeman.'

'You are English policemen?' Radke's red-rimmed blue eyes stared hard at Walker and then at Kent.

'Yes we are. But don't worry. We are not in the least bit interested in theft. We are only interested in murder. We need information and we are willing to pay well for it.' Walker again showed him the bundle of bank notes.

Radke, eyeing the notes, remained silent for a moment before he finally reached a decision. Pointing a finger at Kent, he said, 'He must move away. I will speak to you but I want no witness to what I say.'

Walker nodded to Kent who obligingly rose and moved to a table where he would be unable to hear what Radke had to say.

Kent was pleased to be sitting on his own. He did not want Walker, or Radke, to notice how his hands were shaking. He was also pleased to be sitting because his legs were also shaking and seemed to have weakened considerably. And he was pleased with himself. He may have acted instinctively but at least he had acted. And acted quickly and successfully. Kent smiled as he re-played the action in his mind. Then his smile broadened as the food he had ordered arrived.

'I want five hundred euros for talking to you,' Radke said to Walker.

Walker smiled. He was pleased. Sheen had given permission for him to pay exactly that amount for information and Walker had been prepared to pay more out of his own pocket if necessary. He said, 'I will give you two hundred and fifty euros for talking with me and another two hundred and fifty if you tell me something I don't already know about the man who bought from you the knife and the drawings.'

Radke thought about this and then nodded. Walker counted out two hundred euros and handed them over. 'I've already given you fifty so this makes a total of two hundred and fifty. Now tell me what you know, Herr Radke.'

Radke had been drinking but he was not drunk. He placed the money in the front pocket of a filthy pair of jeans and looked shrewdly at Walker. He didn't trust the Englishman. He thought that whatever information he revealed, this policeman would say he already knew it. So Radke said, 'You tell me all that you know and then, if I find that I know something you don't, I will tell you and you will pay me the other two hundred and fifty euros. Agreed?'

'Agreed,' said Walker who had no objection to Radke's counter-proposal. He leaned forward, trying with difficulty to ignore Radke's odour, and proceeded to tell the German all that he knew.

'The man we are looking for is very tall and has dark hair and very dark eyes. He also has very pale skin – which is why I refer to him as the "Pale Man". Because of this skin he usually wears a hat. He speaks English with a London accent that makes me believe he is English and not German.' Walker paused, waiting to see if Radke would respond.

'Continue,' said Radke.

'I believe,' said Walker, 'that after you stole the stiletto and the drawings you sold them to this pale-skinned man. Your friend Matthius Gruber then stole the drawings from him. The "Pale Man" killed Gruber with the knife when he learned that the four drawings had been passed on to Gruber's brother-in-law. He then travelled to

England and killed several people in order to retrieve the drawings.' Walker took a deep breath. 'What we don't know is the killer's name, where he lives, or why he values the drawings so highly. Why is he so desperate to obtain them?'

Radke leaned back in his chair, folded his arms and looked down at the surface of the table. After several seconds had passed, he looked up at Walker and said, 'I took the drawings from the museum because they refused to give me a reference. And I took the knife because Koppe refused to give me my full pay. Also, I didn't sell the drawings to this "Pale Man". I gave them to Matthius as payment for a gambling debt. And I didn't sell the knife to the "Pale Man" either. He came to my apartment and demanded that I give him the drawings. How he found me I don't know. When I told him I had given the drawings to Matthius he hit me a couple of times and then he searched my apartment. When he saw that I didn't have the drawings, he made me give him Matthius's address. Then he left. He must have taken the knife with him because I never saw it again.'

'Is that all you have to tell me?' said Walker.

'No,' said Radke and he looked slyly at Walker. He smiled and said, 'I think I know something that you don't know. Something that should be worth two hundred and fifty euros.'

'What?' Walker asked. 'Go on. Don't mess about. Tell me!'

'This man, the one you call the "Pale Man". I don't know his name, or where he lives. But I do know why he wants the drawings. He told me that the drawings belonged to his family and that the museum would have returned them to him if they hadn't been stolen.' Radke cast a shrewd glance at Walker. 'That suggests he has been in contact with the museum. Someone there must know his name and address.' Radke sat up straight and looked expectantly at Walker. 'Is that information useful?'

That is indeed useful information, thought Walker. Without speaking, he counted another two hundred and fifty euros and passed them to a grinning Radke.

CHAPTER SIXTY-THREE

After alighting from the tram at Schneiderberg station, Walker and Kent trekked across the broad parkland of Georgengarten towards the solitary, cream-coloured, palatial building with the red roof. This edifice was the Wilhelm Busch museum.

Walker had removed his coat and was holding it draped over his shoulder but Kent didn't seem to mind the heat. He was excited. Ever since he had learned they were to visit Hanover he had been looking forward to visiting the museum again. He was eagerly anticipating viewing the new exhibits. Walker, for once, was not interested in visuals. He was eagerly anticipating hearing the answers to the questions he intended asking of the museum's head curator, Frau Schmidt.

Walker had called Frau Schmidt from the tram to tell her they were coming. At first, she had not sounded too enthusiastic about their visit. Enthusiasm soon appeared in her voice however, when Walker told her he had recovered one of the stolen drawings.

When the two detectives entered the high-ceilinged foyer, Walker showed his identification card to an elderly, uniformed man standing near the reception counter. The man, who had his hands clasped behind his back, barely glanced at the card. When Walker told him they were there to see Frau Schmidt, the guard offered no verbal response and his hands remained behind his back. He simply nodded his head towards a nearby stairway, indicating that Walker should go in that direction.

Much to Kent's delight, he was told by Walker – with the guard's single nod of approval – that he could look around the museum while Walker was speaking with the curator. Kent excitedly crossed the polished wooden floor to enter one of the larger white-walled rooms as Walker climbed the stairs towards the administration offices.

When Walker reached the long, wide corridor the only sound he could hear was a voice speaking quietly in German. The sound was coming from an open doorway to his right.

Walker crossed to the doorway and looked into a large office. There were two women in the room. One of these, a slim, middle-aged woman, seated behind a large desk, was obviously in charge. She was speaking in a quiet, authoritative manner to a stouter, middle-aged woman who was seated on the other side of the desk, writing in a notebook. Both women wore spectacles and both had straight grey hair, but the hair of the woman speaking was shorter, barely covering her ears. This woman was wearing a long sleeved, white blouse, while her companion wore a similarly designed blouse that was pale yellow.

Walker knocked on the doorframe and both women looked towards him.

'Frau Schmidt?'

'Yes?' said the short-haired woman.

'Detective Chief Inspector Walker from England.'

'Oh yes, Chief Inspector. Please come in,' the woman said, rising from behind her desk and revealing herself to be quite tall. When Walker entered she shook his hand and introduced her companion. The stouter woman, who had very noticeable light blue eyes, was named Frau Hinkel. She nodded politely and Frau Schmidt then gestured towards an empty chair, indicating that Walker should join them.

'So, Chief Inspector,' said Frau Schmidt, 'you have found one of the drawings.'

'Yes, ma'am. But I'm afraid we won't be able to return it to the museum right now. The man who has the other three is a murderer and the drawings will have to be presented as evidence at his trial when we arrest him.'

'I understand, Chief Inspector. But I am puzzled. Why are you here if it is not to return the drawing?'

'I'm here because I'm hoping you will be able to help me in identifying the killer.'

'How can I help you? All I know is what I told you on the telephone. That I believe the man who stole the drawings was an ex-employee, Johannes Radke. Do you think he is the killer?'

'No, Frau Schmidt. You may remember that I asked you if Radke was a tall man with very pale skin,' said Walker. 'You described Radke to me and I have since met him. He is not the killer. The man we are looking for, the man who has your other three drawings, is a very tall, dark-haired man with dark eyes and very pale skin. When outdoors he always wears a hat.' Walker paused and watched Frau Schmidt closely as he continued, 'I believe he has made contact with someone at this museum.'

'I've never seen such a man,' said Frau Schmidt.

'I have,' said Frau Hinkel in a soft voice. Her face reddened and she looked down at her lap when Walker and Schmidt stared at her. She said, 'Forgive me for interrupting, Frau Schmidt, but I have seen this man.'

'Where?' asked Frau Schmidt.

'And when?' asked Walker.

Hinkel raised her eyes to look at Walker and said, 'That man came to the museum about four to five months ago. He was a very polite man and asked to see four specific drawings of Max and Moritz. The drawings he described were the ones that went missing over a year earlier. I told him they had been stolen and not recovered. He asked me if I knew anything about the theft.' Hinkel looked downwards again and said quietly and timidly, 'I know I should not have said anything but I gave him Radke's name and last known address.'

'Why?' said Walker.

Hinkel looked at Walker and angrily exclaimed, 'I hated Radke! I'm second in charge at this museum and he never showed me any respect. He was always rude to me. When he was dismissed he asked for a reference. I then lied to him. I told him Frau Schmidt had said he was not to be given one.' She turned to look at Schmidt and said regretfully, 'I'm sorry, Frau Schmidt, for telling him this but I didn't think you would give him a reference.'

'No, I wouldn't have,' said Schmidt, 'but you still should have asked me.'

Hinkel now looked angry again. 'He verbally abused me and pushed me on the shoulder when I told him he would not be getting a reference. And then the four drawings went missing.' She calmed and said, 'So I was pleased to tell this white-skinned man about him.'

Well, that tells me how the killer found Radke, thought Walker. He turned to Schmidt and said, 'According to Radke, the pale-skinned man said that the drawings belonged to his family. How and when did the museum acquire these drawings, Frau Schmidt?'

'They were donated to the museum by a local man named Gustav Braun in the late 1930s, Chief Inspector. Just before the beginning of the war.'

Walker looked at Schmidt for a moment before speaking. 'You must have a good memory to be able to remember the provenance of all of the museum's possessions, Frau Schmidt?'

'I do have a good memory, Chief Inspector, but I don't remember where all of our art works originated. I know about the four Max and Moritz drawings because I had to do some research on them in our archives less than a year ago.'

'Why did you have to do this research when the drawings were stolen a year earlier? Surely the police were no longer interested.'

'No, it wasn't for the police, Chief Inspector. It was for a lawyer representing the family of a holocaust victim.'

'A lawyer?' said Walker. 'And he claimed that the stolen drawings belonged to his client?'

'He wasn't making a claim. He was making inquiries. He didn't know that the drawings he was looking for had been stolen from the museum, Chief Inspector. In fact, he didn't know that the drawings had ever been in the museum's possession.'

'Are you certain that the drawings he was seeking were the ones that were stolen?' Walker asked.

'Yes. He described the drawings accurately,' Schmidt paused and then shrugged before continuing. 'When I received his letter six months ago I passed it on to our legal department. They told me not to reply and that they would not reply either unless an official claim was made. A claim for drawings that we no longer had in our possession might not be so easily dismissed by a court. There always remains the problem of compensation. If the lawyer could prove that they belonged to his client then his client could demand a financial settlement because we lost the drawings.' Schmidt leaned forward and rested her elbows on the desk. 'Our legal department asked me to research the drawings' origin just in case they needed to respond in the future. I did the research, but we never heard from the lawyer again.'

'Do you have the lawyer's name and address?' asked Walker, trying with some difficulty to conceal his excitement.

'No, I don't. But our legal department will have it. Their office is further down the corridor on the right. There is a sign on the door.' As Walker rose, Schmidt said, 'I will let Herr Becker know you are coming.'

Walker thanked the women, and, as he headed for the corridor, Frau Schmidt lifted the receiver of her telephone.

The museum's legal representative was a man of average height and build but with a lot of hair. Thick and wavy, it almost reached his eyebrows at the front and grew past the collar of his light brown suit at the rear. It reminded Walker of a lion's mane. Becker watched Walker closely with dark, intense eyes through gold-framed glasses.

'I don't know that I can help you, Chief Inspector Walker,' Becker said through thin, unsmiling lips.

Walker had expected this response. 'Of course you can, Herr Becker,' Walker said with a smile. 'You're a clever man. This is a murder inquiry and you know that if you don't give me the name of this lawyer, you will eventually have to give it to the German police. And, once they start asking questions, the resulting publicity will attract dozens of new claims – real and false. That would make your life a nightmare. But if you give *me* the lawyer's name this case will be resolved in England without any publicity for your museum.' Walker then gave the man his most sincere expression and said, 'One other thing, Herr Becker. I know you are concerned about possible compensation being sought by this lawyer, but that is never going to happen. The client now has three of the drawings so he has no reason to seek compensation.' Walker paused and frowned. 'This man has killed at least six people, Herr Becker, and your help is needed to catch him. And when I do catch him, I will return all four drawings to you.' Walker now gave the man his most appealing expression and said, 'And there will be no further attempts made by this man to obtain the drawings through the German courts because he will be in a British prison for the rest of his life.'

Becker thought about this. He knew Walker was right. Finally he sighed, stood up, and walked across to a large, wooden filing cabinet.

When he and Kent were outside the museum, Walker rang the office of Julius Meyer, the name given to him by Becker. There was no response. Walker then called a mobile number that had been given to him by Becker. He received an immediate reply. Meyer was in Berlin but would be returning to Hanover the following day. He agreed to meet with the detectives but said it would have to be late in the afternoon.

CHAPTER SIXTY-FOUR

The next day, the temperature was again extremely high but both Walker and Kent were in happy moods. Not only were they making progress on their case, but they had spent most of the morning sitting relaxed at an outdoor restaurant in the city square. Walker had spent the time slowly sipping a highly-satisfying, chilled wheat beer while Kent had opted for a generous serving of Movenpick ice cream.

Kent was feeling happy not only because of the ice cream, but also because of a long distance telephone call; a call he had made not to his mother but to Broadhurst. Although she had teased him, as she usually did, he had been aware of the affection in her voice.

Meyer's office was located near the northern end of the Maschsee, an artificial lake that was shaped like a large letter "P". Although it was not until five p.m. that they were to meet Meyer, Walker and Kent left the centre of the city around one-thirty. They caught a tram to the southern end of the lake, having decided to eat a late lunch there before taking the long walk along the lake's western edge.

After a leisurely meal, Walker and Kent began their slow walk northwards. It was now even hotter than the previous day and both detectives carried a coat over a shoulder. They shared the footpath at the side of the lake with many other slow-moving pedestrians and a few faster moving Nordic walkers and joggers. To their left was a narrow roadway, predominantly used by bell-tinkling cyclists and the occasional silent roller-blader. They whizzed past, often posing a threat to the joggers and Nordic walkers who were forced to overtake the slower moving pedestrians.

Out on the flat-surfaced lake, small, white-sailed boats glided past even smaller, foot operated, brightly coloured paddle boats that churned slowly through the water. Also gliding on the water, but closer to the shore and at a much slower pace, were ducks and their ducklings, and the occasional swan, bobbing their heads in search of food.

Occasionally the narrow strip of land separating the lake's edge from the pedestrian walkway broadened where it was occupied by bike racks and bratwurst and ice-cream stands. There were also boat sheds and restaurants, some of which – like the one in which they had eaten lunch – were open-sided and jutted out on to the water.

As Walker and Kent passed the entrance to a well shaded restaurant, a small red squirrel darted out in front of them and scampered up a nearby tree. Walker stopped and looked up.

'I haven't seen a red squirrel since I was a boy,' he said in amazement.

'The American greys may have overrun the reds in England,' said Kent, stopping and looking up into the tree, 'but they don't yet outnumber the reds in Germany.'

Walker cast a surprised look at Kent. He said, 'Stilettos, Max and Moritz, parades, and now squirrels. Your brain contains some very unusual information, Peter.'

Kent reddened and smiled.

When they eventually reached Meyer's office, Walker and Kent found that there was no secretary in attendance. They were instead greeted by a small, smiling man who Walker estimated would have been in his sixties. He was small not only in height but also in weight and his lean body was attired in an immaculate, expensive, dark suit, a crisp white shirt, and a maroon tie. His thinning, grey-streaked, black hair was brushed back and lay close to his skull, and his dark eyes glinted with a mixture of friendliness and curiosity.

Once greetings were exchanged, an offer of tea, coffee, or a stronger beverage was offered. Walker and Kent politely declined and the three men seated themselves on leather chairs placed in a small semi-circle.

'On the telephone you spoke of theft and murder,' said Meyer. 'Most intriguing.'

'Almost two years ago, four drawings were stolen from the Wilhelm Busch museum,' began Walker. 'A man wanted those drawings very badly and, in the process of hunting for them, has murdered six people.'

'And you have come to Germany looking for this man?' said Meyer.

'Not exactly,' said Walker. 'We have come to Hanover to try and learn the man's name and, hopefully, where he may be hiding in England.'

'What does this man look like, Chief Inspector?'

'He is very tall, has dark hair and eyes, and his skin is extremely white. This makes it necessary for him to wear a hat when he is outdoors.'

'And why have you come to visit me, Chief Inspector?' asked Meyer. His face wore an inscrutable expression.

Walker looked into the man's eyes and said, 'We believe that this man may have been a client of yours, Herr Meyer.'

Unblinking, Meyer returned Walker's stare. With his elbows resting on the arms of his chair, he placed the stiff fingers of both hands on the end of his chin. Eventually he spoke.

'The name of this man you describe, Chief Inspector Walker, is Aaron Jacobson. And he was my client.' Meyer leaned back in his chair and looked up at the ceiling before continuing. 'He first came to this office about six months ago. I think he found me through the Holocaust Assets web-site. He wanted me to trace and lay claim to a set of four Wilhelm Busch drawings that had belonged to his great-grandfather and been confiscated by the Nazis. Aaron hadn't heard of the Wilhelm Busch Museum but I knew of it. So I began my search by taking the obvious step of writing to that museum and giving them the description of the drawings as given to me by Aaron.'

'And they didn't reply to your letter,' said Walker.

'No. But that's not unusual,' said Meyer, again looking into Walker's eyes. 'I know from my work with the World Jewish Congress that European galleries and museums have received many claims since the Second World War and they have become very cautious. I was prepared to wait and then contact the Wilhelm Busch museum again but my client was impatient. He kept calling me and then came into my office for his second, and final, visit four months ago. On his first visit he had been very polite but on this second visit he became abusive. He accused me of taking his money and not doing anything. I told him about having written to the museum and said he must be patient. But he lost his temper. I thought he was going to attack me. He actually turned over my desk which is very heavy. So he is quite strong. Perhaps even a little mad. And he frightens me.' Meyer frowned, paused, and then, giving them a smile that revealed perfect, brilliantly white teeth, said, 'So, Gentlemen, that is why I have no hesitation answering any questions you may have about him.'

'Do you know if he was living in Germany when he came to see you, Herr Meyer? Or was he visiting from England?'

'He was living in Germany when he first came to see me, Chief Inspector. In the town of Celle which is about forty kilometres to the northwest.'

'Do you know if he has family in Celle? Someone who might know where he is staying in England?'

'Aaron told me he was living with his father.'

'His father?' Walker was now excited. 'He may know where in England his son is hiding. Do you mind giving us the father's address, Herr Meyer?'

Meyer rose, went over to his large desk and removed a leather bound book from its top drawer. He opened the book and from it copied an address on to a sheet of paper.

'May I say something?' he said as he handed the paper to Walker and returned to his chair.

'Of course,' said Walker.

'What if you are wrong and Aaron Jacobson is no longer in England? What if he is back in Germany and again living with his father? If you two go knocking on his father's door and Aaron is home, he may attack you. He will most likely be armed and you, of course, will not be carrying weapons. Or, what if you alarm him and he escapes? He could disappear completely. Remember. You don't have the authority to apprehend him here in Germany.' Meyer spread his hands with his palms upwards. 'What will you do?'

'If he *is* here in Germany and we sight him, we'll alert the local police.' Walker paused before continuing, 'But if he's not here, the only way we're going to find out where he's hiding is by talking to his father. We really need to talk to him.'

Meyer shrugged and looked at his watch. 'It's probably too late to visit Celle now. You could take the fast train in the morning. It leaves the Hauptbahnhof at seven-thirty.'

'We'll go tomorrow. And let's hope the father is at home. It will be the only opportunity we'll have to speak with him. We return to England the following day.'

Walker stood and offered his hand to Meyer. 'Thank you for talking to us, Herr Meyer.'

Shaking hands with Walker and then with Kent, the solicitor said, 'I'm pleased to be able to help you, gentlemen. As I said before, Aaron Jacobson frightens me.'

CHAPTER SIXTY-FIVE

The journey from Hanover to Celle by high speed train took only twenty minutes. Walker and Kent were now standing outside Celle station while Kent studied a map that he had purchased from a nearby shop.

'Jacobson's street is not far away, sir. It shouldn't take us long to get there.'

Walker looked around and said, 'I can't see any taxis so we may as well walk. Lead the way, Peter.'

They strode along a narrow street that was lined with colourful, well-maintained, timber-framed houses. Eventually they reached a plaza where cafes and shops were just beginning to open for business. There were a number of other narrow streets leading into this cobble-stoned area so the detectives halted while Kent again consulted his map.

The Jacobson cottage was not far from the plaza. It had taken them only fifteen minutes to reach it after leaving the train station. A small, single-storey, stone building, it sat on a fairly large block of land, bordered on both sides by similar properties and at the rear by a small forest.

Walker stooped to open a low wooden gate.

As Kent followed Walker into the front yard, he said, 'What if the killer's here? As Meyer pointed out, we don't have the authority to arrest him.'

'We'll make a quick reconnoitre before knocking on the door if it will make you feel better, Peter,' said Walker. He moved across the lawn towards a front window that had its heavy curtains closed.

'You take one side of the house and I'll take the other,' whispered Walker. 'If one of the windows has its curtains open we might be able to see who is inside.'

After a few minutes had passed, the detectives turned the rear corner on their respective sides of the building and found themselves facing each other.

'I couldn't see into any of the rooms,' Kent said softly after he had stealthily crossed the grassed area between them.

'Neither could I,' said Walker in an equally quiet voice, 'but I heard a sound. Someone is in there.'

Just then the rear door of the cottage opened. Walker and Kent were readying themselves for possible combat when a plump, elderly woman, wearing an apron and a head-scarf, appeared. She was carrying a wet mop and a bucket.

Jacobson's wife? Walker wondered. Aaron's mother? Even killers had mothers. And mothers would be more likely than fathers to know where their children were. That was something they hadn't thought about. Meyer hadn't mentioned a mother. Meyer hadn't mentioned any woman.

The woman was standing still and staring at the detectives. There was no fear on her face. Only curiosity.

'Do you speak English?' Walker asked in his friendliest voice.

The woman shook her head.

Walker pointed a finger at her and said, 'Frau Jacobson?'

The woman shook her head again.

So. Not Aaron's mother. Maybe Jacobson employed a cleaning woman. Or maybe they had come to the wrong house.

Walker pointed at the house and said, 'Herr Jacobson?'

The woman shook her head again. She said, 'Er ist bei der arbeit.'

'We've got the wrong house,' said Walker.

'No, it's the right house,' said Kent. 'She said he's at work.'

Walker said quietly to Kent, 'I didn't know you understood German?'

'I don't, sir. But I know "arbeit" means "work".'

'That's helpful but it would be more helpful if we knew where he worked.'

It was then that a second person emerged from the doorway; a pretty, flaxen-haired, teenage girl who was also wearing an apron and carrying a mop.

'Can I help you?' the girl spoke English with a strong accent.

Walker smiled at the girl and said, 'We're sorry to disturb you but we are looking for Herr Jacobson.'

'Which one? The father or the son?'

Walker tensed. 'The son is here?' he asked the girl.

'No. He has gone away. Only the father lives here now but he is not at home today. He is at work.'

'Would you mind telling us where he works?'

'He works at the Bergen-Belsen Memorial,' replied the girl.

'And how do we get there?'

'You catch a bus at the station.'

'Celle train station?' asked Walker.

'Of course,' replied the girl. She seemed a little surprised by Walker's ignorance.

Walker smiled and thanked the girl before turning to Kent and indicating that they should leave.

As they exited the property, Walker said to Kent, 'How did you know the German word for "work"?'

'I once saw in a graphic novel that it was one of the three words the Nazis placed above the entrance to a concentration camp. "Arbeit macht frei". "Work sets you free".'

Walker glanced at Kent and said, 'a concentration camp?' Then he added, 'Well, there's a coincidence. It seems we must now visit one of those infamous places if we wish to speak with the "Pale Man's" father.'

When Walker and Kent reached the train station, they learned from a uniformed railway official that the next bus to Bergen-Belsen did not leave for another two hours.

Kent suggested taking a taxi but, after spending some time looking around the train station, they were, surprisingly, unable to find one. They were also unable to learn the location of a taxi stand because none of the German pedestrians they approached could speak English and the English speaking railway official had disappeared. A frustrated Walker suggested that they spend the next two hours wandering around the town.

Normally, Walker would have enjoyed the sights. Celle was one of the few German towns to have avoided serious damage by allied bombing during the war, so most of the centuries old buildings still stood intact and had not required restoration. Today however, Walker was impatient to reach the Bergen-Belsen Memorial and failed to appreciate the town's historic attractions.

Eventually they found themselves back at the plaza. They selected one of the outdoor cafés and seated themselves at a small table. Fortunately the German word "kaffee" sounded enough like its English equivalent for Walker to be able to place an order with a non-English speaking waiter.

While they waited for their "kaffee" to arrive, Walker stretched out his legs, turned his face upwards to the sky, and closed his eyes. Kent made a vain attempt to translate the menu.

CHAPTER SIXTY-SIX

Finally they boarded the bus for their journey to the Bergen-Belsen memorial. It was a journey that was painfully slow and therefore increased Walker's already existing frustration. Time seemed to pass even more slowly because there was little of interest to see. For most of the trip the terrain was flat and consisted mainly of farmland. This monotonous view was broken only occasionally by small clumps of houses.

Walker and Kent spoke little. They both kept their thoughts to themselves as they stared out through the bus window.

When the bus eventually entered a small town, Kent said, 'It won't be long, sir. This is Bergen.'

'How do you know that, Peter?' asked Walker, turning his face away from the window and looking at his companion.

'I just saw a sign on a bread shop window back there. It said "Bergen Backerei".'

Walker smiled. 'Trust you to spot a food shop, Peter.'

Walker's spirits had risen. After their slow-moving vehicle had exited Bergen and passed by an army barracks, he knew that they were finally about to arrive at their destination; a destination where he hoped to finally learn all that he wanted to know. He breathed a deep sigh of satisfaction as the bus came to a halt outside the Bergen-Belsen Memorial.

Nothing remained of the original concentration camp buildings. They had been burned to the ground by a British army intent on preventing the spread of lice-borne typhus. And the memorial building, a plain, two-storey, concrete construction, stood not on the original site of the camp but immediately adjacent to it.

The upper floor of the building contained archives, a library, and a photographic history of the now vanished camp. This photographic display was continued, along with a cinematic one, on the ground floor; a floor that was bisected by a path leading to an outdoor, well maintained, lawn dominated area. The lawn was punctuated by stone monuments and the long, heather-covered mounds of the mass graves.

Upon entering the front of the building, Walker and Kent were faced by an information desk, a bookshop, and a cafeteria. Standing beside the information desk was a man whom the detectives immediately assumed to be the killer's father.

The man's hair may have been grey and his skin sun-tanned, but he was, even though slightly stooped, extremely tall and had, as revealed when he looked up at the approaching detectives, a pair of very dark eyes. There was no doubt in Walker's mind that this was the elder Jacobson.

'May I help you?' the man spoke in English with a distinctive Cockney accent.

Walker, no longer surprised by the assumption that he and Kent were not German, said, 'Herr Jacobson?'

'Yes. I'm Benjamin Jacobson. And you are?' The man looked puzzled.

'My name's Julian Walker and this is Peter Kent. We are police detectives from England and we would like to talk to you about your son.' Walker removed his identification from his coat pocket and held it out for the man to examine.

Jacobson's dark eyes glanced only briefly at Walker's card before returning to look into Walker's eyes. 'My son,' he stated matter-of-factly. Then an expression of understanding appeared on his face. 'Ah! I'll bet he's in trouble because of those bloody drawings. Am I right?'

Walker nodded and said, 'May we go somewhere private, sir?'

Jacobson looked around and signalled to an officious looking woman who was standing outside the bookshop. When she came over to them he spoke some words to her in German and then turned back to face the detectives. 'Come,' he said to Walker as the woman moved behind the counter. 'We can talk as we walk outside.'

They followed the stony path and when they were well away from the building, Jacobson said, 'Gentlemen. Before you tell me of the trouble that my son is involved in, please let me tell you the story of my family. Then you will have a better understanding of my son and those drawings.'

Walker nodded and said, 'Go ahead, sir.'

'My father Isaac was born in Hanover,' Jacobson began. 'In 1938, when he was six years old, he was taken to England by my grandmother. My grandfather Aaron, who my son was named after, planned to join them but was arrested by the Nazis and sent to Auschwitz. He died there.' Jacobson paused and looked at one of the mounds. 'My grandmother, who was born in England, had no trouble with the English government and was allowed to work in a clothing factory in the East End. She also found a small flat there where she and my father could live. After going to school for a few years, Isaac got a job delivering clothes to shops and market stalls. He used an old hand cart. Eventually he owned his own stall and married a young shop girl. Sadly, this girl died giving birth to me.' Jacobson stopped talking as a couple of tourists approached. Once they had passed by, the story continued.

'My grandmother left her job to look after me while my father ran his stall. I went to the same school my father had attended and later got a job as a taxi driver. Soon after that my grandmother died. Several months later I got married.' Walker noticed that the expression on the man's face seemed to harden. 'My wife and I lived with my father in the flat that he and my grandmother had been renting since they arrived in England in 1938. Then Aaron was born.'

Aaron's mother. Walker remembered what he'd been thinking when they'd seen the woman come out of Jacobson's house. He decided to stay quiet for the moment while the older man continued his story.

'Aaron went to a local school. He wasn't happy there even though he was a clever lad. The other kids teased him because of his skin condition – which, incidentally, was examined by many doctors when he was a boy. One of them said it was a form of vitiligo but the last doctor we took him to, a top London skin specialist, disagreed with that and said it was an "as yet unidentifiable genetic skin condition". So nobody knows what it is. Anyway, because of his skin he had to stay indoors and he would spend his lunch hours in the classroom looking through the window at the other kids playing outside. That he was separated from the other children was probably a good thing because if they called him names he would attack them. Even as a child he had an uncontrollable temper.'

'I'm sorry for interrupting,' said Kent, who certainly would not have interrupted without good reason, 'but would you mind if we went inside out of the sun?' Kent was not looking comfortable. His face was very red and heavily perspiring. He may not have recovered fully yet from the knock on his head, thought a concerned Walker.

'Of course not,' said Jacobson. He led them through a doorway, along the main hall and into the cafeteria. After they had seated themselves in a quiet corner of the room, Jacobson again continued telling his story.

'When he got to high school, Aaron would spend his spare time in the library, reading, and in the gym, lifting weights. He got smarter and he got very strong.'

Jacobson sat up straight, looked directly at the detectives, and said, 'Aaron might look like me when we have our clothes on but, believe me, his arms and legs are much bigger than mine.' Jacobson eased back into his seat and looked vacantly up at the ceiling. 'His strength and his temper usually stopped people from bothering him, but there was one older lad who was always bullying him.'

Jacobson's story abruptly came to a halt as a young, blonde-haired woman, wearing an apron, approached their table. She spoke to Jacobson in German. He smiled at her and then turned to the others. He said, 'Would you like some coffee, Gentlemen?' When Walker and Kent nodded, the girl smiled, turned, and hurried away.

Jacobson looked at the detectives and said, 'Where was I?'

Walker said, 'You were telling us about your son being bullied by an older boy.'

'Oh, yes. Well one day this boy made the mistake of calling Aaron "Snowman". Aaron went crazy. He picked the boy up and tossed him down the stairs. Lucky for Aaron, one of his teachers persuaded the headmaster not to expel him.' Jacobson looked at Walker with a serious expression on his face and said, 'It's a bad combination having such strength and such a bad temper.'

Walker said, 'Tell us about the drawings.'

'Right. The drawings. Well, for as long as I can remember, my father would tell me about those four drawings that had been on the wall in his home in Germany. That was about his only memory of his early childhood. He couldn't remember what his father looked like, but he could recall every detail of those damn drawings. The older he got, the more he spoke about them.' Jacobson folded his arms. 'When my son was young, my father would spend hours telling him the same story that he'd told me. Over and over. He told him about how four drawings of two young boys had hung from the wall in his home in Germany. He would then tell him how the four drawings were linked so that they could tell a tale. A tale about how the boys got up to mischief and then were punished. Aaron never seemed to get tired of hearing about them.'

The blonde returned with their coffees and a plate containing three large, heart-shaped pastries. One half of each heart was covered with chocolate. Kent, who had apparently fully recovered from the adverse effects of the sun, eyed them almost lustfully. Thinking for only a moment about why he needed to join a class at the Essex university gym, he reached for the pastry closest to him.

Jacobson took a sip of his coffee and then said, 'When Aaron finished high school he left England to look for work and live in Norway. He reckoned that if he travelled far enough north his skin would be less sensitive and he'd be less noticed. After he left, my father returned to Germany to live. He'd always wanted to come back. But he ended up living in Celle instead of Hanover. Probably because he was able to get a job here at this memorial. Then when he got sick and couldn't work anymore, I came over, moved into his house, and took over his job.'

'And Aaron?' asked Walker, as he added milk to his coffee.

'Aaron loved his grandfather more than anyone and when he learned my father was dying, Aaron came to Celle and lived with us. My father kept on telling him about the drawings and Aaron became as obsessed about them as my father was.' Jacobson paused, took another sip, and lowered his cup to its saucer. He said, 'Because my father had always said that the drawings were linked to tell a story, Aaron figured out easily enough that the drawings were a comic strip. He looked up old German comic strips on the internet and showed them to my father. That's when my father identified the characters and Aaron learned the name of the artist. Aaron then became fanatical about finding them.' Jacobson paused again. 'A few days before my father died, I heard Aaron promise him he would get the drawings back.' Jacobson sighed and then sat up straight. 'I guess he tried,' he said, 'and now he's in trouble. Please tell me about it.'

'Well, your son has managed to retrieve three of the four drawings once owned by your grandfather, Mr. Jacobson,' said Walker as he placed a pastry on his plate.

'Three!' Jacobson looked surprised for a moment. He then lifted his cup and said, 'I'm guessing that he got them illegally and that you're over here to tell me he's in custody and needs my help to pay his bail.'

'No, sir,' said Walker. 'It's true that he obtained the drawings unlawfully but we're not interested in theft. In the process of searching for those drawings, your son killed six people. We're here to ask you where he is.'

Jacobson stared wide-eyed at Walker. His lips parted but he didn't seem capable of speech. He lowered his cup quickly. It clattered on its saucer, spilling coffee on the table.

'Is he staying with you in Celle, Mr. Jacobson?' asked Walker, closely watching the older man's eyes.

Jacobson didn't appear to hear Walker. He looked stunned. He finally found his voice but didn't answer Walker's question. 'Six people? My son? Are you sure?'

'We're certain, Mr. Jacobson, and we need to find him before he kills anyone else. Do you know where he is?'

'No, I don't. He's not staying with me at the moment. The last time I saw him was about three weeks ago. I remember he got real excited about something he saw on his computer. He told me he had to go away for a while. Then he packed some clothes and left. I haven't seen him since.' Jacobson's shoulders slumped as he sat back and stared up at the ceiling. 'Six people,' he said softly.

'Did he drive?' asked Walker.

'No,' said Jacobson. 'Neither of us owns a car. He telephoned for a taxi to take him to the airport.'

'What was he carrying when he left, Mr. Jacobson?'

Jacobson looked at Walker with a puzzled frown on his face. 'He had a suitcase and a small bag.'

Ah, thought Walker. So that's how he took the stiletto into England. It was in the larger check-in bag. If he'd only had a carry-on bag, he would not have been able to take the knife on the plane.

'We think he's still in England, Mr. Jacobson,' said Walker. 'Is there anyone there he knows? Someone with whom he might be staying? A friend? A relative?'

Jacobson shook his head. 'I can't think of anyone.' He spoke sadly.

'What about his mother?' Walker asked. 'Is she still alive?'

Jacobson looked at Walker and frowned. His lips tightened as if he had tasted something sour. 'She's still alive as far as I know.'

Walker could sense the man's growing anger. He asked a question that he guessed would not be well-received. 'What's the story of your wife, Mr. Jacobson?'

Jacobson glared at Walker, but only for an instant. Then he remembered what Walker had told him about his son. He dropped his eyes to the table and slumped in his chair. He let out a long sigh and then, as if finally accepting the circumstances of his life, said, 'My wife ran off with a friend of mine when Aaron was seven. She left Aaron with me and my father. She divorced me and married this so-called friend but he was killed soon afterwards in a work accident. She then met and married a rich fellow. And then he died. Seems she's done quite well for herself.'

'How do you know so much about her? Did she keep in touch with you?'

'No. But she kept in touch with Aaron. When he was younger he used to always tell me what was going on. She wrote to him and always sent him birthday cards with money in them. He didn't see her until he was about sixteen. By then she was married to the rich bloke. Anyway, Aaron went for a visit but got into an argument with her husband and came home with a bruised face. He never went there again until after the husband died. And then, I think, only for a couple of short visits.' He looked up at Walker with a sad expression on his face and said, 'Aaron wasn't telling me much by then but I know she was still sending him birthday cards.'

'Could Aaron be living with her?' Walker asked.

'I don't know.' Jacobson was no longer looking at Walker and spoke resignedly, 'I suppose he could be.'

'Where does she live, Mr. Jacobson?' said Walker.

'I don't know her address,' Jacobson said. 'All I know is that she lives somewhere in the north of London.'

'What's her name?'

'Well, she may have married yet again and my son forgot to mention it,' said Jacobson, pushing his cup and saucer towards the centre of the table, 'but the last I heard, her surname was "Levine". Her first name is "Rachel".'

CHAPTER SIXTY-SEVEN

On the bus ride back to Celle, Walker had called Broadhurst, informed her of their progress, and told her to try and find a North London address for a "Rachel Levine". He had also told her to pass on what they had learned to Superintendent Sheen. Then, before ending the call, he had asked her to meet them at the airport.

Walker had then called Inspector Dietering to inform him that their work was finished and that they would be returning to England the following day. Dietering, who was in a hurry to attend a meeting, had time only to insist that Walker and Kent join him for dinner that evening and tell them that he would pick them up from outside their hotel at half past seven.

At twenty-five past seven, after showering and changing into casual clothes, Walker and Kent were standing on the footpath near the entrance to their hotel. By eight o'clock, they were seated at a small table on the outdoor terrace of a Greek restaurant that was perched on the bank of a narrow canal. It was still light but the air was cool and, thankfully, devoid of flying insects.

'There is something I would like to ask you, Inspector Dietering,' said Walker after they had finished studying the menus.

'And what is that, Chief Inspector Walker,' replied Dietering, giving Walker a curious glance.

'Everyone we speak to in Germany seems to know we are not German. Why is that? Do we have a special odour?'

Dietering laughed. 'It is difficult to say. When I first saw you, I knew you were not German. Why, I do not know. Something about your appearance. But certainly not your smell.'

'And in Hanover, everyone speaks to us in English. In England, very few people speak German,' said Walker

'Most people in Hanover speak English because we learn English in school,' replied Dietering.

'What about American films? Are they shown in English on television?' asked Kent.

'No, American films on television are mostly dubbed in our own language. This is what happens in most European countries – except maybe Sweden. There, the American films are shown in English. That is why the people in Stockholm speak English so easily,' explained Dietering. 'Even if it *is* with an American accent,' Dietering added with a smile.

A smartly dressed waiter appeared at their table and asked, in English, whether they were ready to order.

'So,' said Inspector Dietering, when they had ordered their meals and had drinks in their hands. 'You have ended your quest and are now returning home. I trust that your efforts proved productive and that you did not encounter too many obstacles?'

Walker smiled and said, 'I believe we have achieved our goal. And I would like to thank you for allowing us to roam unsupervised in your territory.' He raised his glass to Dietering.

'You are welcome,' said Dietering, raising his glass in return. 'Obviously you did not need my help and conducted yourselves in a professional and unobtrusive manner.' Dietering then gave them a wry smile and said, 'Of course, I did hear about an incident that occurred while you were visiting Schünemannplatz. But you probably know nothing about that.'

Walker laughed and said, 'Oh, you must be referring to those friends of Radke to whom we made our informal introductions.'

Dietering joined in the laughter and then became serious. He said, 'Do you mind telling me what you have learned while you have been in Hanover?'

'Of course not, Inspector.' Walker placed his glass on the table and leaned back in his chair. 'As you suspected, Radke stole the four Busch drawings from the museum. He gave them to Matthius Gruber to pay off a gambling debt. Radke also stole the stiletto we were looking for from a militaria shop out near Empelde.'

'Ah, yes. Koppe's shop,' said Dietering.

Walker gave Dietering a questioning look but, when there was no response, he continued with his narrative. 'Before the war, the drawings had belonged to a man named Aaron Jacobson. They ended up in the Wilhelm Busch museum. The man we are after, the man with the pale skin, is Aaron Jacobson's great-grandson. His name is also Aaron and he was living with his father, Benjamin Jacobson, and grandfather, Isaac Jacobson, in Celle. When Isaac was dying, the young Aaron promised him he would get the drawings back and went to the museum to see if they had them. When he learned they had been stolen and that the chief suspect was Radke he visited him.'

'Please forgive my interruption,' said Dietering, 'but how did this Jacobson know where Radke lived?'

'Someone working at the museum told him,' Walker replied, before again returning to his story. 'Radke was forced to give Gruber's name and address to Jacobson who then took the stiletto and went to see Gruber. After learning the drawings had been taken to England, he stabbed Gruber. But Jacobson didn't know where in England the drawings were until he came across an English advertisement on the internet. He then travelled to England where he killed five other people while chasing those drawings.'

'And you know where this Aaron Jacobson is now?' asked Dietering.

'We think so,' said Walker, as three plates of slow-roasted lamb were placed on their table. 'We suspect he is hiding in his mother's house in London.'

'How did you learn about the mother?'

'Aaron's father told us,' said Walker as he skewered a piece of lamb with his fork.

'You spoke to the father?' Dietering looked puzzled. 'How did you find him?'

'The killer's solicitor, who we found through our enquiries at the museum, gave us the address of the family home in Celle.'

'Celle?' said Dietering, as he reached for his knife and fork.

'Yes. We were there today,' Walker replied, raising his fork to his mouth.

Dietering carefully returned his eating utensils to their original position at the side of his plate and stared at Walker. In a stern tone of voice, he said, 'What if the killer had been there? What would you have done?'

Walker calmly chewed a piece of lamb and swallowed before replying. 'The killer's solicitor asked me that same question, Inspector.'

'And what did you reply?'

'Why, I told him I would call you of course,' Walker said with a smile.

Dietering shook his head and, lowering his eyes to his plate, once again reached for his knife and fork. 'Give me the address after we have finished our meal. I'll contact the Celle police and have a watch put on the house in case the killer returns.'

CHAPTER SIXTY-EIGHT

Broadhurst was waiting for them when Walker and Kent passed through the automatic exit doors at Stansted airport. Kent, rather self-consciously, handed her one of two rope-handled carry bags containing purchases from the duty-free shop. The other was for his mother.

Broadhurst examined the bag's content and raised her eyebrows when she saw the not inexpensive bottle of red wine. She smiled broadly, said 'Thank you, Peter,' and gave Kent a kiss on the lips. Although this embarrassed him, it also pleased him immensely.

Walker smiled as he imagined receiving a similar reaction from Jenny when he handed over the bottle of wine he had bought for her.

Once they were settled in Broadhurst's Audi – after the passenger seat had been moved back as far as it would go to accommodate Walker – the car began making its way through the parking lot. Walker, who was now reasonably comfortable, asked, 'So! What's happening, Paige?'

'Quite a lot, actually, sir. The London Met nabbed Warren Daniels. Once he was convinced that Haynes had given them his name, he agreed to co-operate. He admitted to his part in the drug dealing and even gave up his mate "Jimmy".'

'What's "Jimmy's" surname?' Walker asked.

'Townsend. He's a small-time hoodlum with a long list of convictions for dealing drugs. He operates south of the Thames. Sells in pubs and clubs. When they found him, he had plenty of coke in his possession so he might testify against Locke for a little consideration.'

'That's welcome news,' said Walker, 'but more importantly, were you able to find out the address of the "Pale Man's" mother?'

'I was saving the best news for last.' Broadhurst smiled. 'There's only one "R. Levine" living in North London, Sir. A "Mrs. R. Levine", living not far from Hampstead Heath in Golders Green.'

'She's probably the one we're looking for,' said Walker. 'Good work, Paige. Did you pass the information on to Superintendent Sheen?'

'Yes, sir. Yesterday afternoon after I found Mrs. Levine's address. The superintendent said he would contact the North London police and ask for their help. He also said he wanted to see you as soon as you got back.'

The parking lot's barrier gate rose and the Audi accelerated towards the main road. Broadhurst said, 'Straight to the station, sir, or did you want to stop off at your place and get your car?'

'I'm not worried about my car. I can get a taxi home later,' said Walker. 'But I would like to make one quick stop on the way to the station if you don't mind, Paige.'

'Where, sir?'

'At the university,' replied Walker. 'I want to call into the library and see Jenny.'

'Yes, sir,' said a smiling Broadhurst.

CHAPTER SIXTY-NINE

It was lunchtime when Walker, carrying the bag containing the bottle of wine, entered the large room on the library's top floor. A thin, elderly, bespectacled woman, dressed in a white blouse and black skirt, looked up from her desk as Walker approached. Walker noted that the adjoining desk, one normally tended by Jenny, was vacant.

'Ah, good afternoon, Chief Inspector,' the woman greeted Walker with a broad smile.

'Hello, Mrs. Price. Nice to see you,' said Walker, returning the woman's smile.

'Jenny's not here at the moment,' the woman said, 'but she's due back soon.'

'Do you mind if I wait?' asked Walker

'Not at all. You may sit at her desk if you wish.' She gestured towards the empty chair.

'Thank you, but I think I'll take in the wonderful view you have from up here.' Walker placed the wine on Jenny's desk and moved towards the large floor to ceiling windows. The still smiling Mrs. Price lowered her head and resumed reading a book that lay open in front of her.

Walker stood close to the window and looked down on the expansive courtyard. Then he momentarily stopped breathing. He was only partly aware of the light-headedness that suddenly overcame him.

Jenny was standing on a pathway almost directly below Walker's window, facing a tall, blonde-headed man and clasping his hands.

Walker gasped as Jenny leant into the man and raised her face to receive a kiss full on the lips. It was a long, tender kiss.

A white-faced Walker turned and headed for the exit. He did not hear the words spoken by a puzzled Mrs. Price as he passed by her desk.

Walker was not to remember descending the building's stairs. And when he emerged into the daylight he was unaware of the bright sun or its intense heat.

All he was vaguely aware of was a constriction in his throat. He walked zombie-like towards the car park.

Broadhurst and Kent could not help but notice the paleness of Walker's face as he approached the car and both knew instinctively that something was wrong. They wisely remained silent as an equally silent Walker opened the car's door and climbed aboard. As he sat gazing unseeingly through the car's front window, Broadhurst turned the key in the ignition.

CHAPTER SEVENTY

Walker, Broadhurst and Kent were in Sheen's office. Sheen was talking but Walker didn't hear a single word that was being said. Walker was thinking of Jenny. They had been apart for less than a week. What had happened? When he'd left for Germany everything had been fine. Had he said or done something wrong on their last night together?

'Chief Inspector!' Sheen's words were loud enough to interrupt Walker's thoughts.

'Yes, sir?'

'Are you with us?'

'Yes, sir. Sorry, sir.'

Sheen gave Walker a quick look of annoyance before continuing. 'I've just been informed by the North London police that our killer is not at his mother's home. They went there early this morning with a search warrant and received full cooperation from Mrs. Levine. There was no indication that our killer had ever been there and Mrs. Levine said she hasn't seen her son for several years.'

'What about the car? Was it there?' asked Walker who was now giving the superintendent his full attention.

Sheen looked down at his uniform and gave his customary flick to an imaginary speck of dust on his sleeve. 'There was a car in the garage. And it was a white Fiesta.'

'So he has been there!' exclaimed Walker.

'The North London police don't think so. It was closely examined as soon as it was found. The only prints found were those of Mrs.

Levine and there was no trace of mud ever having been on either the front or back number plates.'

'Which means it's been cleaned!' Walker was becoming frustrated.

'Maybe it has, Julian,' said Sheen, 'but it could be just a coincidence. Do you know how many people own white Fiestas in this country? I believe that even some of the police in Yorkshire are still using them.' Sheen raised his eyebrows questioningly before quickly continuing. 'Anyway, it wasn't just the condition of the car that convinced the North London police that it hadn't been used by our killer. Mrs. Levine, who is the registered owner, claims that she frequently uses the car. She is currently being treated for cancer and said her car is the only means of transport to the local hospital.' Sheen shifted in his seat and continued quickly before Walker could interrupt. 'And yes, the North London police checked with the hospital. She does have cancer and does go there for regular treatment.'

'Did the North London police speak to her neighbours? Have they seen her driving her car – or maybe getting into a taxi?' asked Walker. 'And have the neighbours been asked if they've seen a tall, pale-skinned man either in the car or entering the Levine house?'

'Of course. The North London police know their job as well as you do. The neighbours haven't seen a tall, pale-skinned man. Nor have they seen Mrs. Levine driving her car for that matter. And no-one's seen a taxi outside her house.'

'She could have arranged to be picked up by a taxi at the end of the street,' Walker said with a snarl.

'Of course she could have,' said Sheen who was obviously trying hard to be patient with Walker. 'The local police have thought of that and they're currently checking with taxi companies. But, as I have already said, the local police are convinced he's not there and hasn't been there. At least not yet.'

'So they are watching the house,' said Walker.

'As well as they are able to.' Sheen looked down at his desk.

'What do you mean?' Walker was now beginning to lose patience with Sheen.

'They don't have someone watching the house continuously.' Sheen looked uncomfortable. 'They've got a terrorist problem down there at the moment and can't spare someone to watch the house twenty-four hours a day.'

'So a police car drives past the place once a day?' Walker said sarcastically.

'Not exactly,' Sheen said quietly and began fiddling with his pen.

'What does that mean?!' Walker was close to losing his temper.

Sheen glared at him. 'The Levine house is situated at the end of a cul-de-sac so a car can't simply "drive by". The house is being observed a couple of times a day by a car passing slowly by the entrance to the cul-de-sac.'

Walker sighed and looked up at the ceiling.

'I'd recommend, Chief Inspector,' said Sheen, placing his pen firmly on his desk and rising from his chair, 'that you and your team continue your search for the killer by following up on the sightings that have come in while you have been away in Germany.'

Clearly, Walker and his team had been dismissed.

CHAPTER SEVENTY-ONE

'I can't believe it!' said Walker as soon as they were outside Sheen's office. 'I'm certain Jacobson's hiding in his mother's house and no-one's watching the place!'

Broadhurst briefly looked over her shoulder at Sheen's open doorway before replying. She spoke quietly. 'Actually, sir, someone is watching Mrs. Levine's house.'

Walker immediately halted and turned to face his sergeant. 'What? Who?'

Broadhurst motioned for him to keep walking until she was certain they could not be heard by Sheen. 'Sam Johnson's watching the house, sir.'

'Sam?' Walker stared at her. 'What's he doing down there?'

'Well, he's been on leave since Stewart's funeral but he's been calling me every day to find out what progress we've made in catching Stewart's killer. He called me late yesterday afternoon and when I told him we'd found the address where the killer could be hiding he begged me to let him help. He asked if he could do surveillance until you got there.' Broadhurst paused. 'We assumed you would be going down there as soon as you returned from Germany. We didn't know at that stage that the superintendent was going to involve the North London police.'

'But the killer knows Sam. If he sees him we may lose him!'

'Johnson's smart, sir. He said he would drive down in his beloved Bentley and wear civvy clothes and a cap. He won't be recognised.'

Walker frowned and said resignedly, 'I hope not.'

As they set off once more down the corridor, Kent said, 'What now, sir? Back to the incident room?'

'No,' Walker replied grimly. 'We're going to North London.'

CHAPTER SEVENTY-TWO

Kent was studying a map on his mobile phone. He had easily found the cul-de-sac in which Mrs. Levine lived. He noted that the Levine house, which was at the very end, was separated from the house on its left by a narrow public walkway. This walkway led to a large public park at the rear of both houses. From the front window of the Levine house, an occupant would have a clear view of the entire length of the street.

Broadhurst was casting an occasional glance at her car's satellite navigation system. She saw that they would soon reach the cul-de-sac.

Walker was looking through the car's front window. He was the first to spot Johnson's car. The ancient, lovingly restored Bentley was parked at the side of the road that ran perpendicular to the cul-de-sac. It sat directly opposite its entrance. Sam would have had no problem seeing anyone emerge from any of the houses in the cul-de-sac but he was far enough away to not be conspicuous. Walker exhaled a relieved sigh.

When Walker, Broadhurst and Kent climbed into the Bentley, Walker had difficulty recognising Sam. He couldn't recall ever having seen the constable in civilian clothes. And Walker thought that the cloth cap Johnson wore not only suited his car but was the perfect finishing touch in his attempt to disguise the fact that he was a policeman.

'Seen anything, Sam?' asked Walker, sniffing the sweat saturated air and noting the food wrappers and two bottles laying on the floor between Johnson's feet. He knew that one of the bottles contained water. He also knew that you didn't have to be Einstein to figure out the contents of the other.

'Only all of the uniforms and detectives that turned up early this morning, sir,' Johnson replied as Walker tried unsuccessfully to get comfortable. The Bentley was spacious but Walker still had trouble with his legs. He couldn't put his seat back any further because the long-legged Broadhurst was sitting directly behind him.

'They didn't see you?' Walker asked Sam.

'Apparently not. And apparently they didn't see our killer either. But I know he's in there.'

'How do you know, Sam?' asked a puzzled Walker.

'Well,' Johnson spoke slowly, 'when it got dark last evening, I took a walk down there. I passed the house and went into the park behind it. Lights were on so I climbed over the back fence and got close to the window.' Johnson saw Walker's frown and quickly added, 'It was pitch black. I couldn't see my hand in front of my face, so no-one inside could see me.'

'Go on,' said Walker.

'Well I heard talking and it wasn't a radio or television set. It was a woman and a man. Yet Sergeant Broadhurst told me that the woman lives alone.'

'So he is in there,' said a grim-faced Walker.

'What's the plan then, sir?' asked Broadhurst from the back seat.

'We wait here until the woman comes out of the house,' replied Walker. 'She'll come out eventually – even if it's just to check her letter box. Then we drive down fast and I'll get into the house before she has a chance to warn her son and he disappears into whatever hiding place he has in there.'

'Shouldn't we get a warrant, sir? Kent asked.

'No. It'd waste too much time and we'd probably have trouble getting it anyway. Remember, one has already been issued and nothing was found.'

'I guess we're not going to call for backup, sir,' said Kent.

'No,' said Walker. 'There's four of us. We should be able to handle him.'

'Don't forget he's armed, sir,' said Broadhurst. 'He's got that stiletto and he has no qualms about using it.'

'We'll be armed too,' said Walker. 'Sam and Paige, do you have your expandable batons in the boots of your cars?'

When they both confirmed that they had, they were instructed by Walker to take not only the batons from the boots, but also the iron tools normally used to remove their car hub caps; the same tool that Walker had used to open Locke's garage door.

Once all four of them held a weapon that was expected to prove effective against a knife, Walker said to Broadhurst, 'Do you have a torch, Paige?'

Broadhurst nodded and began rummaging in her bag. She soon found what she was looking for and handed a small torch to Walker. He placed it in an inside pocket of his coat as he gave further instructions. 'When Mrs. Levine appears, drive down quickly and park across the driveway, Sam. Then you and Peter hurry along that side pathway and wait in the park. If Aaron attempts to escape over the back fence, you'll be waiting.' Walker then spoke to Broadhurst. 'You keep watch out front, Paige. I'll go inside with or without Mrs. Levine.'

CHAPTER SEVENTY-THREE

The front door was eventually opened and a short, plump woman emerged. She had jet black hair and wore a gold coloured, pant suit. After looking around her, she began walking down the driveway.

'Go!' shouted Walker.

When the Bentley came to a sudden halt across her driveway and four people jumped out, the woman's heavily made-up face revealed a mixture of fear and concern. She cast a quick look back at the house.

'Is your son here, Mrs. Levine?' Walker asked, holding up his identification card.

'No, he's not,' she replied. She spoke unconvincingly in a loud, high-pitched voice.

'Wait just outside the door, Sergeant,' said Walker, grasping his tyre iron firmly in his right hand. Then, closely followed by the loudly protesting Mrs. Levine, he strode purposefully towards the open front door.

Johnson and Kent had already disappeared down the side lane but Broadhurst hadn't noticed. Her attention was fully on Walker. She knew that if the son was not here then Walker was going to be in trouble. Big trouble.

Once inside the house, Walker quickly took in his surroundings. The foyer was large with a floor that was tiled and bare of ornaments. Directly in front of him a wide staircase with balustrades led up to the next floor. To both Walker's left and right were open doorways.

Approaching the doorway on his left, Walker soon saw that it led to a study. It contained a large desk, an upholstered swivel chair, and a couple of low bookcases. There was no place in this room where a person could hide.

Walker crossed the foyer and cautiously entered the other doorway. He found himself in a large, opulently furnished lounge room. He quickly determined there was no-one hiding in this room and headed towards another doorway at the rear. He knew that Mrs. Levine was close behind him.

Walker passed swiftly through a wide dining room and entered a kitchen. After carefully opening a number of doors in a passageway leading off the kitchen, Walker had located a laundry, a small room containing a wash basin and lavatory, and an exit leading to a terrace that overlooked a small, professionally maintained backyard. A quick survey of the yard revealed that there was no place of concealment. He noted that Kent and Johnson were in position outside the rear fence.

Returning to the kitchen, and excusing himself as he brushed past Mrs. Levine, Walker moved quickly towards the door at the other end of the kitchen. It was the final downstairs door and once again Walker exercised extreme caution as he opened it.

This door led to a garage. It contained a white Ford Fiesta.

'Your car, Mrs. Levine?' Walker asked.

'Of course! I've already told that to the other police when they came this morning. Who else's car would it be?'

Walker didn't respond. He entered the garage and looked through the side windows of the Fiesta at the front and back seats. No-one was hiding in there.

Both side walls of the garage were bare and the rear wall held only shelves and a small cupboard; a cupboard far too small to conceal a person, even someone much shorter than Jacobson.

Now, Walker said to himself, it's time to look upstairs.

Walker quickly ascended the staircase. He was closely followed by a now loudly puffing Mrs. Levine.

Walker thoroughly and very cautiously searched three upstairs bedrooms and two bathrooms but didn't find Aaron or, rather annoyingly, any indication that he had ever been there. In one of the bathrooms Walker had noted a trapdoor in the ceiling but, after standing on the end of the bath, removing the trapdoor's cover, and using the torch provided by Broadhurst, he quickly determined that no-one was hiding in the small, narrow area under the roof.

Walker now approached the open doorway of the only room he had not yet searched. He realised, just as Broadhurst had realised earlier, that if Jacobson wasn't hiding in this room then he, Walker, was in big trouble. Mrs. Levine, who was now complaining loudly, would almost certainly file a complaint for illegal entry and trespass. If not dismissed from the force, at the very least he would probably be suspended. That, plus the loss of Jenny, would mean his life was ruined.

These thoughts were momentarily pushed aside by the sight of the room's contents. Walker's eyes opened wide in amazement. There were dozens – if not hundreds – of swords and knives on display. Row upon row were hanging from all of the high walls and they were also resting on black satin in low, glass-topped show cases that covered most of the bare, timber floor. The room looked like it belonged in the British museum.

The swords on the walls included many foils, sabres and epees that Walker recognised because of the time he'd spent watching a girlfriend fence during his university days. But there were also claymores and numerous other broadswords, one of which resembled a drawing Walker had once seen of King Arthur's "Excalibur". There was even a scimitar.

This is a valuable collection, thought Walker. Like Nigel Clement, the other collector associated with this case, the late Mr. Levine obviously had plenty of money to spend on his hobby.

Walker recalled reading a psychologist's article in which it was claimed that the typical collector was a single, middle-aged, sexually frustrated male. Maybe I should become a collector, he mused. I certainly qualify now that Jenny's gone. Then he shook his head angrily. Forget all that, he told himself. Focus on the case.

Walker forced his attention back on the room. He noticed that against the back wall stood three high cabinets. All were tall enough to hold a man but two of them had clear glass doors, revealing that their only contents were shelves holding knives. The third cabinet, the one in the middle, had two solid wooden doors, and this was the one that now interested Walker.

Walker began walking towards the cabinet, still closely followed by Mrs. Devine. He glanced briefly at the woman and noted her worried expression and the intense stare she was focusing on the cabinet they were approaching.

CHAPTER SEVENTY-FOUR

Walker quickly opened the cabinet doors and, just as quickly, stepped back. It was wasted effort. The cabinet was empty. Not only was there no Jacobson but nothing else was stored in there. Apart from a bare floor and walls, all that could be seen were three coat hooks, each attached to one of the three wooden panels that made up the shallow, rear wall of the cabinet.

Feeling defeated, Walker was about to turn away when something caught his eye. One of the coat hooks, the one on the centre panel, was much shinier than the other two. Walker reached forward and touched it. He quickly discovered that it turned and in doing so made an unlatching sound. The panel moved and an entrance to a rear area was revealed.

Walker turned on his torch. The first thing the thin ray of light revealed was a cord hanging just inside the opening. Walker risked quickly reaching for it, giving it a sharp tug, and, just as quickly, withdrawing his hand. The recess behind the cabinet was now bathed in light. It was a long narrow room. There was no-one hiding there.

Initially, apart from the absence of the killer, Walker noticed only a safe. It had probably been used by Mr. Devine to hold cash necessary for quick purchases. And maybe for holding small, jewel encrusted daggers. The safe was quickly forgotten however, when Walker saw what else was in the small room. On the floor was a sleeping bag and an open suitcase. And in the suitcase, on top of a few items of crumpled clothing, was a rusted stiletto. Walker smiled.

Jacobson might not be in the room now, but he had certainly been in there not too long ago.

Walker donned a glove and picked up the knife. He then turned to face Mrs. Levine who was standing in front of the cabinet, trembling, with her hands clasped to her ample chest, and her dark eyes cast downwards. Holding the knife up in front of the woman, Walker asked, 'Where's your son, Mrs. Levine?'

'I won't tell you,' she said quietly, slowly raising her eyes and looking piteously at Walker. 'For whatever trouble he's in, I am responsible. I abandoned him as a baby and left him living with his crazy grandfather. Silly drawings were all he ever talked about. No!' She now raised her voice. 'I will not betray him! For whatever bad things he's done, it is me you must punish.' Mascara-stained tears began running down her plump, highly rouged cheeks.

Walker said no more to her. He stepped out of the cabinet and tried to figure out where the killer might be. He may have been in another part of the house when the detectives arrived and Walker's sudden and unexpected appearance could have prevented him from returning to this hiding place. But where was he? Walker believed his search had been thorough.

Maybe, thought Walker, Jacobson had left the house before they arrived. But was that likely? The car was still here. Would he have ventured outside on foot? And his bag and knife were still here. But, Walker suddenly realised, there was only the suitcase here. Where was his other bag? And maybe he no longer needed the stiletto because he had replaced it with something from his step-father's collection room. Fortunately, Mr. Levine's collection had not included fire-arms.

Walker was carefully searching the walls and cabinets for a vacant space, when he heard the faint sound of a collision – metal striking metal – followed by a yell from Broadhurst. Walker turned and raced down the stairs.

Broadhurst was standing just outside the house's entrance and pointing up the street. She said, 'He just went around the corner, sir.

He was driving the white Fiesta. I didn't hear the garage door open but I heard him drive out. I saw him clip Sam's car as he veered and drove over the grass. The car then bounced on to the road and sped away.'

Walker stepped on to the stone path leading from the house and looked towards the end of the street. He then looked at the broad expanse of grass that lay between the Levine's front brick fence and the road. He immediately realised he had made a stupid mistake. In order to effectively block the Fiesta's exit, he should have had Sam park his car right up in the driveway instead of simply parking across it.

'Call the Metropolitan police and have them get their response cars looking for him. Did you get the car's plate number?' Walker said to Broadhurst as Kent and a heavily breathing Johnson emerged from the walkway leading to the park.

'I did, sir,' said Broadhurst, immediately pressing buttons on her mobile phone.

Kent was now attempting to console a sobbing Mrs. Levine while Johnson was looking aghast at the Bentley's broken tail light.

Walker began silently cursing himself not only for failing to have the driveway blocked, but also for neglecting to look under the car when he was in the garage. It was now obvious to him where the killer had been hiding.

'They haven't forgotten that the driver is wanted for the murder of a young policeman,' said Broadhurst who had finished her call and was now placing her mobile in her bag. 'So don't worry, sir. They'll make sure they find him.'

'Let's hope so,' Walker said quietly.

CHAPTER SEVENTY-FIVE

The Audi was on the A12 heading north-east. Broadhurst sat silently behind the steering wheel. She glanced into her rear-view mirror to see if the Bentley was still behind them. It was gone. Maybe Johnson had decided to take a different route back to Wivenhoe. Broadhurst could imagine him spending the entire journey muttering angrily to himself about the damage done to his beloved car.

Walker was also silent. He hadn't spoken a single word since they'd left Mrs. Levine's house. He was still annoyed with himself. After all of the time and effort they'd spent determining his whereabouts, Aaron Jacobson had managed to elude them once again. And all because of Walker's mistakes; mistakes he was convinced he wouldn't have made if he had not been so preoccupied with thoughts of Jenny.

Kent was using his mobile phone. He was talking to a Metropolitan police officer whom he had met and befriended while attending the police radio training school several years ago. Suddenly he became excited. 'What?' he said. 'That's great news, Jim. Thanks. I'll speak to you soon.' He closed his phone and announced, 'They've just found the Fiesta!'

Walker's annoyance instantly evaporated. 'Where?' he asked.

'In London. In Praed Street.'

'They certainly found it quickly,' said Broadhurst.

'It was easy to find. Jacobson abandoned it right outside Paddington Station. The Fiesta was blocking all the traffic.'

'Get off this road the first chance you get, Paige,' said Walker.

An exit sign appeared up ahead and Broadhurst moved into the left lane. As the Audi began to slow, Broadhurst looked into her mirror. There was no sign of the Bentley. Johnson had definitely gone a different way.

Once they were on a side road, Walker said, 'Pull over, Paige.'

'What do we do now?' Broadhurst asked, after she had brought the car to a halt.

Walker didn't reply. He was staring through the front window, obviously deep in thought.

'Now that Jacobson's gotten rid of the Fiesta, how is he getting around?' said Broadhurst. 'Has he stolen another car or is he walking, riding a bus, a taxi, or, most likely, a train?'

'Yes. The Fiesta was found outside Paddington station so he's probably on a train,' said Kent. 'But what train? Where is he going? Is he going North, South or West? Is he headed for a sea port or an airport?'

Finally, Walker spoke. He quietly said, 'He's headed for Heathrow.'

Broadhurst and Kent said nothing. They watched Walker and patiently waited for him to say something else.

Walker shook himself out of his reverie and turned to face Kent. He said, 'Ring Heathrow and find out when the next flight leaves for Norway.'

CHAPTER SEVENTY-SIX

The detectives were lucky. The last flight of the day from Heathrow to Oslo had departed at half past three that afternoon. There was no way that Jacobson could have reached the airport in time to catch that flight.

Kent had also learned that the next flight to Oslo did not leave until ten to eight the following morning. That gave the detectives time to return to Wivenhoe.

On the journey, Walker gave his colleagues precise instructions. Broadhurst was to drive Walker and Kent to their respective homes so that they might have a shower, a meal, and catch a few hours of sleep. They would meet at his home the following morning at three a.m. and then travel in Walker's car to Heathrow. Walker intended that they arrive at the airport before the desk for baggage handling, passport checking, and seat allocation, was opened.

'Are you going to inform the superintendent about what has happened and what we plan on doing, sir?' said Kent as the Audi approached Ardleigh.

'No,' Walker replied sharply. He saw that Broadhurst was dropping him off first. It would have saved her many kilometres by going to Kent's house first. Walker managed to restrain himself from commenting on this. Instead he said, 'We'll keep well away from the station and not respond to any calls that are identified as coming from Superintendent Sheen.'

'He'll be pretty upset if he doesn't hear from us,' said Broadhurst.

'He'll hear from us once we've caught that pale-skinned, murdering bastard.' Walker spoke angrily.

'Whatever you say, sir,' said Broadhurst and, when Walker turned to open the passenger door, she raised her eyebrows at Kent. Kent shrugged. Like Broadhurst, he knew why Walker was angry. He was still blaming himself for the killer's escape.

As Walker climbed out of the car, he said rather stiffly to Broadhurst, 'I'll just get my things out of the boot.'

Broadhurst and Kent sat silently while Walker retrieved his travelling bag. They heard the boot slam shut and soon after Walker appeared on the driver's side of the car. Both Broadhurst and Kent watched as he bent down to gaze in at them through the driver's open window. Softness had now replaced the previous hardness in his features.

'I'm sorry for snapping at you, Paige.' Walker spoke gently, both his voice and penetrating eyes expressing his regret. 'I'm just so annoyed with myself for allowing Jacobson to get away.'

Broadhurst smiled. 'That's alright, sir. And don't worry. We'll catch him.'

Walker smiled back. 'I hope so,' he said wearily. 'I'll see you both here early in the morning.' Then, as he was about to move away, he added with a grin, 'And in case you're wondering, Paige, I did notice that you've dropped me off first. Just make sure you both get *some* sleep tonight. We will all need to be fully alert tomorrow.'

Walker knew that *he* wouldn't get any sleep that night. He would be awake thinking of Jenny. Should he call her, he asked himself, and get the answers to the questions that kept surfacing in his mind? No, he resolved. That could wait until after they'd captured the killer.

CHAPTER SEVENTY-SEVEN

It was now just before five a.m., and nineteen days after Anna Gruber had been murdered. As Walker positioned himself against the wall so that he had a clear view of those beginning to queue with their bags and passports, he hoped that this was to be the day the killer was finally caught.

Kent and Broadhurst were standing directly opposite Walker, against the far wall, at the other end of the long, broad passageway that separated the weigh-in counters of the various airlines. Unlike Walker, they were armed. They each carried an expandable baton concealed inside a folded newspaper.

By five-thirty, enough luggage-carrying people had joined the unmoving Oslo queue to make it long enough to require being turned twice, forming three parallel rows. Each row was separated by a bright red cord attached to the tops of strategically spaced, vertical, chrome poles. The snake-like queue reminded Walker of those he had seen outside rides at Disneyland, which he had visited when in Paris several years ago.

Three uniformed women were now at the luggage weigh-in/passport-checking counters preparing their computers. So far, they had ignored the queue; a queue headed by a patiently waiting elderly couple who, until summoned, dared not cross the red line clearly marked on the floor.

Walker was tired of observing this scene. Jacobson was not in the queue. He may have disguised his skin but, as Walker had stated previously, it would be difficult to disguise his height. He looked towards Kent and Broadhurst and slowly turned his head from side to side. They responded with similar head movements.

Walker glanced along the main corridor. There was a group of about a dozen people moving quickly towards him. He watched as all but one of them turned into an adjacent check-in bay.

The lone, grey-haired figure now coming towards Walker was carrying an overnight bag and wearing dated, ill-fitting clothes. He was supporting himself with a walking stick and walking very awkwardly.

As the man came closer Walker thought he recognised him. No, he thought again. He didn't know him. Then he realised that the man closely resembled someone he did know. Benjamin Jacobson. But Ben, like his son, was much taller. It couldn't be him.

Then full realisation struck Walker. It was Aaron Jacobson. He'd dyed his hair grey as well as tanning his skin. And he was walking with a crouch to disguise his height. The fact that his legs were bent was concealed by the very baggy trousers he was wearing; trousers he'd probably taken, with the rest of his clothes, from his deceased step-father's wardrobe. And, Walker further realised, he'd dyed his hair not just to disguise himself but also to deliberately make himself look like his father. He had his father's passport and intended using it to get to Norway.

Just then this grey-haired man, who had been walking with his head lowered, looked up. Walker saw dark eyes glaring at him. The killer had now recognised Walker.

When he realised, because of the intensity of Walker's stare, that the detective knew who he was, Jacobson dropped his bag and rose to his full height. He then turned and raced down the passageway towards Kent and Broadhurst. Walker noticed that Jacobson had not dropped the walking stick.

Walker casually followed Jacobson. He was in no hurry. Kent and Broadhurst had seen him coming towards them. The killer was trapped.

Some of the people in the queue were watching. A few of them were curious. Others were amused by the sight of a man running in baggy trousers that had cuffs reaching just below his knees. This figure of fun however, was not to remain funny for long.

When he saw Broadhurst and Kent, now with fully extended batons in their hands, Jacobson came to a halt. He cast a quick glance over his shoulder to see how close Walker was and grasped his walking stick in two hands. Then, with a twist of the handle, Jacobson withdrew from the stick something that was long and shiny.

Walker also came to a halt. The killer had found a replacement for the stiletto in the Levine collection. A weapon that Walker recognised as being a nineteenth century cane-sword. A very sharp and lethal weapon.

Jacobson's audience was growing. Those in the queue who had witnessed the unsheathing of the sword nudged those who hadn't. Perhaps, many thought, a movie was being made.

The killer advanced on Kent and Broadhurst. Broadhurst swung her baton at the outstretched sword but missed. Jacobson then made a thrust and the point of his sword entered Broadhurst's shoulder. Kent dragged her back and moved in front of her. He held his baton out at full length and pointed it at the killer, hoping to hold him at bay. Walker knew that it was a useless gesture. The sword was longer than the baton.

A woman in the crowd screamed. She had noticed the blood that was beginning to appear on Broadhurst's jacket. Other screams followed and the people who had once been standing in an organised queue pushed and shoved to distance themselves from Jacobson. They had finally realised that this was not the making of a movie.

Walker knew he had to do something. And do it quickly.

'Hey! Snowman!' he shouted.

The killer froze for just a moment. Then, with maniacal rage in his eyes and a bestial howl emanating from his mouth, he turned and charged at Walker.

Jacobson was fast but Walker was faster. As the sword arm lunged at him Walker deftly stepped aside, grabbed Jacobson's wrist with his right hand, twisted it, and slammed a left palm into the elbow. The loud, sickening sound of bone breaking was followed by a high pitched scream. Jacobson dropped the sword and sank to his knees.

Walker looked towards his colleagues. Broadhurst was leaning against Kent who had an arm wrapped protectively around her and a handkerchief pressed against her wound. She was pale-faced but the white handkerchief was not completely stained, indicating that the sword had not pierced an artery. Broadhurst looked at Walker and gave him a weak smile.

Walker's responding smile was one that expressed both relief and affection. For a few seconds, he gazed fondly – and perhaps a little enviously – at his fellow detectives. He then turned his attention to the moaning figure laying on the floor.